CW01429557

TWO RINGS AROUND THE MOON

KENT BAKER
Copyright Kent Baker 2014

If some of the characters and places seem familiar to those who read my earlier work - "THE SECRET WAR "DAIRIES OF JOEY MULDOON" You are not imagining things. We are back in Craggs Bottom. I couldn't bring myself to abandon the beautiful moors and the ugly slag heaps. I was also not quite prepared to leave that period - The second World War with it's restricted way of life,"all in this together" attitude and basic if somewhat rationed values. If this offends please forgive me, I'll try not to do it next time. But I can't promise!

KB.

ACKNOWLEDGEMENTS

"Agnes Lightfoot" aka Ellie Clapworthy: Who dragged me kicking and screaming from a dull world of ignorance. Taught me that life was a Ball and most poor sods never even got taken to the local hop!. She knew, she knew, she knew!

Bill Thompson: Fearless war hero and great guy. Ex fighter pilot and daredevil he cheered me through some tough times. Bill laughed a lot and it was contagious!

Ray Duffill: A good and loyal friend. Accomplished and gifted he generously spread his talents around. To my everlasting indebtedness some of it fell my way.

Colin Wright: Faithful, and encouraging he and his lovely wife Vickie are a big plus in my life.

Jason Flint: For his infinite patience which I will be eternally grateful. He persevered and finally got me able to switch on my new PC! No small achievement...thanks Jason!

Ravishan Gamage: Alongside Jason, Ravi showed great forbearance and kindness. Eventually enabling me to conquer the impossible procedure of copying onto my Memory Stick! His patience is heroic"... thanks Ravi!

Kate and Daniel: Where would I have been without the kindness and encouragement of my two fabulous neighbours? Don't answer that!

Thanks also to **Networkx**

DEDICATED TO

Rosie Baker my Mam. Who taught
me how to make the rations stretch
the whole week, how to iron a shirt,
and ..er... spacing?

Right from wrong... ?

Not to be cheeky...?

To keep me nose clean, me bowels
open, me socks up and trust in the Lord...?

Hold on! There was something else...

Oh yeah, I remember - how to time a gag!

To my dear cousin
Brenda ... cousin twice
removed but closen
affection. Love
Kent xx

CONTENTS

ELENORA CLAPWORTHY

Snow clouds, dark and heavy had been gathering for over a week. Not a single snowflake was set loose to hint at the transformation about to take place. Until during the hours of sleep on the Saturday night, then – Voilà!

The hill top village of Craggs Bottom awoke to the muted sounds of a world buried beneath deep drifts of snow. Broad brush strokes of intense white topped the dry stone walls and crowned the tired hassocks of the rugged moor land grass. Well before the first call to Matins – by word of mouth these days since all church bells were now a war time restriction, only to be sounded in the event of victory or invasion by the all powerful Nazi War Machine.

Through the tiny bubble glass panes of the ancient window Elenora Clapworthy looked with delight to see for miles across Grantham Hill. To her left, towards Thornton and beyond to the Haworth moors, the sweep of the hills brought to mind the 1939 version of *"Wuthering Heights"*. The film's over the top Hollywood version of English countryside for once compared fairly accurately with this - the real thing.

Up the steep hill ahead of her, the stout little millstone cottages of Craggs Bottom huddled together bearing with defiance every cutting blast thrown at them. It occurred to Elenora, not for the first time since she settled here some twenty odd years earlier, that it was one of the endearing peculiarities of these stoical North Country folk to have named the village *"Craggs Bottom"* and not more correctly as *"Craggs **Top**"*. A glaring anomaly seeing as the ancient cottages all clustered together at the very top of the steep mountain.

Oblivious to any man made threat the early morning sun broke triumphantly through prompting Elenora to fling open the blackout curtains of her bedroom window and let out a mad screech of delight which reverberated around the hills ages after the emission. To those who heard Elenora's madcap hoot of delight, and that must have been everybody in every household on the mountainside who was not totally deaf, registered little surprise. Normally quick to frown on such exuberance, especially *"first thing of a Sunda' morning"*, Her spontaneous shriek of unrestrained glee ricocheted around the hills evoking nothing more than a wry smile of acceptance and a slow shake of the head. For Elenora had a tacit understanding, an almost divine permission to disregard the strict no nonsense rules of behaviour. Miss Clapworthy, the rare exception around these parts was after all, coming from the south of England as she did, was lets face it, *"a foreigner"* The villagers were also quick to recognise that Elenora's childlike – no-one mistook it for "child*ish"* – behaviour was part of a multi-gifted personality. Admired with open mouthed wonder for her seemingly bottomless list of talents. Qualified Veterinarian, occasional Magistrate, dog breeder, leader of a successful Jazz band, and unofficial champion of the underdog were amongst her known attributes. In each of these roles she appeared to take on a different personality. The nosier villagers did sometimes wonder at her actual date of birth. Not that she was coquettish in any way, but in the unlikely event that anyone would deem it necessary to press her further on the subject, she would gladly admit to being aged *"...somewhere between forty five and a decent burial"* This brief explanation was usually enough to put a block on any further inquiries about her age.

The excited yelps from the pups housed in one of the low out buildings drew Elenora away from the window and into the ancient shower to scream once again at the onslaught of the icy deluge. She couldn't help but chuckle to herself as she thought of what her dear old Aunt Drusilla would say of her insistence on having a cold shower in the middle of Yorkshire's Arctic winter.

Aunt Dee had long ago stopped voicing her despair at Elenora's choice of habitat,having raised her beloved niece herself in the picture book cottage situated in the gentle Home Counties after the sudden and tragic death of both the little girl's parents".

"With your qualifications," Aunt Dee reasoned more than once in her weekly letters to her niece, *"you could have had your pick of any number of practices in the civilised world. Instead of which you chose to live and work in the most unhealthy place on the face of the earth! Bronte Country! Is there any wonder all the sisters died of consumption and the brother Branwell became a hopeless drug addict and drunk?"*

Both women understood however, the event that had forced Elenora to abandon the successful practice she had established in her original village some twenty years earlier. They adopted a tacit understanding not to dwell on it.

` It was an uphill slog for Elenora between her house/surgery/kennels and Minnie Clegg's cottage but one she looked forward to every Sunday morning. She knew the reception would be as always, warm and welcoming, with some little home baked treat made by Minnie in spite of Lord Woolton, the Food Minister's stringent wartime rationing. It was almost a ritual, to call on her unlikely friend Minnie to swap the latest village gossip. Especially now since the little cottage Hospital had expanded into a Military Convalescent Unit covering most of what had previously been a large slice of Thornton Moor

Wrapped up well against the glorious cold morning Elenora paused in her climb to sit with her legs dangling over the edge of the massive bare rock, known famously hereabouts as *"The Cragg."* from which the village took its name. The keen northern wind that had prevented the previous night's snowfall settling on the Craggs flat surface was now stilled and the winter sun shone joyously in celebration. Wrapped up well in her cord trousers, lined Aquascutum classical raincoat, knitted comforter and flat cap Elenora cut a stylish, attractive figure that would sit well in any glossy fashion magazine. The Cragg, a gigantic slab of granite, a leftover from the fourth ice age formed a natural platform commanding a spectacular view over the city of Bradford and beyond to seemingly endless stretches of moor lands. There were some ancient villagers still alive who swore on the Bible their own grand parents had gathered beneath the flat shelf to hear the great John Wesley deliver his sermon to the multitude gathered on the scattered rocks some forty feet below.

From her vantage point, she took in the City spread below her. The woollen industry had won the battle for space and crammed the valley with ugly mills and row after row of back to back housing for the workers. From up here the grimy woollen mills with their individually shaped tall chimneys, now elegantly topped in a beautiful crown of white, were a world away from the isolated little village of Craggs Bottom.

Although in reality merely a district of the city, the village considered itself very much apart with its little private shops, it's very own Co-op Emporium – The

Craggs Bottom Industrial Society Limited. A rather underused Police Station or *"cop shop"*, two or three pubs, two doctors, one fried fish shop. a Pea and Pie Salon and one flea pit cinema – all jostled together silhouetted against the skyline at the very top of the mountain with nothing but bleak skies above as if to shut out the rest of the world.

In spite of the war-time upheavals the many varieties of churches and chapels from C of E. through every variation of splinter groups from Methodist to Seventh Day Adventists still seemed to thrive. Townsend's Textiles, the dominant building on the skyline was the one and only mill to make it to the top of Grantham Hill. Without hope of shelter from the strong winds that rarely ceased in these parts. This stark industrial building (unlike the ones down below in Bradford) Townsend's Textiles never quite turned into the stereotypical *Dark Satanic Mill* Blake so vividly immortalized in his magnificent hymn, Jerusalem.

Elenora had come to love the Village and the people, the Cragg, the uncompromising countryside and now even the new Council Housing estate. This recently built development on the edge of the village in what was the Co-operative Society's old farmland did not, as it did with many, diminish her fondness for the place.

This particular Sunday morning however, the view over Bradford City, commanded all her attention. The snow had worked the miracle of giving even the mills below a striking beauty and she was loath to move on. Relaxing, Elenora removed her man's tweed flat cap and threw her head back to let the fresh air tousle her still natural ash blond hair. Although she welcomed this break, unlike her strange mongrel companion she was not really in need of a rest. Elenora's energy seemed boundless. Heinz, her beloved canine friend – Heinz, as in 57

Varieties - welcomed any opportunity to flop inelegantly, as he did now, his incongruous delicate head resting on her lap.

"Heinz, you old fake!" Elenora fondled the dog's ears as he gazed up at her with a half self pitying half besotted look. "We've only done a few hundred yards. Don't get too comfortable my old love, we're only going to take five, then it's up that hill we go to Craggs Bum."

Her words of chastisement elicited a pitiful whine of protest from Heinz, (she swore he understood every word) "Oh! OK, don't keep on at me, another few minutes then, alright?" In any case she was quite content to sit a little longer watching as away to her left the Municipal tramcar with its snow-plough attachment laboriously climbed the almost impossibly steep main road to the terminus on the very peak. She allowed herself to drift into a contemplative mood.

It seemed to her again, not for the first time, every significant thing that had ever happened in her years on earth had happened under a heavy covering of snow. It was here, sitting in this very spot when she first arrived in Yorkshire some twenty years earlier that she felt, no, not merely felt – *knew,* for certain she had at last found solace and her true home?

From the depths of her despair all those years ago she realized that if there were to be any place on earth where she might have some kind of life, some chance to recover the shattered remains of her heart and mind it was here in this most unlikely setting. She never expected to love again, but she had every intention to live and even more importantly – laugh again!

On an impulse all those years ago she had answered the advert to take over whilst old Jim Caruthers, the regular Veterinary Surgeon at Ambler Thorn recovered from a bout of pneumonia. After his recovery she stayed on to share the practice, not noticing how quickly the months turned into years. Before she knew it she was so much a part of the practice and the community, any thoughts of returning to the South of England was no longer an option. After Jim Caruthers retirement and eventual death, it only seemed natural she take over the practice herself, much to Aunt Dee's grave misgivings.

Elenora knew the minute she saw the old Manor House and learned the Bronte-like title - *Ambler Thorn*, Monolithic , bleak yet snug and comfortable in its few acres of land; with out buildings, barns, kennels and ample space for a surgery she had found her spiritual home. Aunt Dee, back home in the more gentle countryside of Surrey suffered sleepless nights unable to comprehend how her darling niece could lose her heart to this most unlikely rugged part of England that couldn't make up its mind whether to remain rural, or keep up with the Industrial Revolution.

Looking out over the snow covered valley Elenora allowed herself to be carried back on a wave of pure nostalgic joy to an earlier landscape. Back to the treasured memory she knew without doubt her thoughts would home in on as she breathed her last on this earth. Back to that enchanted winter when, as a twenty year old student, together with a group of like minded girls struck out boldly against convention and booked one months accommodation in a desperately faded therefore affordable Hotel, a small unfashionable resort in the French Alps. One whole month! Un-chaperoned!

"...*the only 'grand' thing about "Le Grand Hotel Mont Blank" is its name."* she wrote excitedly on the back of the multi – scene postcard. *"Oh, and Aunt Dee, the proprietor is a gorgeous little character. His name is Monsieur Claude Chirac. In his top hat, waxed mustachio and haughty manner I swear he has fallen straight from a poster by Toulouse Laurence. On our first day here the girls and I created perhaps a bit too much mayhem for the genteel clientele, but when I offered an apology M. Chirac, belying his prissy façade said, "au contraire, it is of no consequence... a leetle joi de vive is most welcome! Mademoiselle, sous are a long temps Mort!" The snow is pure and fine, ideal I'm told for skiing. More later, love, love, love, Ellie"*

Elenora's thumbnail sketch of M Claude Chevalier-Chirac was bang on. A dapper little gentleman with an outwardly snooty manner; inwardly as soft as blancmange, positively fluttering with delight at having such well bred and vivacious guests in his modest pension. His delight knew no bounds when he learned of their musical abilities, gladly giving them free access to the palm bedecked raised dais which served as a modest concert platform. Elenora, torn between a musical career and her veterinary calling decided, knowing she would be incapable of abandoning either, to follow both. Aunt Dee was left to do the worrying. Since her niece's early childhood Aunt Dee had always been the one who cared and loved and yes, worried over all the normal pitfalls that lay in the path of the bright, beautiful child.

After Elenora's parents were killed in a climbing accident in the Alps. It was Aunt Dee who vowed to make the child's life as happy as was humanly possible. This she had done with honours. But now, here she was, poor worried Aunt Dee, once more plunged into deep concern as her beloved niece sought to kick over yet more social traces.

Elenora's group of girl musicians had formed over a year earlier when they gravitated towards each other at the start of their degree course at university. As performers, although not up to Elenora's standard, the other girls were all competent musicians capable of knocking out a more than passable tune on violin, big bass, drums, banjo, trumpet and a couple of ukuleles. Separately they were all fun loving, pretty and talented amateur musicians, playing together they were a mild sensation.

The Hotel's afternoon entertainment was in the hands of the resident trio of elderly lady musicians – "*Le Trio Arcadia*". The three matrons were so long established they had become part of the furniture of the hotel, blending perfectly with the shabby décor. On a given cue they would sweep grandly onto the podium in a cloud of Essence of Violets. Their ancient dresses – black, jet encrusted taffeta for their leader Madame Chevrolet on pianoforte. Coffee lace over ivory satin for Madame Calvert on cello, and deep emerald green shot silk for Madame Gavin on violin. All their necks were weighed down with numerous strings of beads, their fingers ditto with rings of every description.

"*...Especially showy,*" Elenora wrote on one of her daily postcards to Aunt Dee, "*are the gigantic paste dress rings which make the Koh-e-nor look miserly. Through which is threaded an enormous chiffon handkerchief anchored to each of the ladies little fingers. Not always matching the fussiness, of the osprey and ostrich plumes clustered haphazardly and abundantly on their heads. Voluminous feather boas of marabou, again not necessarily matching are draped around their shoulders. Collectively they look, like a explosion on a poultry farm! After milking dry the last dregs of the sparse applause on their entrance the three old dears then make a lengthy show of removing the boas and chiffon before embarking on another lengthy ritual of getting comfortable. Then comes the stretching of knuckles, waxing strings and tuning their various instruments. Finally satisfied they are* *perfectly in tune (to their standards) Madame Calvert gives the other two ladies a nodded count in and they strike up."*

Elenora's description although kindly meant was pretty accurate for not only were they excruciatingly off key but also jarringly out of tempo. Offenbach, Tosti and other previously much loved and admired melodies would thereafter forever have an entirely and not unwelcome new appeal to Elenora's highly developed sense of pitch and humour.

M Chirac, a kindly man could not find it his heart to give the Trio Arcadia the boot. All he could hope for was that they try to emulate the spirit if not the musicianship of the English youngsters who under the leadership of Mademoiselle Elenora brought some very welcome contemporary magic each evening to his staid little pension.

For the girls part, after filling the daylight hour's sleighing, skiing, and skating with unladylike abandon, had fallen into the habit, of taking over each evening the little stage to provide *"a quick shot of Honky-tonk"*.

Bursting with boundless energy the young English girls would blast the latest jazz, rag time and Tin-pan-alley tunes into the deepest corners of the dingy palm strewn salon as if they had come hot from New Orleans rather than the genteel Home Counties of Edwardian England. The stuffy wood-panelled lounge with its dingy leaded lights, threadbare carpets and wicker bath chairs, more accustomed to hushed tones, lowered voices and gentle snoring now fairly throbbed nightly to the beat of the *'One Step'*, the *Hoochy - Coochy* and the *'Grizzly Bear'* Swelling with pride, his waxed moustaches fairly bristling with excitement M. Chirac proudly announced his new young friends.

16

"Mesdames et Messieurs's! Jail longueur de sous presenter mes infant de jazz!" Elenora, eager to get her hot little group into the mood picked up their cue with professional timing. Keeping up the pace they held the evening on a breathtaking level until propriety and consideration for the older clientele prompted them to reluctantly call a halt.

Talk spread quickly around the little resort, the girl's fame increased, as did their applause. By the third night of their holiday this had risen to a tumultuous ovation causing the dull crystal chandelier drops to shed many years of accumulated dust over a delighted audience. M Chirac experienced a glow of satisfaction and joy he had never known. In the morning sunshine whilst the cleaners removed the evidence of the previous night's celebrations M. Chirac set off with a sprightly spring in his step to face his fellow hoteliers at the local coffee shop with newly found optimism, and why not? After all, since the arrival of *"Mes infants de Jazz"* his personal stock in the town was riding high and every one was going to know it!

"...not only are they paying guests, they are young, beautiful, they entertain for free and are scrupulously respectable!" Wallowing in hyperbole he would round off his glowing commercial with the sweeping assertion that... "...all who come within the orbit of Mlle Elenora and her young friends cannot fail to be charmed, excited, smitten!" How right he was!

Of those who came within Elenora's orbit, none could have been more charmed, excited and smitten than John Clapworthy. He was a medical student in his final year who had arrived with a group of English male University students who had booked in at a rival Hotel. Even before they had unpacked, news of the phenomenal *"Girl Band"* reached their ears. The boys made a beeline to the Hotel Mont Plonk. Elenora's name for the hotel had become common usage.

Johnny Clapworthy stood both literally and figuratively head and shoulders above the eager youngsters gathered around the bandstand. He would indeed have stood out in the collective beauty of ancient Greece and Modern Hollywood put together. Such masculine physical perfection in one man might have been suspect had it not been for the mischievous smile that immediately put paid to any hint of conceit. On their fifth evening on the bandstand, after a rousing big finish to the last chorus of *"Georgia Camp Meeting"* Elenora, turning to acknowledge the applause, was instantly taken captive. Her cornflower blue eyes gazed into the intense deep violet of Johnny's and remained locked there.

And that was that ! Undying Love!

If, previous to their meeting she had been bursting with life, now she was positively supercharged. Unable in later years to recall being formally introduced – for, being a well brought up young girl, she knew there must have been such an introduction - the actual moment forever eluded her. She would of course never forget Johnny's wonderful, heartbreakingly madcap proposal which happened extremely soon after their meeting.

"Ellie, you do know don't you what has happened to us? You do know I want to spend all my life with you? I want us to grow old together and..." He tried to think of a romantic and memorable way of saying it, but if he tried he knew her well enough already to know they would both be reduced to a fit of giggles. Instead he took her head gently in his hands and kissed her tenderly leaving no need for words.

"Johnny Clapworthy! You think you are getting away with it so easily? Oh no! I want a traditional proposal in the time honoured way!"

"Down on my knees, *in the snow?*

"Down on your knees. In the snow!   She demanded,

"Right, It's a deal!   But you must provide the incidental music."

"No trouble." She replied, quick as a flash. "What would you like? I can lah–lah anything you name from *"After the Ball" to "Come Into the Garden Maude"*

"You must lah-lah our own special tune – *"Georgia Camp Meeting"*

"That's a rag time tune, hardly a romantic ballad!"

"It doesn't matter; it'll always be our own special tune."

"Right oh, you got it! *"Georgia Camp Meeting"* it is!"   Elenora began to lah-lah the lively tune, as dramatically, as much in the style of a silent movie pianist as she could. John went down on one knee, adopted a bad squint as much like Jimmy Donaldson's from the Keystone Kops as he could manage and to the lah-lah-ed accompaniment he went into his act.

"…Lodestone of my heart!! I want you! I must have you for my wife!"

"Desist, Sir!" Elenora's line in ham acting more than equalled his. "Pray, what would your wife want with me?"

"You misunderstand me Oh Light of the Moon!" , his cod desperation mounting, "Beloved, I beg you, I implore you – change your name to mine!"

"Change my name to John?" What would the neighbours think" She feigned maidenly vapours.

"No my lurve you misunderstand again – Clapworthy!"

"You certainly are sir, worthy even of a standing ovation!"

"I don't mean worthy of a clap beloved – The name I wish to share is "Clapworthy!" Johnny placed the back of his hand on his forehead in mock despair and threw himself headlong into the snow and began thrashing about in idiotic delirium. He grabbed her ankle and pulled her down beside him. They rolled around screaming with laughter, the passion not entirely theatrical. He lifted her to her feet, both of them coated from head to toe in fine alpine snow. Suddenly the comic melodrama evaporated to be replaced by a genuine kiss so sincere and deep it could not be measured in earthly time.

"You will marry me, won't you Ellie?" he breathed tenderly.

Conformation, if any were needed was in the passionate embrace that followed. The remaining days and hours of that enchanting winter holiday, were lived in an aura of love that charmed everyone around them.

....

M. Chirac wept unashamedly as the English youngsters boarded the train, making them promise to return. This they did on the condition that he would come to Surrey for the wedding.

Two years went by. Their love for each other deepened. John secured a partnership in a family practice in the picture postcard village of Gosling near Dorking Almost simultaneously Elenora, now a fully qualified Veterinary Surgeon took a position with a well established local practice in the same locale. The marriage was planned for the following spring.

Aunt Dee was in her element, putting herself in charge of the reception, the flowers, the guest list, the invitations, the hiring of the marquee and the million and one things a society wedding entails.

Both Elenora and Johnny harboured slight misgivings about the increasing grandness of the occasion. Afraid the formality of the affair might interfere with the fun, yet unable and unwilling to put a brake on Aunt Dee's enthusiasm.

"Now I understand Ellie dear how much you love modern music," Aunt Dee gingerly broached the delicate subject, "...and by all means after the meal, for dancing, a Jazz type band might be appropriate, but don't you think that during the meal we might hire a respectable..."

"Aunt Dee," Elenora anticipated what was coming, "before you suggest it, the answer is no."

"But darling..."

"No chance Aunt Dee. Definitely Not! No parlour or chamber music!"

"I don't mean anything heavy dear, just something gentle, soothing, tuneful, a light orchestral trio for atmospheric background..."

"Absolutely - NO!" Elenora said with finality. Then out of the blue inspiration burst upon her. **"Yes!** Absolutely - **YES!"** Elenora kissed the surprised Aunt Dee, lifted her up and swung her around in a whirl of delight."You are dead right my old sweetheart!"

"Am I dear? Dead right?"

"...One hundred percent right! How could I have been so wrong, a light orchestral trio! And I know just the musicians to fill the bill."

"You do dear...? Aunt Dee was never quite prepared for one of her nieces bursts of exuberance.

"Have you sent M. Chirac his invitation, and his instructions as to his duties as substitute father of the bride yet?"

"Not yet dear?

"Well when you do ask him if Mesdames Chebrolet, Calvert and Gavin – *"Le Trio Arcadie"* would like to come to the wedding, and bring their instruments. Tell him we'll put them up and pay them top rates. They'll fill the bill perfectly Aunt Dee, perfectly!"

"Do they play light classical.... ? "

"Like you've never heard before, they'll be a sensation! You're a genius, my old love" releasing her characteristic war whoop Elenora left it at that.

From the moment he alighted from the train M. Chirac seemed disorientated and overawed at the thoughts of meeting English gentry face to face.

Having been asked to officiate in such an important role as surrogate father of the bride, Claude Chirac was moved to tears with pride. However nothing could take away the fear that outside of his own safe home territory he would be a heap of insecurity.

At last the big day arrived. In a cloudless sky the unrestricted sun had full access to the beautiful bride as she arrived by horse drawn open carriage The landau, tastefully accoutred fore and aft with small bunches of early wild flowers tied with ribbon catching what little breeze there was fluttered joyously. On arrival at the ancient church, the same girls, who had shared that never to be forgotten holiday in the French Alps were all in high spirited attendance now in the role of bridesmaids.

Heavy with the smell of fresias and jonquils the congregation inside the crowded church, smiled with admiring approval as the dashing bridegroom accompanied by his best man stood to take their places at the business end of the aisle. Also in attendance in the roles of grooms-men and ushers were the same group of young bloods who had witnessed the romantic meeting of the two lovers. All under orders to lavish extra attendance upon the three French ladies, *"The Trio Arcadie"* who preened coquettishly as the handsome tail coated boys escorted them to their seats alongside the cream of the County.

The happy buzz of whispered conversation died down in anticipation as the highly charged moment drew near for the entrance of the Bride on the arm of the extremely nervous old French hotelier.

The bridesmaids lined up ready for the signal to fall in step. The organ faded on the gentle background music. A hush fell over the congregation. One mighty chord from the organ heralded the onset of Mendelssohn's triumphant Wedding March. This sudden crescendo was all it took to put paid to M. Chirac's efforts to keep a grip on his stage fright. He went down in a heavy swoon.

The little church porch was a flurry of taffeta, silks and nets as thirteen pairs of hands all leapt in to resuscitate this most important player in the ceremony. Someone produced smelling salts which had immediate if only temporary results.

"Claude, it's me Ellie. Are you with us darling?"

"Oh, Mon petite, I am so ashamed. I 'ave let you down.."

"Ellie, you are supposed to be halfway down the aisle by now..." one of the Bridesmaids whispered urgently. "Shall I get Charlie to stand in for Claude?"

"No, wouldn't hear of it. Claude will be fine in a minute," she smiled as she cradled the old man's head. "You heard that Claude honey? That was our music cue. Time we went down the aisle, and I'm not going without you. Come on, sweetheart, on your feet." She stood the pale faced Claude back onto his feet, gave him a quick peck on his cheek forced a substantial gulp of brandy down his throat from a hastily produced flask. Then, dabbing away the sweat which threatened to melt the wax in his moustaches, she took him firmly by the arm and set off down the aisle.

So far the bulk of the congregation had no idea the beautiful smiling bride was bodily supporting the light headed Frenchman all the while whispering encouraging words Elenora added, "...not far to go now...nearly there...you'll make it Claude...Smile!" She was mistaken. Clause's legs lost what remaining strength they had and he went down for a second time.

With no more ado, the bride lifted him bodily and carried him the rest of the way down the aisle, sat him gently without fuss on a hastily provided chair, checked to see he was conscious, gave him another peck on his cheek and took her place beside the groom.

The Groom and the Minister, having had the best view of the drama as it unfolded were both unable to subdue the laugh that unless acknowledged and released threatened to cause internal explosions. The humour spread through the entire gathering removing any remaining tension as well as the jelly from M. Chirac's knees. It was probably the happiest wedding there had ever been in the ancient church.

By the time the bride and groom had welcomed the last of their guests to the reception M. Chirac had recovered his composure enough to wander around chatting to the *"gentry"* he had previously so feared. He was even composed enough to mount the podium to announce the *"Arcadie Trio"* in perfect (or near enough) English.

"Mesdames et Messieurs's, or should I say, my Lords, Ladies and Gentlemen, from out of my own country, I am pride to present with a selection of – how you say it in England – Jewels from the shows – *"Le trio Arcadie"* which contains Madame Chevrolet, Madame Calvert et last but least of all – Madame Gavin"

After their usual elaborate display of doffing their surplus feathers and coffee lace and tuning up their instruments they were ready to begin. Eventually the three ladies went into a selection from "Choo *Chin Chow"* blissfully unaware how excruciatingly off key, they were. Scraping away at their instruments happy in the knowledge they had brought a measure of Gallic culture to the proceedings they blissfully sawed away at their instruments until the meal was over and the speeches were about to begin. Most of the guests, unfamiliar with their work, either didn't register the Trio had been so off key they were unable to recognize the tune or didn't care one way or the other. Either way the gathering was completely won over. A warm and prolonged round of applause, all errant notes and mistiming either overlooked or un-noticed made the day perhaps the most warmly remembered in the lives of the three old musicians.

"They were truly charming Ellie," Aunt Dee confided later, "but am I right in thinking they were just occasionally slightly off key?"

"Not so you notice darling." Elenora replied with a straight face.

The afternoon moved on and inevitably pressure was being brought to bear from the younger guests for some livelier entertainments. Aunt Dee thought it not quite proper for the bride to take part in such entertainment. Still the voice of youth demanded some *"red hot jazz"* and even Aunt Dee could not deny such a force for long.

Of course it was no accident that all the girls had brought their instruments along and within seconds of them striking up with their opening number – *"Bill Bailey Won't You Please Come Home"* the real party began. It went on unabated until the small hours when they closed with *"Georgia Camp Meeting"* and the guests departed. The three French ladies, glowing with satisfaction retired, confident they had done their country proud. The bridal couple set off to honeymoon in Scotland leaving Aunt Dee and Claude Chirac to enjoy a final glass of Champagne before turning in.

"It has been a perfect day M. Chirac, don't you think?"

"Perfect, Miss Gowan I did not wish it to end."

"Ah, Monsieur, we have a saying in our country – "all good things must come to an end.""

"We also share that – how you say – homily. Let us drink to the wish that the joy this day has given us may never come to an end"

"Amen to that!" The two friends' clinked glasses smiled wistfully not knowing how prophetic their toast had been. For it was the late spring of 1914.

....

In August of that year John received a commission in the Cavalry. The already crowded train that was to take him away pulled in to the platform at Dorking Station. It was a scene that was being enacted simultaneously in many parts of the country on that warm autumn evening. Strikingly handsome in his new uniform he stooped for one last kiss before boarding. The smoke and steam belching from the engine, together with the flickering gas mantles in the station platform lamps momentarily suggested a dark dream she had once had and until now had never recalled. It passed as soon as it came and yet it cast a chill over Elenora that she would recall until the day she died. Shaking off her bad dream she smiled and looked deep into her husband's violet eyes. A shutter clicked inside her head as she gazed at him and a picture was taken to be permanently stored in her memory.

26

Notification from the War Office was brief. Her husband had died honourably for King, Country and Empire. A posthumous decoration was to be awarded. The telegram offered no apology for the evil insanity of the Warlords who caused this wholesale waste of young lives.

Inconsolable, unable and unwilling to shake off the black despair that held her in its grip Elenora went about her work in the surgery tending the animals as if in a trance. Weeks turned into months, until one January afternoon as the meagre daylight faded suddenly she knew that time was doing nothing to heal her loss and she knew it never would.

The resolve came to her coldly and fully formed. She would be done with contemplating the long years that lay ahead without John by her side. She had the means to hand and certainly had the courage. She would put an end to her unbearable misery. The heavy skies of the winter twilight seemed to strengthen her resolve. Coldly and clinically she opened the drawer and took out the hypodermic syringe.

Was it John's voice she heard or merely the remembrance of some shared joke that held them helpless with laughter? She would never know, but something made her look up from the dreadful task in hand.

Through the window of her surgery she saw gentle snow flakes falling so slowly they hung suspended in the winter air.

In her mind and heart she was being swept irresistibly back to that enchanted evening. That special evening when the snow had so completely covered their embrace and there was no discern-able demarcation line between their two bodies. For how long she watched the falling snow that evening she never could account for in later years, but somehow during this time she began to see a way through the hell she had endured since that telegram arrived. The unbearable weight of her loss mercifully began to lift. Replacing the hypodermic syringe safely in its place in the drawer. Her eyes brimming with tears for the first time since his death she was able to summon the treasured memory of John's dark handsome features smiling optimistically down at her. The following day her life began again.

....

ARNOLD WILKINSON

"Good-morning Miss Clapworthy!" Police Sergeant Arnold Wilkinson's cheerful voice roused Elenora from her trawl through those cherished memories of her past life. The cheery greeting came with a suddenness that might have been an unpleasant jolt had it come from anyone else. But Elenora like most people in the village admired, trusted nay loved Arnold to distraction in spite of the fact that he was the *"Law around here"* - or was it because of it? Women especially could forgive Arnold anything. His great sense of humour, not to mention his Women's Magazine good looks were irresistible to them.

On top of this, his easy-going method of keeping the law was unique unto himself. He would do almost anything to avoid writing out a charge sheet. Arnold believed leniency and kindness got him better results than all the tough armed techniques in the book. Of course this didn't go down well with Chief Inspector Oswald Cartwright who considered such doings as dereliction of duty.

"Arnold!" Elenora, now fully roused from her mental trip into her past, greeted the friendly copper warmly, "you're up and about early aren't you?"

"Well, I just thought I'd go down the hill and see how the old ladies in Stephenson's Fold are coping with last nights snow fall."

"I thought you were off duty on Sunday?"

29

"I am," Arnold answered, "Archie minds the shop on Sunday as a rule."

"So how come you're not still in bed?"

"Oh, me life wouldn't be worth living if I didn't call in on 'em, to check if they're all still alive and kicking."

"You mean you do courtesy calls out of love not duty...on your day off? You're just a big softie aren't you Sergeant Wilkinson." Elenora said with a teasing smile, "Are you sure you're tough enough for the job of law enforcer?"

"Well...I won't say anything if you don't." Arnold replied, flashing a cheeky smile back over his shoulder as he carried on down the steep snow covered mountain side to the ancient cottages of Stephenson's Fold. Arnold had to admit if only to himself, that Miss Clapworthy was dead right about him.

Having a chronic aversion to charging miscreants was a definite drawback to his career as police officer in charge of Craggs Bottom's main and only sub station. Not that he intended changing his ways or lose a minute's sleep, for he knew he was in no way lax in keeping the peace, even though his methods often meant bending the law to force it. For instance, if things got out of hand at chucking out time at the "Feathers" Arnold was not averse to kicking a few arses and chucking the offender in the cell to sleep it off. But arrest them? Oh, come on! It made much more sense to him to see the old folks were warm and secure and their blackout curtains were in place than to wait until they had a light showing and then slap a fine on them. Or call round to check that old Harry Petty hadn't nodded off in his outside khazi during the cold weather which was his habit whilst in his cups. And surely a blind eye was in order if somebody could wangle a bob's worth of under the counter offal now and then? There was the time when Arnold saved Ada Clough's dress making business by directing a bit of mysteriously acquired parachute silk her way. His unconventional methods even extended to taking on the role of a Chicago hit man to put the shits up the local SPIV - Arthur (Slimy) Slickey for trying to pull a nasty little extortion scam on one of the old age pensioners. I mean, come on – the only one who ever suffered was Chief Superintendent Cartwright whose nerves rattled a bit whenever he paid one of his infrequent visits to chastise Arnold on the pitiful amount of arrests on the Craggs Bottom's Substation's weekly charge sheet! Odd   policing perhaps, but come on – nobody _nice_ ever suffered. Not if Arnold Wilkinson had anything to do with it. But it wasn't only the lack of notches on Arnold's gun that worried head office. There was the casual homeliness of the little Cop Shop itself. More like a social drop in centre than a place of hard justice. The fact that the substation, requisitioned at the outbreak of war, was in one of the pretty little cottages on Primrose Row. That didn't do anything to toughen the image either. The two holding cells, (originally the bedrooms) rarely housed any prisoners and still had the floral wallpaper and chintz curtains they had before old Mrs Bellamy, the previous occupant, had died. Arnold couldn't bring himself to change them. It would have been an insult to the old girls memory.

The handsome good natured flatfoot was no fool though and fully aware that were it not for the shortage of manpower due to the call up, he would have been given the elbow long ago – and the community would have been much the worse for it. Why then with all these qualities in his favour and his pick of the eligible Craggs bottom maidens was he not blissfully conjoined?

Minnie Clegg who had been present at his birth and cared for him like a sort of belligerent mother since his own parents _"passed over"_ knew the answer to that one. It was because the beautiful young widow and now chief barmaid at the "Feathers",Sally Hancock filled Arnold's heart and soul every waking moment, and gave him even less peace in his dreams. Sadly all Arnold's longing and dreaming of a future with Sally went for nothing, since she still pined desperately for her dead husband. Which was why she had packed in her lucrative job in the office at Townsend's Textiles, on Minnie's advice to take the barmaid job, in order to meet folk and *"bring her out of herself"* Even if Arnold were to have had the courage to plight his troth, which he most certainly didn't, he believed his declaration of the truest kind of love would have fallen on deaf ears.

"Arnold lad, tha'll have to make a move soon," Minnie declared without pulling her punches, "...else some other bugger' ll snap her up."

"Aye well, I'll have to take my chances on that happening, won't I Minnie?"

"Don't thee think it won't happen norther," Minnie replied, getting agitated, "she won't keep on turning yon Yankee lads down forever, and they'll not stop pestering – asking her." Arnold leapt upon the word,

"Pestering? How do you mean Minnie, do they pester her?"

"Now then, keep your flannel shirt on – I didn't mean *bothering* her..." Minnie came back like lightening in defence of the GI's. "...no nothing, like that. Most on 'em is politeness itself, proper gentlemen. Make no mistake I don't mind telling you, if I were forty years – twenty - years younger, they could pester me to their hearts content!" Minnie screamed with laughter at her own outrageousness giving the police sergeant a playful prod with her elbow.

"Minnie Clegg, if tha' were forty – twenty – years younger, I Might even pester thee me self." Arnold loved these moments of banter with his beloved old adversary.

"Is that right? An' if tha' had forty – twenty – times more brass in the bank I might welcome thy attention. Now take notice of what I tell thee – make a move with Sally else tha'll be too late. Besides, it's gone way beyond the time that lass had a lovely fellow in her life. And in spite of the fact that sometimes I feel fit to strangle thee, you Arnold Wilkinson are namely, the said lovely fellow! So make a move!"

Arnold of course, did not make a move on Sally and Minnie did not stop badgering him to do so.

....

BIG NELLIE

Alf Ryan, a master French Polisher for Hopkinson's Quality Household Furniture had hoped the depression of the earlier part of the 1930's would pass them by but that was not to be. Along with Gordon Watson and Desmond Mundy he was finally handed his cards, the three of them having held on to their jobs longer than most in that late summer of 1937.

Hopkinson's had always valued Alfred as a master of his trade and were reluctant to let him go but, *"when money gets tight Alfred lad, folk can always manage without a beautifully polished sideboard"*. Alfred knew this and there were no hard feelings. He knew that when things began to look up he would be welcomed back. In the meantime the three men had heard there was work to be had in the ship building trade in the race to win the Blue Riband of the Atlantic run.

"Well Alf, if it means either going to Liverpool to find a job or sticking around here and going on Public Assistance I don't see as how you have much choice..." Rosie Ryan's voice remained steady having expected something like this for the past few weeks. "When will you go?" She asked, looking anywhere but directly into her husband's eyes.

"Tomorrow morning."

"How will you get to Liverpool?" Rosie asked holding her anxiety in check for fear she made the situation worse for her husband.

"We'll get a lift in a truck," Alfred said, trying without much success to hide the trepidation in his own voice. "...Desmond knows a driver who goes that way every week"

"I'll make you some sandwiches." Rosie sliced through the flat cake she had baked that morning. Not a cake at all really, but a loaf of soda bread rolled out flat, spread with dripping and sprinkled with salt and pepper. Stuffing it into his tin lunch box she put it on the window sill where she left his "*jock*" every evening for him to pick up the following morning as he left for work. Only tomorrow was to be no ordinary morning. He would be gone for God knows how long to some strange part of the country with no certainty of work at the other end of his journey.

"You'd better take this ten bob," she said reaching for the tea caddy on the mantelpiece, in which she kept the house keeping money. "and drop us a postcard whenever you can."

"I will, you know I will," he said, hiding his face, "...and hopefully by next weekend there'll be a bit of brass in an envelope."

With three children to feed and only her cleaning money and whatever the kids could bring in through running errands and selling firewood, Rosie could just about manage to make ends meet. That was before Alfred got laid off. Now the strain was really on. It was going to be tough but applying to the Panel for Public Assistance was out of the question. Rosie was of proud stock and loathed the thoughts of having "*handouts from anyone*".

From Liverpool the three men moved north to Barrow in Furness then to Glasgow where they had heard that work was to be had. Three weekends passed and Rosie received the odd postcard from Alfred during that time, each one progressively losing hope of ever finding work, but no *"envelope"* arrived. Rosie gathered her three little boys around her to explain the lie of the land,

"Now you know your Dad's off looking for work and it won't be long before he gets fixed up and we will get some money in the post, but in the meantime the rent has to be paid," Rosie kept any uncertainty and fear she was feeling well out of her announcement.

"So you see boys, I will have to get another job, happen charring, seeing as there isn't much going in the mills these days.

Still I've done it before and there's no problem there. Together with that and taking in more washing we should make enough to pay the rent. That's the essential thing, the rent – that must be our main priority."

"Then Mick, with you running errands and hawking your kindling, we will have enough to feed ourselves and if there's any spare cash we can send your Dad a bob or two until he gets a job. But if you can think of anything else that might earn us a bob or two it would be grand. What do you think?"

Mick going on eight years of age knew things were not quite as his Mam said, he suspected desperation was closer to the surface, but his younger brothers, Terry at six, and little Danny at five years of age were too young to realise the full gravity of their situation.

Mick was only too aware their mothers religious pride would not allow them to be beholden to anybody, least of all would she allow them to beg. Already he held down three errand jobs and one paper round, not to mention the small income from his firewood customers.

The middle brother Terry had a tidy little earner. Seeing he was a way above average reader for his age he would collect the library books for a pair of old maiden ladies with fading eyesight, then sit and read the books to them. Of course this sort of diligence Rosie heartily approved. This was money honourably acquired – but hand-outs? Never!

Long before his Dad had been laid off and times were comparatively good, Mick had been aware that his little brother Danny had film - star looks and a certain magical charm that reduced women to pulp, especially older women. Could there be some way to harness this gift that might earn a bit extra? After all, Mick had seen with his own eyes how mature ladies behaved when they beheld his little brother. They would *"Oooooh!"* and *"Aaah"!* They would sigh and gurn. They would search for words of endearment they would never dream of bestowing on their own kith and kin, but little Danny Ryan? "Ah, little Danny's smile melted the hardest heart, forced roses to bloom through a blizzard and rhubarb to ripen in November..."

A sample encounter went something like this in Mick's imagined scenario...

"...whenever did tha' see such a bonny little lad?Mrs Armistead" the first matron would bleat, almost in a swoon.

"...nay Mrs Rawson, it should be agen' the law for any lad to be so lovely! There's no other word for it – he's an Angel!

"...he is - a proper Angel, straight from off the ceiling of the cistern Chapel."

Mick's exciting dream to exploit Danny's beauty was that when all these accolades were showered upon his younger brother Danny the infant himself was to utter not a word. This, Mick felt, enhanced the cherubim's

37

attraction. The little boy merely smiled ever more beguilingly, the dimples in his cheeks sending the matrons into even deeper raptures, prompting them to delve into the deepest corners of their purses to find a few coppers or a three penny bit as a gift; an offering to the little Heavenly creature, who would then, (following Mick's instructions) slowly but even more bewitchingly shake his head in what looked like a charming refusal. Mick would then supply an answer.

"Our Mam say's he isn't allowed to take charity,"

"Oh, God love his little cotton socks." The Matron would say (or words carrying a similar apologetic tone) "It isn't charity doy; it's just a little treat, a present for being so damned gorgeous! Do let him have it"

"Oh, all right then" Mick would concede allowing the offering to be made, satisfied there wasn't any suggestion of alms, or begging entering into the transaction. All this of course was but yet an imagined outcome. The reality had yet to be proved.

Saturday nights when closing the shop for the weekend Mrs Driver the greengrocer's wife would gather together all the fruit and vegetables that were past their best and give them to whoever hung about - and there was always a good crowd hoping for such a bounty. Mick made sure that Danny, oozing charm fit to break his face was prominent in the crowd.

"Laddie, ask thy Mammy if she would be good enough to take these bits and pieces off me hands and make use of them. I can't abide chucking 'em out. Waste is a sin." Mrs Driver pleaded. With no defence against Danny's all conquering enchantment she would bestow her gifts on him alone with a pat on the cheek, and an adoring sigh, then add, "… hold on a minute sweetheart, here's a copper or two for thi'sen". Mick of course, would convince his mother she was doing the kind greengrocer's wife a favour. Content the fine line his Mam toed in regard to charity remained intact he continued to perfect his methods of increasing their income.

Due to these little leg-ups the Ryan's managed to stay afloat, but only just. The rent, being the main item was covered, leaving little over for food and running repairs, plus that increasingly vital bob or two to send to their father. Mick, always with an eye wide open for the main chance began formulating another plan in his head, a bold one, but certainly not by any means a dishonest one, for that was never an option in the Ryan family's book. It did veer dangerously close to what his mother rated as equally unacceptable – that ever present bogeyman – charity! But Mick intended stepping up the exploitation of his baby brother's obvious charms to further their financial advantage.

To this end the boys increased their workload, especially on Friday and Saturday evenings when the main street of the village thronged with shoppers all *"buying in"*. Seeking bargains from the traders before they closed their businesses for the weekend.

Mick would spot a likely lady with her shopping bags full and sidle up with his bogey cart – a soap box mounted on a set of old pram wheels,

"Nah then Mrs Barraclough, you'll need a help with your bags?" Mick would offer, "...for three pence we'll even unload 'em for you once we get you home?"

If Mrs Barraclough turned out to be a bit of a tight wad and declined their offer, that's when Danny was brought in. His task was to charm the lady into submission. He would stand with his head slightly on one side, look shyly into his victim's eyes, turn on his smile and she would (most times) be a gonner. There would usually be an extra bonus of a copper or two for the smiling cherub. The scheme was increasingly successful as the weeks went by, and their takings helped swell the Postal Order Flossie was able to send off to her husband as he sought work in some strange town in Scotland.

There was however one source of earnings in the village Mick had not yet managed to tap into. Until now the leading lady of this proposed enterprise was a very unlikely subject. She was suspected of having no sense of beauty, no kindness, no feelings in fact no heart at all therefore a waste of Danny's charms. If the boys were able to win her over it would be a true masterstroke. After all she was the notorious – Big Nellie Fawcett! An amazon, a female Genghis Kahn, a terrifying creature from everyone's worst nightmares.

Standing almost six feet tall, as broad across her shoulders as the biggest wool bail humper in the West Riding, Nellie had, according to the description attributed to her from the men in the tap room at the *"Feathers"* *"...a bottom as big as the Titanic's boiler"* (This group of "Tap-room Lawyers" held a definitive opinion on all the women in the village, if not the Universe).

It has to be said however their unkind description of Nellie was pretty accurate. Over a pair of rolled down knitted stockings Nellie wore a pair of size ten, broad fitting studded working boots – *"like a pair of reinforced fiddle cases"* (the *"taproom lawyers"* again.) Her constant threats of death aimed at almost everyone deserving or not came from the depths of the roughest voice box imaginable, Her gin blossomed large blue veined nose was said to be the result of some advice she got in mythical times when she was a trainee Gorgon *"...Nellie, you want a cure for your red nose? - Drink till its blue -* which may, or may not have alluded to her gargantuan intake of mother's ruin

If at first sight Big Nellie's physical appearance drained the breath from one's lungs, that was merely the start. Once the vision was allied to her frighteningly belligerent attitude, the experience was something from an "H" (*for Horror*) Certificate by the Board of Film Censors. The last word on Nellie's effect on the locals was this oft repeated joke originally told by a club comic to a drunken Saturday night audience, "...*Nellie Fawcett complained there was a rapist sex maniac persistently banging on her bedroom door. In the end she had to get up and let him out.*" A hardly likely scenario to have any basis in truth, as it was hard to envisage any sex maniac brave enough to try anything on with Big Nellie.

The astonishing thing was, in spite of the above description being accurate, Nellie turned out the most unbelievably delicious, delicate, light, home baked bread, pastries cakes and delicacies the world has ever known. Her Victoria sponges, ginger parkin, Simnel and Banbury Cakes left folks speechless with admiration. Her Angel Cake was truly aptly named, the icing and delicate piping on her Birthday and Wedding Cakes were way outside even the posh folk of Undercliffe's frame of reference, as Nellie's order books lay witness to – always chock full! That there was a permanent demand for her products was testament to the queue that formed to clear her shelves every Friday night. This almost fevered adoration for her works of confectionery art from her tiny home bakery belied the fact that the lady herself was far from the delicate, fragile creature one would have supposed from her output.

Every Friday night in Nellie's little front yard crowds would gather enticed by the glorious aroma of baked bread. Creating a buzz of excitement akin to a Broadway opening night. After the last batch of golden crusted loaves were laid out to cool on the trestle tables and covered by immaculately laundered tea towels outside her tiny cottage, she would put the final sprinkling of icing sugar over the fruit pies. Casting a critical eye over the magnificent array of exquisite creations of confectionery which covered every shelf and surface of the interior of her cottage. Finally she would take a deep swig of gin from the half bottle she kept in her vast apron pocket. Then came that magic moment when the aroma of her exquisite creations had lured the queue into an aching nostalgia for a time when everyone was young and the whole world smelled of newly baked bread. After that, and only when she was ready, Nellie would glower belligerently upon her admirers - shattering their dreams of a Utopia that never was by berating them unmercifully for no reason at all.

"You'd better all have the right change," her menacing growl making even the toughest man quake, **"I'll not be bothered with anyone who hasn't the sense to have the right change...and form a decent queue, and be quiet!"** When she was satisfied everyone was locked in a terrified gloom, Nellie would begin to serve them. Deftly she would wrap the gorgeous bread in frothy white tissue paper. Place the fancy cakes and more delicate confectionery carefully and lovingly into stiff paper cartons to keep them perfect in transit. The transactions would take place in terrified silence with only the occasional grunt of disapproval from Nellie when someone would be foolish enough to offer a nicety about the weather. A spontaneous remark on the sheer beauty of one of her products would illicit a mouthful of invective that would make the recipient squirm and hurry off with their purchase to the safety of their home.

"What do you mean me meringues are exquisite?" She'd explode, **"course they're bloody exquisite. I don't make owt that's not bloody exquisite."**

"Sorry, I just meant to say..."

"Well don't! Keep your opinions to yourself."
Then addressing the queue, **"and if any of you lot have owt to say, wait till you bloody well get home to say it! Next!**

Many of them would of course, have forgotten Nellie's belligerence by the following week and return for much of the same treatment.

But there were some folk Mick knew, still smarting from the roasting she had given them, and didn't want to forget their grievance. Of course they could have forgone patronising Nellie altogether, but that was never a consideration. These were the potential customers Mick wished to cultivate.

If only he could offer a *"shopping service"* for the more timid or thinly skinned customer, someone who would dearly love to avoid that weekly tongue lashing from Nellie. With hope in his heart he and Danny hung around Nellie's yard until the queue began to ease off.

"What do you young tykes think you're up to?" Nellie bellowed, **"Hanging about with that bogey cart?"** Mick wondered if it would be politically in order to tell her the truth, after all it would be no skin off her nose if he touted for custom from her customers once she had finished with them. On second thoughts he figured it wiser not to.

"We was just waiting to be served." Mick answered.

"Well get at the end of the damned queue then, and wait your turn." Nellie bellowed.

Mick did exactly that whilst he tried to decide whether or not to expand on his new idea and offer his delivery service to Nellie herself. Or would that be tempting the fury of the Underworld to which Nellie surely belonged? Better not. Not yet anyway - too dangerous!

Mick hustled his little brother forward in the queue to face the fray.

"Turn the full charm on Danny," he whispered, "this is your toughest one yet." Danny knew exactly what was required of him. He began to radiate enough charm to melt the Arctic ice cap.

"Right then come on you lot," Nellie looked disgustedly straight at Mick, completely ignoring Danny who was working overtime on his technique d' allure, **"come on, I haven't no time to waste on you lot. What do you want?"**

"I wondered if you had any broken buns...er...damaged cakes or anything going cheap, seeing as its nearly closing time..." The shocked silence that followed this outrageous violation, as she saw it was worse than the fall of Man. It didn't last quite as long though. Nellie soon found a voice.

"I do **NOT** have as a rule, any *"broken buns"* or *"damaged cakes"* nor do I ever have anything *"going cheap!" Is that clear?"* Another death filled pause, then she added, **"How much brass have you got? I don't run a charity"**

"We're not asking for charity." Mick answered courageously, "We have some money."

Hastily counting the coppers in his hand, "Five pence" He answered. Then to forestall the next tirade he added, "...our Danny has four pence that's nine pence altogether."

"Nine pence?" she snarled, **"What do you expect to get for nine pence? And what's this little 'un grinning at?** She asked, completely immune to Danny's razzle-dazzle."

"He isn't grinning Mrs Fawcett, he's only smiling at you, friendly like."

"Well tell him not to."

44

"He can't help it." Mick answered, becoming annoyed, "It's just his way. Don't you get nasty with my little brother, If you don't want our custom, say so and we'll be off"

"...CUSTOM? *YOUR* CUSTOM?!" She exploded, "**DO YOU THINK I NEED YOUR CUSTOM –** *NINE PENCE?* **DO YOU THINK I'D GO BANKRUPT OVER** *NINEPENCE...?*

Fearing he'd unlocked the gates of hell Mick began to steer Danny out of danger. When they reached the top of the yard an almighty bellow from Nellie stopped them in their tracks.

"Hold on you little tykes! Did you or did you not ask for nine penn'orth of my goods?"

The reply to this demand sent everyone into a deep trauma. From whom it came was an even deeper shock. For the voice that shattered belief belonged to none other than Danny Ryan! Yes, (**yes Danny!)** the beautiful cherubim answered - clear as a bell...

"Nellie, You know where you can stick your... " It would be indecent, if not illegal to reveal the rest of the reply.

The stunned silence was obliterated by an even bigger shock – a spontaneous, awesomely jolly burst of heavy metallic laughter from the depths of Big Nellie Fawcett herself. – Laughter that had been locked away since the Dark Ages, now finally set free. Years later when this story had matured into folklore people swore blind that Danny's outspoken resistance to the tyrant stopped traffic on the main road as far away as Baildon.

The boys got their nine pennyworth's of confectionery and a lot more besides, and Nellie refused to take their money. Mick got lots of new clients that night. Also the promise from Nellie that he could deliver the weekend orders for the detached houses up Buckingham Avenue.

It would be nice to be able to say that beautiful little Danny's advice to *"...stick her goods etc."* had given Nellie the ability to laugh again, transforming the monster into a benign gentle soul. But everyone knew in their hearts that would have been an unnatural outcome. Nellie continues to audibly beat up anyone who hasn't the balls to fight back – but, as she learned that fateful Friday night, that most certainly does **not** include little Danny Ryan.

....

WASHDAY BLUES

It was a dreary, dreary Monday morning.

By tradition Monday was the only permissible day for decent folk to do laundry but the Ryan's did not come into that category, it was wash day every day at their house seeing as Rosie Ryan took in washing to keep the wolf from the door. Setting light to the gas ring under the big iron saucepan she made steaming helpings of porridge for her three boys. Looking out of the window, the sky hung heavy and threatening. There was no point in stringing the clothesline across the Fold, even if the weather were to "take up" there was little chance of it being a "good drying day". Resignedly she brought inside the bundles of dirty washing that had been left on the doorstep by her clients.

It was the school holidays and grossly unfair of the skies to open up and rain on the holidays but life is like that and it started to come down in torrents. The three boys' disappointment was really no worse than their Mam's for she relied on Mickie, to take the younger ones, Danny and Terry out from under her feet in order to enable her to tackle the mountain of washing she took in to supplement the housekeeping.

"Come on boys!" she called up to them, "come and get your breakfast. "You're not going to be able to go out

47

to day it's starting to teem down. Looks like its set in for the day." Since the entire living space in the little cottage would be filled with clothes lines full of wet sheets there would be no place for them to play. The only solution was for her to let them join her in the wash scullery and allot them various tasks.

One might be forgiven for thinking this would have been a cause for rebellion on the part of three young boys but the Ryan's were well used to doing jobs to keep the family afloat. What is more, due to Rosie's kind nature and sense of fun those tasks were carried out with a good heart and no dissent or at least, very little.

Half an hour later, washed, dressed and fed found Mick winding the mangle, Terry manning the posser, (a sort of cone on the end of pole which caused a suction when it pounded into the wet clothes), Danny the youngest boy helping Mam fold the sheets ready for the mangle, but mostly keeping them all entertained with his latest burst of his own unique brand of the English language.

Danny had learned to talk very early and at five years of age was highly articulate, even if his rules of grammar and syntax were known only unto himself. There were some who thought his grasp of English bizarre, not their Mam of course or his teacher Miss Bishop. Never the less when Mam called at the infant's school to discuss Danny's end of term report she broached the subject of his peculiar turn of phrase.

"Oh that," Miss Bishop smiled, "nothing to worry about there Mrs Ryan."

"Well it doesn't worry me so much as wonder where he got it from." Mam answered, "It isn't that we can't understand him either, but some of the things he comes out with -- "Famishlicated" when he's hungry and "unhungrified" when he's had enough. He saw me unpacking Mrs Raistrick's laundry and he remarked how "bigly-bummed" and "Titanic-ally--titted" she must be to wear such "colossal combinational's"

"Oh, but that's wonderful Mrs Ryan," laughing heartily Miss Bishop replied. "Enjoy it while it lasts my dear. He loves words, never has his nose out of the Dictionary, and even if he gets it wrong he's merely trying out words that are new to him, and I wouldn't be surprised if he isn't aware of how entertaining his inventions are. Besides he's in good company; when Mark Twain was a young boy and asked to spell "Mississippi" he replied that he knew how to spell it, he just didn't know when to stop."

It was nice for Rosie to get confirmation that her youngest son was on the right track linguistically. But it has to be said Miss Bishop was biased in his favour. Along with most of the female population of Craggs Bottom who thought Danny so beautiful they would have forgiven him anything short of mass murder.

"In any case," Miss Bishop said as she and Rosie parted company, "he was dead right about Mrs Raistrick's build, I couldn't have put it better myself."

Back to that wet Monday morning when they were well into their chores. Mick was the one who started the discussion.

"How often should you change the bedclothes Mam?" he asked, prompted by the heavy weight when wet of the expensive bedding belonging to Mrs Dracup who he figured that to be able afford such quality sheets Mrs Dracup must not be short of a bob or two.

"As often as it needs changing..." his Mam replied, as she loaded another shovel full of coke into the furnace under the copper boiler

"Yeah, but how often is that?"

49

"Every week," Mam answered decisively as she turned her attention to energetically beating the grime out of Mr Dracup's flannel Union shirt.

"If I had my way," Terry, the middle brother known for being too fastidious for his own good, answered, "I'd have clean sheets every night."

"You wouldn't if you had to wash 'em yourself." His Mam answered, "What about you Danny, How often would you change your sheets?"

"If I had my way I'd never change em!" Danny answered emphatically.

"Wouldn't you Danny!" Mam asked. "You wouldn't ever change your bedding?"

"No! Not ever." Danny sang out with conviction, "I wouldn't wash anything, especially bedclothes-es, sock-es, handkerchiefses and the back of my neck. I hate to abolutionise my neck."

"Wouldn't you wash your neck Danny love?" Mam asked gently. But I love you when you're all scrubbed clean and bonny"

"Does that mean you don't love me when I'm mucky?"

"Course not ..."

"There you are then! What's the point in washing my neck?"

"But you love it when I put you in this tub every night, up to your chin in hot water,"

"Oh yeah, but that's different! I get slopperific when I'm in the tub."

"Don't you mean soporific?" Mick corrected,

"No - slopperific!" Danny insists, "I come over all sloppy like as if my joints have all got loosenified and my muscles were melterating. So I never think about washing the back of my neck. Why should I? No-body ever sees it but me Mam."

"But I wash your neck when you are in the tub and you don't mind. In fact you love it." Rosie replied.

"Ah yeah, but when you do I'm too luxurianated to notice."

"Luxurianated? What does that mean?"

"It means I'm overcome with weakliness... sleepy and dozy with soakating in the hot water."

"You're not too dozy to have a pee in the tub though are you?" Mick asks.

"Oh no, course not! I have to have a little pee! That's all part of the luxurianisation..."

Disgustedly Terry springs to life. "...In the water...? "You mean to say you pee when you're in the tub?"

"'Course, doesn't everybody?

"No they don't! Do you realise I have to follow you into the tub and Mick has to follow me?"

"Alright boys, that's enough." Rosie said, trying in vain to hide her smile, "Remember there's a lady present." Rosie was right. There was a sudden urgency to get the conversation away from what happens in the privacy of the tub and buckle down to getting through Mrs Dracup's laundry.

Work done for the day, Rosie fed the boys rolled out the same Peggy tub that had done such sterling work throughout the day, and placed it in front of the fire. Filled almost to the brim with hot water, she threw in a generous handful of Lux Soap Flakes. One after the other, in order of age, youngest first, the boys willingly jumped through the gorgeous foam into the hot water. After the loofah had done its brutal but effective worst on necks and knees she would allow the boys to luxurianate until their eyelids were too heavy to bear. It was truly the most glorious, cherished part of their day.

After a brisk rub down with well boiled Hessian towelling they were willingly tucked up in bed. No sooner had his head hit the pillow than Danny was well on his journey to the land of Word-ology-fication. As Mick was about to sink into oblivion Mam came to tuck them in. The last thing he heard before he dropped off was Terry whisper in his mother's ear.

"Mam, I have a confession to make…"

"Shhh! if it's what I think you did and you did it in the tub – you're forgiven…"

"…but Mam…

"..its alright Terry love, I don't need to know the details. That would be what our Tony would call *"Too much informational-isation."* Shhh! Go to sleep now love."

. . . .

THE PRIDE OF OUR ALLEY

Old men sitting on the bench outside the Wesley Chapel discussing the state of the world stopped mid sentence, painfully engaging their core muscles in order to sit up just that little bit taller whenever young Sally Lodge walked by. Old women sighed, plundering their own distant, often false memories to dredge up a picture from their own prime when they too had some of Sally's radiance. Young mill girls, especially those prone to bitchiness tried hard but couldn't find a wrong thing to say about her. All they were left with was to try to emulate her – smile like her – walk, talk like her. Be her.

By the time she was coming up to fourteen years old the local lads, hair slicked back with large dollops of Yardley's Brilliantine, their Sunday boots buffed to an impossible shine prowled, paced and lolled hopelessly. Waiting in front of the bleak orphanage where she had been raised since infancy hoping for the merest glance in their direction. A waste of their time, Sally had eyes for only one boy. If Billy Hancock was aware of his phenomenal good fortune in being Sally's chosen one, there was no conceit, no edge to him. For he knew no other love, and it wasn't optional, he had no say in the matter.

From the age of five when he was sent to the Lodge - The Craggs Bottom home for Destitute Children, Sally and he gravitated towards each other. There had never been a time in his memory when she had not been his main reason for living.

In the first half of the twentieth century for the majority of the male population of Craggs Bottom the most life offered was fifty odd years service with Townsend's Textiles - with time out to fight the Establishment's pointless wars. After which, providing they didn't snuff it in the meantime, they might be spared a couple of years growing rhubarb and spuds or perhaps try for a prize chrysanthemum in the allotments annual competition before Samuel Hogg the Co-op undertaker, committed their remains to the heavy soil of Clayton Depths Cemetery.

If this was all the village kids could expect out of life there was an even narrower window of opportunity for the boys and girls from the orphanage. For these unfortunates, on reaching their fourteenth birthday, a job would be found appropriate to their achieved educational level, which in most cases was very basic. Providing they had not already fallen foul of the law, they were considered adult enough to face the world under their own steam. In other words they were given the heave-oh from the only home most of them had ever known and sent out into the world to live in approved digs under the often cold impersonal eye of the Magistrate's Bench. On reaching the age of sixteen the bureaucratic umbilical was finally severed. Now considered responsible adults they had to make their way as best they could. Having been strictly disciplined by the many rules and regulations of the orphanage they usually emerged at the age of fourteen well mannered and subservient. Institutionalized! Ideal mill fodder!

Mr Herbert Townsend the mill owner saw these kids as a double bonus *(a.*By giving employment to these *"unfortunates"* he felt it made him look like a magnanimous benefactor, which he most certainly was **not.** *(b.* They would remain longer in the menial posts (on the lowest pay) far longer than the village kids from the Housing estate. On both counts be was often misled for he did not take into account that not all the Magistrates on the bench were like his wife. There were some, like Elenora Clapworthy who kept a kindly eye on these vulnerable juveniles. Likewise, once the kids arrived on the shop floor the over lookers and some of the old hands guided any promising kid in the right direction - towards betterment and the knowledge there was a life to be had beyond the mill walls. At fourteen years and two days Billy reached this milestone in his life and took a room at Mrs Firth's, a clean but impersonal boarding house at the top of the village. To be joined by Sally the following year when she reached the age of fourteen – separate rooms of course. Hers was in the attic above Billy's, small but perfectly adequate box room. Not that it mattered how modest the room was. They had each other, what more could they wish for?

Sally Lodge and Billy Hancock were especially dear to Elenora Clapworthy, who in her role as occasional Magistrate had intervened in their favour against the more mean minded members of the bench; like the detestable mill owner's wife Mrs Townsend who wanted to separate the pair when they first left the orphanage as teenagers. She insisted Billy take lodgings separate from Sally. Miss Clapworthy's reply was swift and devastating...

"...Please madam chairman, do not include me in your unkind assessment of the young persons in question. Personally I can only imagine this particular young couple being a great strength to each other, unlike

your proposal *seemingly only able to see the worst outcome."* Elenora's motion was delivered with such rightful disgust. It was seconded and immediately entered into the minutes of the meeting. To substantiate her case for the defence Elenora also called upon Sergeant Wilkinson, Mrs Firth the kid's landlady and other kind hearted villagers to vouch for the youngsters, thereby shooting down the evil minded Mrs Townsend into the bargain. End of debate.

From that day forth Sally and Billy found, not one but two guardian angels. Elenora was one, the other just as formidable was Leah Stead. Said to be the one of the oldest inhabitants in Craggs Bottom.

Leah had no intentions of allowing the usual pattern expected from the ex-inmates of the Lodge to be foisted upon Billy and Sally. Once under her tough old wing, Leah put it into their heads that it was alright - **more than alright**, to want to make something of their lives – education, or as she put it…

"H'edication! Tha' must let **h'edication'** be thy driving motive. Both on yer! Not just thee Billy, thee an' all Sally lass!" On Leah's advice, or was it a command? They both enrolled for evening classes diligently applying themselves plus any odd moment they could for study during lunch break or before lights out. Sunday afternoons, weather permitting were left free for *"walking out"* usually across the fields below the village to the Cragg before returning to Leah's tiny cottage for tea.

On the Monday morning it would start all over again, but for the two of them it was not the dull routine it might have been had they not had the drive to stick to the programme they set themselves. Although neither of them looked for approval or encouragement, having never had that luxury as children in the Lodge, it was nice to get it and Leah Stead supplied it in abundance. Every Sunday over tea she would demand they give her a progress report .

For most people in the West Riding The Cragg was a popular beauty spot. For some a holy place. For some the Cragg was a place of solace. For those in despair it was a place to end it all. But for courting couples it was created by Mother Nature for romance. It was here Billy and his sweetheart had played together as children. Here they had fallen in love, and here they had first consummated that love.

They would sit, their feet dangling over the edge of the chasm, looking over the grimy city in the middle distance and beyond to the moors, dreaming the same dream lovers have done since time began. Then with a good heart they would start their crowded weekly routine all over again on the Monday morning, Billy at six a.m. in the engine room of the mill, Sally at nine a.m. in the office.

Their application and industry soon began to pay off. By the time Billy was eighteen he was put in charge of maintenance. This kick upstairs, defied the strict pecking order set by Mr Townsend the Mill owner was soundly defended by Len Gateley the works manager.

Len had enough clout, due to his intimate and exclusive knowledge of the ancient machinery to over ride his boss and give the promotion to Billy strictly on ability and not favouritism. Billy took to his new status eagerly with good grace.

For Billy - like Sally - was also *"made of the right stuff – that lass'll get on, thee mark my words"*, Leah repeated often enough to anyone who showed interest. Sally's abilities were quickly recognised in the workplace and in spite of reluctance on the part of Herbert Townsend it wasn't long before she was in charge of the typing pool. Sally's popularity was extraordinary. Responsible for the dozen or so typists, most of whom were older than her. None resented her rapid rise in the ranks however; the girls would do anything and work all hours to make her job easier. Quite an achievement in a room full of women brought together from different walks of life and levels of education many of whom were vying to attain a safe civilian post to avoid call up, if the rumours of another war with Germany came to fruition.

The sudden availability of a small rented cottage in Smithy Fold was the catalyst prompting them to set the date for their wedding in the spring of 1938. Two days after Sally's eighteenth birthday. Leah was as excited as the young couple and took it upon herself to scrub the floors, polish the windows and black lead the range until the newly rented cottage sparkled.

The church was full of well wishers all bearing sensible and useful presents for the house, though what the newly-weds were to do with four clothes horses, three fireside companion sets, and a couple of twenty four piece tea services was a problem they decided to put on the back burner for another time. One year later their deep love for each other bore fruit, Billy got a place at Leeds University and Sally became pregnant.

"Of course I'll have to forget all about University now," Billy said with some concern, aware of his responsibilities to his unborn child, "with just one wage and another mouth ..."

"...Oh no, Billy Hancock! You won't forget about university," Sally interrupted, "you'll keep on going and get your degree just the way we planned it".

"But how will we manage on just your wage?" Billy protested.

"Tell me something sweetheart," Sally asked with a tantalising grin, "How do you rate our standard of living for the past year? Since we got married? Have we gone short?"

"Not at all, we have lived like the landed gentry we are!"

"There you are then, proves my point!"

"Yes, but", Billy answered, "That was on *both* our wages combined"

Knowing she was hiding a delicious secret Sally almost danced across the living room to the sideboard where, eyes flashing with mischief she produced from the furthest recess of the drawer a Craggs Bottom Industrial Society share book. She stood before her husband beaming as he scanned the deposit column. Wide-eyed with delight he discovered that since the day they had married Sally had banked all of his pay. Realizing that this meant university was secure Billy whooped like a Republic Studio's Apache, picked up his wife and whirled her around in sheer elation. "I'm beginning to realize what a treasure I got in thee, Sally Hancock!"

"It's just as well," Sally replied alluringly, "seeing the condition you've got me in"

"Oh yeah, there is that. Well then I suppose I'd better do the honourable thing, I suppose I'd better marry thee."

"I think you'd better…oh, come to think of it, you already did…"

"Did what…?" he asked dreamily, their embrace reaching a higher level of intensity as she began to melt in his arms.

"…marry me!"

"So I did. That was a smart move on my part," he said, as they headed for the stairs to the tiny bedroom. "Ah, the landed gentry have nothing on us this night kid," he whispered as, shutting out the rest of the world, he gently closed the bedroom door.

The next two years flew by. The hard slog of work and study was, for both of them no more than a pleasurable routine. After the graduation ceremony Billy had a formal photograph taken at Jerome's Photographers in his mortar board and gown, proudly brandishing his newly won degree. They then had a picture less formal, with his wife and little son Brandon; another, for framing to stand on Leah's mantelpiece. Finally a happy group picture including friends from work, like Len Gateley and the girls from the typing pool. Elenora Clapworthy, Police Sergeant Arnold Wilkinson, Minnie Clegg and Mrs Firth all posed holding their glasses high toasting Billy's great achievement.

A sunny Saturday afternoon following their visit to the photographer, Sally booked a table for three at the famed Collision's Café on Tyrell Street in Bradford for a celebratory outing. A long established restaurant with the dubious attraction of the Palm Court Trio - three lady musicians who like the Arcadia Trio of a generation earlier, sawed blissfully away on their stringed instruments oblivious to the fact their musical tribute was, like the trio of old, almost unrecognisable. Far from being a turn off and bad for business, Bradfordian's adored them. The collection plate, set prominently on the edge of the podium - almost always overflowing - offered ample testimony to their popularity.

"Now Billy..." Sally said, giggling at the intrusively off key, off tempo music as she poured a second cup of "*fine selection*" tea and got down to the business in hand, "...stop laughing at the orchestra, you'll be old and tone deaf yourself one day - and concentrate! I have an announcement to make. I intend to carry on with on with my studies at home, I've no intention of chucking it in, but university can wait a little longer for me. In any case I want to spend as much time as I can with Brandon whilst he's little."

"It doesn't seem fair on you though," Billy protested, "after all it was your wages that kept us afloat all the time I was at uni..."

"Never mind "fair", we must do what's sensible," Sally went on determinedly, "if, as you say, your degree can get you a good post in the Merchant Navy. You take it."

"The Merchant Navy...?"

"Yes! The way things are going on, if they bring in conscription like they did last time, you won't have the choice much longer. I don't fancy the idea of you digging trenches in the infantry, you're too gorgeous." She said flirting shamelessly with her husband.

"...too gorgeous Daddy..." Brandon put in mischievously, forcing a delighted smile from two old ladies at the next table.

"But Sal, haven't you heard? Mr Chamberlain's straightened it all out with Hitler – appeasement! Peace in our time!"

"I know! We saw him on the newsreel reel didn't we, waving that bit of paper, but we haven't been issued with gas masks and air raid shelters for no reason."

"But the Merchant Navy Sally..." Billy protested half-heartedly, "what made you dream that up? If I gave it any thought at all, I always pictured myself in the RAF."

"I don't know," Sally offered, "The Merchant Navy just seems safer somehow, not being a fighting service."

"You have done your homework, haven't you?" He smiled and took her hand in his.

"Well, yes I want my man to come back to me safe and sound. Besides I think I'll fancy you in bell-bottoms."

"Merchant Navy personnel don't wear bell-bottoms..."

"I'll fancy you anyway."

On a sudden rush of pride and happiness, Sally leaned across the table, disregarding the fragility of the ageing clientèle's sensibilities, kissed her husband long and lovingly. She then hugged her little boy and tickled him until his squeals of delight threatened apoplexy amongst the aforementioned ladies. Laughing gaily at her own exuberance her eyes met Billy's and she realized that there never would be a moment as full of joy as this one. A moment that seemed more precious than ever now as the threat of war came closer by the day.

Billy was occasionally, but only occasionally, torn between his own desire to join the RAF and Sally's convincing argument that he would be better out of the front line. One thing was certain, he would be called up eventually whichever service he chose. Anyway, the Merchant Navy or the RAF wasn't much of a contest – and how could he deny Sally anything?

After initial training he was to join his first ship at Liverpool the first week in August 1939. The goodbyes were cheerful as Billy boarded the train at Bradford Exchange Station that was to take him first to Liverpool then – who knew where? He guessed that since his departure was from Liverpool, it would be along the usual shipping routes to the America's. That was as much as he knew - as much as anyone knew. Already the world was cowering under a cloak of secrecy.

Due to massive losses of manpower at Dunkirk, conscription accelerated to include all but the very old and physically unfit. Sally could now justifiably take consolation with the thought that Billy was comparatively safe, far from the European theatre of war where most of the danger was. What she hadn't reckoned on was the might of the U-Boats of the German Navy.

The notification, when it came was brief.   Her husband's ship had gone down with all hands.   He was missing, presumed dead. Lost at sea.

To all outward appearances Sally took the unthinkable news stoically.   Friends and neighbours called to offer condolences.   The girls in her charge at the office wept in sympathy and marveled at her superhuman control.

As ever Sergeant Wilkinson was on hand to offer practical help like arranging a memorial service at St John's C.O.E. church.

Len Gateley, Billy's old boss at the mill wept openly. Elenora too, showed special concern, recognizing that Sally's loss even now weeks after the initial shock was much the same as hers had been in that other, earlier war.   Sally received their kind wishes in a quietly dignified but distant dry-eyed manner.

A couple of months into her bereavement and Sally was still running the office efficiently and smoothly as she always had; dropping Brandon off at the junior school and collecting picking him up from the child minder after work.

She kept her little cottage as spotless as she had in the past and, apart from not wanting anyone near her appeared to be picking up the pieces of her life as well and courageously as many other young wives all over the country were doing. Only Leah Stead recognised the devastation deep inside the heart of this young girl she adored.   Yet even Leah wasn't allowed to break through the wall Sally had built between herself and the world. The old lady respected Sally's need to be alone but hoped time, that great healer, would come to the rescue sooner rather than later.

Early November and the nights began to draw in. Bleak winds and rain blew up from the moors and whistled around the mill yard and engine room where Billy had served his apprenticeship. To Sally, the engine room had never been anything but a place of grease, grime and extreme joy, for inside the dirty, coke fume and sulphur smelling confines there had been a light radiating from that shining boy who had been so much a part of her.

The crisis that Leah feared came late one afternoon. It had been necessary for Sally to go across the mill yard to the engine room to ask Len for his weekly time sheet. As she crossed the wet cobblestones of the yard Len came to the door to greet her. Standing in the doorway where Billy had often stood, with the light behind him suddenly, in her mind's eye the older man metamorphosed into Billy. This was not the first time this phenomenon had happened since the notification of Billy's death. She would see his likeness in the most unlikely people; always his imagined image would be smiling and radiating love. Not this time. Now he appeared infinitely sad and almost accusingly. As if rooted to the spot she stopped dead in her tracks oblivious of the bitter rain lashing into her face. The false vision didn't last long, no more than a fleeting second but she would have traded her soul at that moment just to turn and run rather than enter that place that had held such delight in the past. But now Len replaced the image of Billy once more and it was too late to turn back.

"Sally lass, come in out of the rain."

"Can't stop Len," she answered her voice casual and controlled belying the fact that her inner emotions were in melt down, "I just want your time sheets for this week. You couldn't do me a favour could you and send 'em up to the office? Ta."

Striving desperately to control her turbulent emotions Sally returned to the typing pool where the girls were covering their typewriters signalling the end of another day. With superhuman effort she remained coherent long enough to bid the girls "goodnight" and ask of her friend, "Betty, will you call in at the baby minders for me and tell Mrs Clark I'll be a little late calling for Brandon to-night?"

There was no moon, no stars hardly any light at all. The icy cold rain driven by a sharp cutting north wind sliced into her as she struggled blindly over rugged tussocks of coarse moor-land grass towards the Cragg. In a trance- like state she paused perilously close to the edge of the chasm. A dreadful, un-natural calm descended upon her. Praying aloud she begged for forgiveness, not for what she was about to do, for that, she had no choice. The forgiveness she sought was for her selfishness in sending Billy to his death. For wasn't it at her insistence Billy who wanted to join the RAF was dead? It was as much her fault as the torpedo that sent him to the bottom of the ocean. She inched nearer to the edge of the chasm. As she peered into the blackness prior to the leap that would put an end to her torment Police Sergeant Wilkinson's voice came as a brutal intrusion.

"Sally? Is that you?" The kindly copper was behind her in the darkness. "Nay, I was just going down to Stephenson's Fold to look in on the old ladies..." his lie was gentle and his motive transparent,"takin' a short cut,,, I suppose that's what you were doin' eh? ...takin' a short cut? He kept talking, gently and saying nothing of importance, but his presence was enough to reach through Sally's misery and partly bring her back to the present. He didn't move any closer he merely kept up his one way conversation, content for the moment that she didn't move closer to the edge of the Cragg. "Mind you it's a lousy evening to be out over the Cragg, you and me must be round the bend... well, I mean it's common knowledge that I am – round the bend I mean..." Sally heard Sergeant Wilkinson's voice as if he were talking from the opposite end of a long tunnel, but gradually his words got through to her and sanity brought with it the return of her grief. Arnold's voice rambled on...

"...Oh by the way, I'm glad I've seen you, there's a bit of a foot ball match next Saturday after noon on the Reck, I promised I'd take your little Brandon along if it's alright with thee..."

Suddenly the mention of her little boy evoked a vivid image of Billy. But this time it was not Billy as he was when she last saw him alive. It was as he had been as a four-year-old waif when he had first come to live at the orphanage. The same age as Brandon was now... Brandon!

With the blinding rain lashing into her face she turned from the edge and began to run with frantic urgency from the Cragg.

"Thank you Arnold." She heard herself calling over her shoulder in an oddly normal voice as she stumbled recklessly over the wet grass, "Yes, Brandon would love to go with you to the football, thank you...!" Her priority was suddenly now to be with her little boy – Billy's little boy. Arnold watched as she ran blindly away from the imminent danger. Soaked to the skin he followed her and from a distance watched as she picked up her son from the baby minder and headed for her own little cottage.

....

In spite of the foul weather Leah opened the door in answer to the loud urgent knocking. "What... the deary me?! Arnold, tha' looks like a drownded rat, come in and get up to't fire..."

"...I don't want to panic thee Leah," Arnold said, "but this is something I can't handle on me own..."

"Well get on with it lad what is it?"

"It's Sally..."

"I thought it might be..." Leah said as she began to don her coat and shawl. "She's taken a right beating lad, and disappeared inside herself since Billy was killed. Kept everyone at arms length – even me, well by the look of thy face things have come to something of a head..."

"She's alright – at the moment – but she's in an awful state. I thought summat was wrong when I saw her heading for the Cragg after work. So I followed her. She was - well... she was standing right on the edge." Arnold's concern showed vividly in his normally laughing eyes "I managed to talk to her and she seemed to come down to earth. After a bit she went to Mrs Clark's to pick up little Brandon and take him home."

"Come on then Arnold, we'd better get round there sharpish..."

"If you don't mind, I'll walk you round to Sally's, but I won't come in." Arnold said, "I don't want her to think I was spying on her, you see..."

"Aye, right enough," Leah replied knowingly, "if she's come to her senses she might well wonder what you were doing on the Cragg on a night like this. It wouldn't do for her to know she has somebody like you minding what happens to her, now would it lad?"

"Well, nay... I mean..."

"You're a grand lad Arnold." Leah said,

"But tha' must promise me tha' won't tell her I sent thee round, will tha'?"

"You have the kindest heart of anyone I've ever known Arnold lad, and one day Sally'll be grateful." Leah spoke her line as if she were quoting a passage from the

Bible, as she gathered together some home baked bread and various treats for the little boy.

The energetic knock on the door seemed an intrusion to Sally.   She was annoyed.   No-one was welcome.

"Sally...!" Leah shouted through the letterbox, "...are you there?" From the doorstep Leah heard the excited footsteps of the little boy as he ran to open the door.

"Leah!" Brandon squealed, his eyes bright and excited, "Mammy! It's Leah Stead come to see us!"

"Well, don't leave her standing on the doorstep love, ask her in," The usually beautiful vivacious girl was distant, pallid and taut as a steel spring.

Normally not thrown by any situation tough old Leah was for once shocked by Sally's appearance; it was a moment or two before she could find a voice

"I've been doing a bit of baking" Leah began, somewhat lamely for her, as her sharp old eyes scanned the room.   The house was as neat as ever.   There was nothing wrong with the bairn physically - outwardly happy and curious, but perhaps a little edgy. He climbed onto Leah's lap and clamped his arms around her neck with an almost imperceptible desperation. Then with a brave effort to show everything was fine he became slightly over playful and sneaked a look in her shopping basket.

"Mammy," he squealed, "Leah has made me a Ginger-parkin man, and a flat-cake for you and she's brought me the "Dandy!"

"You mustn't be nosy sweetheart, Sally said sweetly, "how do you know the parkin-man is for you? Leah used to make parkin-men for me when I was little. Now say thank you and go put it in the pantry to save for after your supper." Brandon scampered from the room with his spoils. "It's lovely to see you Leah sorry I haven't

68

been good company lately." Sally said after an awkward pause, then she added awkwardly, "How are you?".

"I'm as right as a bobbin," Leah replied, "It's thee I'm concerned about."

"I'm fine," Sally said, carefully avoiding Leah's eyes. "I'm absolutely fine!"

"You're **not** fine!" Leah replied, shooting from the hip, determined to confront Sally's misery head on. "Thou'rt far from bein' *fine!* Aye, me bonny lass, I realize tha's had a tremendous knock, but tha' shouldn't look the way tha' does, I'd feel much better if I saw thy eyes red raw with crying rather than the way they look now, all dry eyed and stony faced" Sally turned to avoid Leah's blunt but accurate assessment.

"Don't turn away." Leah swung the young girl around to face her. "Listen hard to what I have to say. Denying thi'self the right to mourn and shuttin' thi'self off from life just won't do!"

"...I go to work everyday..." Sally protested, in spite of Leah's firm grip on her shoulders she remained rigid with her eyes tightly closed to prevent the older woman access to what might been seen behind her eyes. "and Brandon wants for nothing..."

"Oh, I can see that" Leah replied forcefully, "he's thriving right enough. But he's wound up like a Swiss watch with the tension coming from thee. It's been weeks now lass, and apart from work nobody's seen neither hide nor hair on thi' outside work."

"I'm better on my own Leah...!" Sally violently broke away from the hold on her arms and turned away. Leah, ancient though she was, moved like a whippet, caught the younger woman in a tight maternal embrace ignoring the struggle and although she felt cruel doing so did not relent until the tension subsided a little. Then gently rocking her like a mother would a heartbroken child Leah said her piece.

"It's gone on long enough Sally. I don't want to sound hard, but you aren't the only one what's lost her man. Now come on doy and give way to your grief. Until you do, you'll not be able to pick thi'sen up and carry on with your life."

"You don't understand Leah." Sally replied, her eyes still tightly closed to avoid Leah's relentless honesty.

"What's to understand?" Leah gave no quarter, "What's happened to thee doy is as old as the Bible."

Sally couldn't hold back the awful admission any longer. **"But I'm to *blame* for Billy's death! Can't you see Leah? It was my fault!"** The desperation in Sally's voice revealed that she really did believe she was responsible for her husband's death.

"Nay Sally love, talk sense. How on earth was it thy fault?"

"It was me who made him go to sea Leah!" The dreadful statement of guilt burst from Sally in a hysterical outpouring that had festered since receiving the telegram.

"He didn't want to join the Merchant Navy! He would have gone in the RAF if he'd had his choice. I knew he would have done anything to please me. Anything Leah! I persuaded him he would be safer. *Safer!* It was my stupidity...my fault..."

"So that's it?" Leah said, "tha's been blamin' thi'sen all this time..? Now listen to me. Get it into your head that it wasn't your fault. It was not your fault! You no'but have to look in the Telegraph and Argus every single damn night to see that it wasn't thy fault". Leah reached frantically for the newspaper from the fireside rack. There was a passionate urgency in the old woman's actions as she tore through the paper to find the War Casualties section.

"Nah, then - there! Just thee look at that!" She thrust the paper in front of the girls face, but Sally turned her head away. "Don't turn away lass, face it! Look there, one after the other! RAF dead...RAF dead... RAF missing... missing... Missing believed dead!" Leah

70

jabbed the column with her finger as she went down the list. "There's as many young lads killed every night in the Air Force as there are in any other of the services. This bloody cruel war isn't choosy..." She forced the young woman to read the dreadful list.

Sally sank to her knees. A low pitched moan more alarming than a scream escaped from deep within her.

"Oh doy, I don't mean to be cruel, you know that, but **tha' has to   realize it's not thy fault...!** Now then come on, convince me that you believe it's not your fault...Come on, say it out loud!" Sally was still on her knees, but gradually the message permeated her mistaken belief and got through. After a while she took the proffered newspaper and through the tears streaming down her face she at last acknowledged she was not culpable, Leah had been showing her the truth.

"...I see..." her whisper was only just audible

"See what? Come on **say it**!" Leah insisted.

Sally finally managed to utter the few words that were to free her of any blame. "I see it...it's not my fault!" Leah sank to her knees beside her and gently held her in her strong old arms as Brandon, eyes wide in panic, came running in from the bedroom. Sally's instinct to protect her son from her own grief came into play.

"Go back upstairs Brandon darling and read your comic..." she made a half-hearted attempt to disengage his arms from around her neck.

"Let him stay!" Leah said sharply, "It's his loss too. Billy was his daddy as well as your man. He's old enough to understand."

"Oh, Leah I only want to protect him..." Sally said weakening to the little boy's embrace.

"I know you do lass, but tha' must let him stay and give thee comfort. Leah insisted.

"He needs to cry as much as thee. You must share your grief". Leah gently led mother and son to the couch and laid them both down.

"Sally love," Leah said as she tenderly covered the pair with a blanket, "I know right now, at this moment you're wondering how you'll be able to stand the pain in all the long years that lie ahead. But believe me lass, It will get easier, there never will be a time when it feels worse than it is at this moment; you have been blessed with your little lad, hang on to him. Hang on to one another, it will, I promise you, get better".

Leah banked up the fire, lowered the gaslight and quietly let herself out of the cottage leaving Sally and her son holding each other until they ran out of tears and a healing sleep settled over them.

....

CARRY ON AND CARRY OUT!

If there was anything Ada Shepherd liked better than a glass of draught Bass of a Sunday morning, it was two or even three. Especially whilst beating air into the Yorkshire pudding. It was an essential ritual. Her puddings would have been flat as a fart without a glass of draught Bass on the side.

Of course it would never have done for a respectable widow woman to be seen *"carrying out"* from the off licence shop in broad daylight with a wash-hand jug in her hand? Out of the question! In Mrs Shepherd's book – second only to her glass of draught Bass – decorum was all. So the pact of secrecy between herself and young Terry Ryan who did the off licence run every week was shared by no-one, except perhaps everybody who lived in Stephenson's Fold. Never the less the cloak and dagger charade was followed religiously every Sunday morning.

"Terry, I've told you time and time again, it's against the law." Rosie Ryan warned her middle son, even though it was only a half hearted warning, for in all fairness she herself couldn't for the life in her see any harm in it. "You're only a minor. If you get copped you, me, Mrs Shepherd and Mr Cullinder at the off licence will all end up in Armley gaol."

"But Mam, Mrs Shepherd says it isn't right for a lady to be *"carrying out"* herself, somebody has to." Terry's strange logic made little sense but he said it with such conviction his Mam didn't argue any further. "Besides if anybody asks what the jug is for I tell them I'm fetching a jug of milk."

Rosie Ryan was not totally convinced. But lovely old Mrs Shepherd did love her Bass and it was only on Sunday, and like Terry said somebody had to fetch it for her. The thing that would have made Rosie put her foot down, had she known, Terry was becoming very skilful at having a "good slurp" from the jug on his way back without disturbing the froth.

Things came to a head that sunny Sunday morning as he turned into the snicket with his two slurps less than the original three-pint consignment, when his younger brother Danny joined him.

"What have you got it the jug Terry?" He asked.

"Milk"

"You lie! It's beer." Danny answered.

"If you know why did you ask then?"

"Everybody knows. You fetch it every Sunday…"

"Alright! Alright! Its draught Bass for Mrs Shepherd," Terry answered in hushed tones, "but keep your voice down, else we'll all be in trouble. Technically it's against the law."

"How come?" Danny asked, "You didn't nick it did you?"

"Of course I didn't nick it, but Albert Cullinder is not supposed to sell it to me, because I'm still a minor."

"I won't tell anybody," Danny said slyly," if you let me have a sup."

"You're not used to supping ale, it'll make you dizzy."

"Have you ever had a taste Terry?" Danny asked with gravity,

"I have a taste every Sunday," Terry boasted, "I just nip down Sunders Snicket and have the quick slurp on me way back with it."

"Oh let me have a sup Terry, will yer? Will yer?"

"Well just a drop then. Watch me first. Watch how I sift it through me teeth so that I don't disturb the froth on top. That way old Ma Shepherd doesn't know there's any missing."

The younger boy watched eagerly as his brother gently poured the precious liquid into his mouth. Taking the jug in both hands young Danny was far too eager. The weight was more than his little arms expected and before Terry could restrain him the froth together with a good helping of the precious liquid disappeared down Danny's gullet.

"You dozy ha'p'orth! I told you to sift it through your teeth," Terry protested, "Now I'll have to give it a good shake to bring the Froth back up again." Terry swilled the jug around vigorously. A bit too vigorously. A sizable portion swirled out of the jug and spilled onto the ground. By the time he had another taster a good half of the original shipment was gone.

"That's your fault," Terry said, "How can I go back now with all that missing?"

"Tell her you spilled some." Danny offered, "It's true, in a way."

"I can't tell her that. I tried that once before and she said, '...aye, and I know where you spilled it – down your throttle!' So you see, she's on to me."

"No! The only thing I can do is to say I emptied it down the drain because Sergeant Wilkinson got s'picious and started to follow me." His voice was beginning to betray the effects of the many slurps.

"Right-o!" Danny squealed, "Look there's a drain over there!"

"Do you think I'm barmy? You don't think I'm really going to pour it down the drain do you? Good Health!" Between the two of them Terry and his younger brother polished off what remained of the golden liquid. At least Terry did. Danny's eyes began to water, and after one tiny quaff, burping and gurning he threw in the towel leaving what remained of the precious brew to his elder brother.

With his eyes shining like a couple of Toc-H lamps, Terry's cockiness reached an unusual high level as he announced expansively, "By the living'! That was a drop of good stuff!" Wiping his mouth with the back of his hand, as he had seen Victor McLaughlin do to great effect in "Gunga Din," he carried on with unnatural confidence. "Now we got to sustanshate our story, get me?" Terry usually did a fairly good imitation of Jimmy Cagney, but to-day, considering... "Listen to me kid, there's a tap over there at the side of the garage, go wash this jug out. That way we'll wash away any trace of edivance that could 'criminate us. The old Dame'll think were pretty smart guys. Get it?"

"Why are you talking funny like that Terry?" Danny asked, slightly alarmed.

"You poor, dumb, crazy hoodlum!" Terry went on, his befuddled mind still lost somewhere in any one of a dozen Warner Bros. gangster movies. "Stick with me kid. Do as I say, you'll be OK. Cross me and you'll end up in some back alley with a slug in the head." The younger brother would have been more alarmed had he not been used to the fact that Terry was often given to wild dramatic flights of fantasy – even without the aid of stimulants.

"Sometimes…" Terry now in the persona of WC Fields pondered philosophically as he watched seemingly unconcerned as Constable Barker approached suspicion written all over him.

"If my eyes don't deceive me, that person walking towards us is an officer of the law" Danny's eyes almost popped out of his bonny face as he handed the now empty jug back to his brother. For it was true, not merely a figment of his brother's Booze induced imagination. There coming towards them, in the flesh, Constable Archie Barker was bearing down on them. Terry grabbed the empty jug from his little brother and quickly slipped the beaded doily - provided by Mrs Shepherd for just such an emergency – over the jug and stood looking, in spite of his inebriated state the picture of innocence as the constable arrived. Terry felt confident in this crisis. After all, someone must be watching over him for hadn't God sent Constable Barker and not Sergeant Wilkinson? Everyone knew Archie Barker was a bit a of a 'Do-lah-lee.' and Arnold Wilkinson was as sharp as a Sheffield darning needle besides there really was no case to answer was there? After all the jug was empty! Terry had never felt, nor would ever again feel so smug and arrogant as he felt at that moment.

What have you got in that jug Lad?" Archie asked in his most officious tone.

"What jug?" Terry answered the picture of hurt innocence.

"The wash-hand jug you have in your hand."

"I see no jug!" Terry retorted with a face like stone. For a instant, there was a flicker of confusion pass across the face of the none too bright cop as he doubted his own sanity.

"I'm talking about the jug with the doyley over the top!"

"Oh! This jug!" Terry answered with growing confidence, causing his younger brother to squirm with unease. You mean this jug constable! What was the question again?"

"I asked you what was in it!" Archie answered, getting more irritated and cross by the minute.

"Nowt! Nothing! Zilch! Not a thing!" Terry answered cheekily.

"Right, well I'll just take a gander then." The policeman replied with increasing frustration. Somewhere from deep beneath his newly found Dutch courage Terry knew he was pushing his luck to a dangerous level. He knew it was against all his upbringing and indeed his nature to be so foolhardy. But he was in the grip of the devil and enjoying himself immensely.

"Come on let me have a look in that there jug." Constable Barker reached out to remove the doyley, as Terry, pushing his luck to the limit, drew it back out of the constables reach.

"First let me see your search warrant! Terry demanded.

"Search warrant my arse!" Constable Barker replied as he whipped the doyley from the jug.

"I'm going to have a look, come 'ere!" Of course the jug was empty. He even sniffed it. Nothing!

"There you are!" Terry was triumphant.

"Right, well er…. I'll let you off this time" Constable Barker replied, having made something of a fool of himself. "Only next time we can do without so much impudence from you!"

Pushing his luck way past the limit and putting the fear of God into his little brother, Terry couldn't leave it at that and replied with cringing audacity,

"*You'll* let *me* off!! I'm not sure *I'll* let *you* off!" Terry said in his best but flawed Charles Laughton. "This is far from the end of the matter. Expect to hear from my lawyers for this blatant intrusion into my privacy, make no mistake I shall see you hanging from the highest yardarm in the British Navy..." Without more ado, a sharp slap on the side of his head, put paid to his histrionics.

"Hold that you cheeky little bugger," the affronted copper retorted, "and get off home before you feel my boot toe up your backside!" Terry didn't need twice telling.

"Why did you cheek him back like that" Danny asked, obviously shaken by their encounter with the law, even if it only was Constable Barker. "You came near to getting your arse kicked you know?" Terry however, detected a note of admiration in his brother's admonition.

"You what!?"Terry answered with a victorious swagger, "It was more than his job was worth. He knew he daren't go too far. Ugh! I would have had him thrown out of the force!" Danny looked at his brother with a mixture of admiration, apprehension and for all his tender years, a feeling of concern. "We ought to go play in the graveyard till you sober up a bit Terry." Danny's words of good sense fell on deaf ears.

"All in good time my good man..."

"Do you like being drunk Terry?" Danny asked, "Is it nice?"

"Do I like being drunk!? " Terry replied, "Do I like being drunken sir? I wouldn't know my good man; I've never touched a drop in my life..."

"Well you're drunk now." Danny said.

"Am I?" Terry replied genuinely surprised.

"Honestly our kid. You're paralectric. What does it feel like?"

"Feel like? Feel like? Fantastic

The two boys proceeded vaguely in the direction of Mrs Shepherd's cottage via the graveyard, where Danny hoped his elder brother would tarry long enough to discard his many alter egos and become himself once again. The power of the hops however had not yet quite done with our hero, and the higgledy-piggledy headstones of the graveyard beckoned invitingly suggesting still one more exciting scenario for Terry's booze powered imagination.

With the ease of a well-oiled Thespian he slipped effortlessly into the part of Robin Hood as played by Errol Flynn. Leaping from one gravestone to the next, still with the empty jug in his hand, only now the jug was an unspecified weapon with which to subdue the evil Guy of Gisbourne as played by Basil Rathbone. One moment the jug was a trusty sword the next it was a shattered piece of pottery strewn over the last resting place of Esther Partridge 1801 – 1854.

Terry Ryan came to earth with a jolt. Mrs Shepherds booze was gone, and now her precious wash-hand jug in a million pathetic pieces. The only evidence it ever existed was the handle gripped in his guilty right hand...

"Oh, shit Terry! You've broken Mrs Shepherd's precious wash-hand jug!" Danny wailed, "Now what are you going to do?"

"Do? Do?" Terry pondered trying to think of some witty defiant retort but none came to mind.

"Mrs Shepherd'll go bonkers!" Danny offered unhelpfully.

"Ma Shepherd. Poor old Ma Shepherd!" Terry replied, his rapidly evaporating bravado giving way to alcoholic remorse. In his befuddled imagination he could hear a lush Max Steiner score behind his words. Words that, he believed, should be spoken by the great Paul Muni – at least!

"Poor old Ma Shepherd! First she loses her ale, then her beautiful floral wash-hand jug – and do you know, she never did a lousy turn to anyone in all her life. But who cares? Not any of you rabble for a start. Its fate, fate I tell you fate! Cruel, cruel fate..."

"Terry, stop acting. You have to think of something to tell her.

"...asking little from life, just the odd jug of booze of a Sunday morning, deprived of even this little pleasure..." Suddenly Terry came out of his fantasy world and for the first time spoke sensibly. "I know what I'll do! Do you know what I'm going to do our Danny?"

"You're going to sing..."

"No seriously. I mean about the jug and the Bass."

"No what?"

"I'm going to tell old Mrs Shepherd the entire unexpregra... un- exasperated...un,,,thing-ummy-gig TRUTH!"

"Christ!" Danny gasped.

"I want you to go straight home Danny." From somewhere Terry got his act together enough to send Danny home warning him to say nothing about their escapade. Then Terry set off manfully trying to walk in a straight line towards Mrs Shepherd's front gate. By this time the booze that had been his crutch had lost much of it's strength. Even, his bombast had evaporated to be replaced by very genuine contrition and shame. He stumbled up the path to where Mrs Shepherd stood on the doorstep.

"Where have you been all this time doy?" she asked gently, full of concern, "I thought you got yourself knocked down with a motor car, else arrested or summat. Are you alright?"

Owing to the weight of his shame Terry was unable to lift his eyes higher than his clogs, After some laboured throat clearing and a genuine attempt to find a voice, this time his own if possible, he began.

"Mrs Shepherd, I have summat to tell you," he began haltingly, then suddenly seemingly of its own volition his confession blurted out in one non-stop lump, "I-supped-all-the-bass-from-the-jug-then-I-broke-your-lovely old-piece-of-China-to-smithereens! All except the handle – here it is."

"Dear Lord Help us all!" The old lady, staggered back against the doorpost, "Three pints! You never supped three pints on your own?"

"I did Mrs Shepherd. Well I spilled some of it. I'm ever so sorry."

"You never did!"

"I did Mrs Shepherd. Before when I've told you I spilled it, you never believed me, you said I supped it. Now when I tell you I supped it, you still don't believe me."

"Well I never did!"

"Mrs Shepherd, I'm very sorry I supped all your ale and broke your lovely wash-hand jug. I'd better be off now. Good afternoon!" On automatic pilot Terry turned and started to weave down the pathway to face the music at home.

"Mam I've summat to tell you," Terry stumbled through the doorway and stood wavering in the centre of the wash scullery. Rosie looked up from the Peggy tub where she was pounding a fortnight's grime out of a pair of Mrs Lodge's flannel combinations. Drying her hands on her apron Rosie took in the sorry state of her son. She said nothing. One look told her all she needed to know. Terry wished he had positioned himself nearer the wringing machine and not in the middle of the room so he would have had a steady prop before he embarked on his momentous confrontation.

"Mam, as you can see I'm on the road to ruin..." Once started the whole sad tale of his downfall began to pour out. How it all got started with him having a little slurp – then another – and another – spilling some - being cheeky to Constable Barker – quaffing the rest and thinking up the lie to cover his tracks –breaking the wash-hand jug in the graveyard – the look on Mrs Shepherds face when he told her she was bereft of both ale and jug. The only thing he left out from his admission of his fall from Grace was his younger brother's part in the sorry occurrence. All this while Rosie merely stood and listened, slowly she began to walk towards him. Screwing his eyes tightly shut Terry stood his ground to take whatever punishment his mother might dole out – and he knew it could be awesome. It was awesome too, only not in the way he expected. She didn't shout at him. She didn't even speak. She didn't give him the pasting he knew he deserved. As his knees were about to buckle beneath him she brushed his hair back and gently placed her hand on his forehead, as she would when any of her kids were feverish. The last thing he was aware of before he fell into a stupor was being carried upstairs and put to bed, and a cold flannel being applied to his reeling skull.

Terry slept like the dead throughout the rest of that day and night, awaking just after six on the Monday morning. That's if it could be described as waking for he had the Mount Vesuvius of all hangovers.

Downstairs he found his mother ironing the pile of Mrs Lodges washing she had slavishly laboured over the day before.

"How do you feel sweetheart?" She smiled as she placed her hand on his forehead in the same way she had before he passed out.

He couldn't believe it! Here he was an undeniable drunkard, and she didn't turn a hair. Had she not heard his confession? Didn't she realise how wicked he was? Had he just dreamed the whole thing? That was not possible. But why didn't she whip the living daylights out of him. That really worried him.

"I feel terrible Mam!"

"You will do for a while. It's what's called a 'hangover' love"

"But what about Mrs Shepherd," Terry asked, "how am I going to face her?"

"Nay love, don't ask me. That's something you'll have to work out for yourself."

The Mrs Shepherd problem continued to worry him throughout the day. As soon as school was over he went straight to the local shops and cadged some empty boxes which he immediately took home, chopped up, put into bundles, then onto the bogey cart and took them round to the old lady's cottage. As quietly as he could he left the sack of kindling on her yellow scoured doorstep. As he was slinking away the door opened and she called after him.

"What's this Terry love, firewood?" she asked in a kindly voice, "Well that's right grand, just what I need! How much is it?"

"Has the whole world gone barmy?" he wondered, didn't she realise he had cheated her out of her draught Bass and dashed her best piece of china to bits?

"No charge, Mrs Shepherd," he said, still unable to look her in the eye. "I owe it to you, in part repayment for what I did yesterday. I'm fair shamed for what I did."

"Oh aye, you must be," She said dolefully, accepting the whole shameful incident with philosophical resignation.

"Will you let me know how much your jug was worth and I'll run errands for you until I've earned enough to pay for it?"

"Oh, the jug was part of a set. I could never match it up it with another."

"It was priceless then?"

"Well lad." She answered mournfully, "Let's just say you couldn't put a price on it."

"That's a pity…"

"It is lad.   It's a right pity," she droned in her melancholic way, "Still I might be able to get another, similar, from the junk shop where I got the one you broke."

Terry stood for a moment, lost for words before he turned to slink away.

"Hey Terry lad, just a minute," She called after him, "You like ginger moggy don't you?"

"Yes…" he answered in trepidation.

"Well I've just made a baking tin full." She said, "You'd better come inside and cut yourself a piece, while I side this firewood into the low cupboard."

It took Terry a minute or two before he realised that neither his Mam nor Mrs Shepherd were going to pursue the matter any further. His only punishment was his shame. That he must handle on his own. Well, he could do that all right, no bother! Unable to deny the smile of relief that threatened to split his face in two he cut himself a wedge of warm ginger moggy.

"Oh, and you will come round next Sunday morning, won't you doy?   I'll find another jug from somewhere" she said conspiratorially, "You will come won't you? It would never do for lady to be seen "carrying out" from the off licence."

……………………………

CUT ON THE CROSS

"There's nothing else for it Edgar love, I shall have to get a cleaning job."

Ada Clough, a widow of many years and well used to making decisions for both her and her delicate, mollycoddled son was in a terrible state. Having managed all these years to protect him from the world she was now at her wits end.

"Nay, Mam! Talk sense, you can't work in the Mill at your time of life. I'll see if they'll take me on at Townsend's in't weaving."

"Don't talk soft Edgar! You big lump! You wouldn't last two minutes in't mill!" Ada replied impatiently.

The reason for their despondency was the Government's latest plea to the women of Britain to support the "*Make Do and Mend*" campaign. That was cruel enough on Ada Clough's fragile income. But the introduction of clothes rationing as well promised to be the absolute death knell of her one woman industry. As the hand written notice in the window of Ada's front parlour explained...

ADELA GOWNS

YOUR OWN CLOTH MADE UP TO

HUNDREDS OF YOUR OWN CHOICE OF

BEAUTIFUL PATTERNS FROM OUR

EXTENSIVE CATALOGUE.

This present crisis was one of many in Ada's life. Her only child was the cause of most of them. School had been a constant torment for Edgar, a fey, effeminate lad from his childhood showing no interest in male designated subjects like woodwork and handicrafts. He would fall into a muck sweat at the mere thought of any sort of field sports and almost scream out loud at the suggestion of swimming lessons. Afraid of his own shadow he would shuffle around the playground lonely and friendless trying not to be noticed, a perfect soft target for all the bullies. The little girls in his class were, to him totally alien. He scored even worse with his own gender.

As those few adults who showed any compassion at all kindly put it – "*a bit of a backward lad*" or "*summat of a do-lah-lee*"

These remarks, although sometimes well meant hurt Ada deeply causing her sleepless nights worrying over his future. Only one incredible thing saved him being sent to a special institution – his sketch book.

This closely guarded portfolio contained page after page of beautifully detailed fashion drawings. Awesomely glamorous, these minor masterpieces were disregarded as nothing more than an idiots scribbling to most people. Yet had they ever come before a tutored eye, they would have been recognised as minor works of genius. As a young teenager, occasionally one of the girls in his class at school would speak kindly to him. In return, too shy and awkward to engage her in conversation he would deftly create a flattering lightening sketch of his giggling benefactress. Bestowing upon her a beauty and elegance she would never attain in real life. Only to have his clever offering heartlessly discarded, dumped in the waste paper basket and forgotten within minutes.

When conscription was introduced mercifully he was declared unfit to serve in His Majesty's Forces, Now, due to the dramatic drop in the profits of his mother's dress-making business he sat sadly gazing into space, sharing his mother's concern but unable to offer a solution.

Now balding, podgy and fast approaching middle age, cursed with every kind of minor ailment real and imagined, he sank even deeper into the springs of the shabby armchair in deep terminal despair. A sad friendless man, he felt himself to be, if ever there was one.

Friendless he was, that is with the notable exception of Arnold Wilkinson. The two boys were born - Edgar's mother was always proud to tell - on the same hour of the same day on the same street. There the similarity ended.

Arnold was everything Edgar was not, bursting from every pore with boundless charisma, handsome, athletic, popular with the girls but without the slightest touch of conceit. Arnold was, in the new wartime vernacular *"one hell of a hunk"*. Such was Arnold's confidence and command, he was, without the slightest trace of embarrassment able to treat Edgar with human decency without any one daring to cast doubts on his own sexuality. Arnold was Edgar's idol and protector.

This kindness and loyalty to his coeval was steadfast throughout their adolescence and into adulthood. Whenever Edgar floundered, his mother would send for Arnold, and he would always take time out from his joyous errand through life to dispense cheer and instil enough confidence in his childhood friend to make him *"Buck up! Come on you big lump, buck up and get on with it"*. Through the years this friendship never waned. On the other hand it never waxed very much either, for it was obvious to all that Arnold's pace was far too fast to carry passengers. As a Young recruit to the constabulary Arnold was warned often enough that his admittance into the Police Force might be in serious jeopardy if he continued to turn a blind eye and continued to associate with his bizarre friend.

"Tha' knows Arnold," went the doom laden warning, "he's a queer stick is yon' Edgar Clough, it's rumoured he makes wimmin's frocks! Some say he wears 'em".

"Well I'll be buggered if I can see owt much wrong wi' that. What he does behind his own front door doesn't harm nobody else," Arnold reasoned, "I've never seen him in a frock meself, besides I'll bet he looks a damn sight more comely than some of the sights that pass for real women round here!"

Edgar was totally discrete about his fascination with fashion and his mother believed his solitary pastime kept him marginally on the right side of sanity. After all, she reasoned, he didn't ask much, there were only a few other pleasures he got from life. Accompanying her to the Women's Institute Sewing Circle was one. He also held the title of Wardrobe Master for the CADS – Craggs Bottom Amateur Dramatic Society, although he was never present during performances – too bashful to be present when the performers changed their clothes for costumes.

The high spot of his week was when he and his Mam paid their visit to the Elysian Palace Picturedrome. The bright, lavish musicals from Hollywood with the mouth watering designs by Adrian and the slick talking comedies from the Warner Studio's with dresses by Orry Kelly and Edith Head held Edgar in thrall. He would memorise every detail. Not one frill, panel or stitch went unrecorded in his memory. After the movie he would rush straight home, not even stopping for fish and chips in his hurry to sketch the dresses, or better still his own version of them in his precious book of fantasy gowns.

Apart from this clandestine pastime of Edgar's there was another even bigger secret he and his mother shared. The creative brains behind ADELA GOWNS were not Ada's, as everyone thought, they were Edgar's! A tacit understanding between the two of them deemed it necessary he should forever remain anonymous. That he could never claim credit for his creations was grossly unfair but something he just had to live with. After all, it would never do to have a male dressmaker in a place like Craggs Bottom - Heaven forbid!

Their little deception was simplicity itself but completely fooled the ladies of the village who swore that Ada's creations could stand against the best Leeds could offer, even better than some London's couturier's. Ada herself would conduct the initial interview/fitting in her front parlour discussing at great length over many cups of tea which style, fabric and colour would best suit the clients' particular skin tone and figure. Finally feeling pampered and flattered at the elaborate attention the client would stand to leave. At this point Edgar would just *"happen"* to pass through the room. One bashfully stolen glance at the customer as he scurried through the parlour and her height, width, contours and peculiarities were stamped indelibly on his brain. Ada's lengthy obsequious sales patter had been no more than a front. Almost before the customer was out of the door Edgar had repaired to his workshop - the back bedroom, rolled out the material and expertly cut out the garment. His assessment was hardly ever wrong. The finished dress would rarely need adjustment. The creation would be exquisite in every detail. There was never a dis-satisfied customer. All this of course was before the shortage of cloth, the crisis they now faced. Things had never looked so bad for ADELA GOWNS. Mother and son were in despair.

They might have known that Arnold, now Police Sergeant Arnold Wilkinson in charge of the little sub station, would be the first to recognise their predicament and like the knight in shining armour that he was, would come charging to their rescue.

"Now then Ada, I believe things aren't too good at the moment?"

"Oh, Arnold lad, how did you know/"

"Shortage of material for your frocks? Is that right lass?"

"Aye love, that's right." Ada replied mournfully, "But you see love, I have to rely on me customers bringing their own dress lengths these days and they haven't the coupons to spare. Christmas comin' on an' all, I don't know what were going to do if I can't get a cleaning job."

"Could you use some good quality raw silk? White only? Would that be any use?"

"Oh, Arnold doy, that would be a Godsend if only I could get a permit. Oh, Arnold what are we going to do. I'm at me wits end..?"

Touching the side of his nose in a sign of conspiracy Arnold replied with a knowing smile,
"Mum's the word Ada!"

"But Arnold love, how much will it cost, I'm a bit hard–up at the moment..."

"We'll talk about that when you win the Irish Sweepstake. I'm off now, give us a smile!"

The following morning Ada found a large parcel on her doorstep. Excitedly tearing it open she found inside – a parachute! Her initial reaction was disappointment but that was soon dispelled when Edgar's expert eye assessed the magnitude of the godsend as it spilled out, tumbling into the furthest corners of the tiny room like a burst of summer cloud on a cold November morning.

"Mam, this is right bloody champion!" Edgar was shrill with excitement. "I've heard tell of folk getting their hands on one panel, but this ere's a full chute! That's twenty eight panels! I could dress a Busby Berkeley musical with this lot. Where on earth did you manage to get 'old of it?"

"Never thee mind where I got it from. There's a little note came with it that says there' plenty more where it came from! Start unpicking! Were back in business mi little cock sparrer!"

With the application of various dyes and inspired cutting Edgar brought enchantment back into the lives of the war weary mill lasses. Full-skirted creations that would not have looked out of place on the catwalk now graced the Saturday hop at the mill canteen. Word spread like wildfire. Thereafter no young war bride went down the aisle in drab uniform or civvies; they floated altar-wards in fairy tale creations the like of which they had only ever seen in the movies.

It says much for the loyalty of the community that the source of all this splendour remained a tight secret. For it was, as every one knew, strictly speaking, an illegal transaction to purchase any item of clothing without coupons. But there was no one stupid or mean enough to spoil such a good thing, was there? Well, maybe there was – one - Mrs Drusilla Townsend JP!

Now that things were back on a level pegging at Adela Gowns Edgar and his Mam felt they were able again to attend The Ladies Sewing Circle every Tuesday evening with an easy heart. The current project the ladies had set themselves was to enter the Yorkshire quilt making competition in aid of the starving Russians. A mission of such importance to the war effort the committee decided to turn a blind eye to Edgar's gender – whatever that was – and allow him to enter the contest under his own name. It soon became obvious to the circle that Edgar's fine needlework and intricate design was of a very high standard. Although covered in embarrassment at the attention he was secretly aglow with pride for it was the first time in his life he had ever received credit for his talents. There was though, that one afore mentioned member of the group positively imploding with envy at the adulation being showered on Edgar's exquisite work on his quilt. The mean spirited Mrs Drusilla Townsend JP the local mill owner's wife! A perfect match for her bloated, greedy husband Mrs Townsend was seething with indignation. Unable to bring herself to mention Edgar by name, feeling soiled merely by association, she set about his downfall with a will. After all she reasoned to herself *"as chairwoman of the sewing circle, was not I the one who proposed entering the competition in the first place? Most galling of all, with the exception of this pervert wasn't*

I myself the strongest contender for the first prize, at least for our own branch? A prize I had set my heart on winning! Well, I shall see about this!" I'm not a leading member of the Magistrate's bench for nothing.

Very early the next morning an urgent knocking on the door of the Police Sergeant's bachelor quarter's roused him from sleep and brought him bare footed to answer the door.

"Ada lass, what's up? Come in..."

"She's had our Edgar kicked out of the Sewing circle!"

"Who? What?" Arnold, still partly asleep asked in bewilderment.

"She has, that mean awful cow..."

"Which mean awful cow Ada...?

"I'll swing for her, I will! I'll do her in!"

"Well before you do, put the kettle on and make us both a cup of tea...."I'll just go across the yard to the lavatory, I'm nearly busting, then you can tell me all about it." Arnold's calm and casual manner brought little comfort to the distraught old lady.

Ada unable to fight back the tears greeted Arnold on his return from his trip down the yard. "Just when he was making such headway with the competition an' all..."

"Who's had him kicked out?"

"Mrs Townsend, the nasty old sod! She said it was no place for a man. She made all sorts of incinerations about him..."

"Calm down Ada," Arnold said soothingly, "it can't be as bad as all that."

"**It is** as bad as that Arnold" Ada said, her panic rising even further, "The old witch said he'd been breaking the law by making Black Market garments and that if he didn't leave the sewing circle it would be the worse for him. Then she said even if he did leave she felt that it was

94

her duty as a pillar of the Community to bring it to the notice of the Magistrate's bench!"

"Oh, she did, did she? Arnold looked grim but determined, "we'll see about that. Stay here Ada, pour yourself another cup of tea, I'm off for a private word with your Edgar. While I'm gone if you feel like it you can wash that heap of mucky pots for me. Some of them have been piling up in that sink since last Easter."

It was no surprise to Arnold to hear of such despicable behaviour coming from the House of Townsend. Both husband and wife, Arnold knew, were known to hit below the belt, and used their position of privilege to do so.   "Well, hold on to your hat Mrs Drusilla Townsend!" Arnold thought, "you are about to smirk on the other sides of your two faces."

....

Having invented his plan of retribution on the way round to Edgar's house Arnold was bursting with energy and raring to put it into action.   His excitement was evident in the spirited banging he delivered on Ada Clough's front door. "Edgar! Buck up! You big lump" Pull thi'self together, and listen to me."   Edgar didn't need twice telling, anything Arnold said always lifted his gloom and warmed his heart. He was immediately all ears.

"Nah then Edgar, can you make me up a couple of white silk shirts out of that parachute your Mam got hold of. Big enough to fit somebody like Herbert Townsend, and can you do it by tonight?"

"Aye, no bother, but who're they for...?"

"Never thee mind who they're for," Arnold said, "The less tha' knows the better.

"Right-oh!" Edgar answered starry eyed.   If the handsome copper had told him to jump in the Mucky

Beck, he would have obeyed without question - Arnold's word was Edgar's command.

"I want you to do 'em up right bonny wi' tishy paper and all the posh trimming's you can think of — and most important — *don't forget to sew* an "**Adela Gowns"** *trade label inside the collar.*

"Right oh! I'll get cracking straight away." The now bucked up Edgar was filled with a renewed spirit. For although he had no idea what Arnold's plan was, whatever it was could only be on a par with an Act of God.

"Ta-ra, then Edgar lad, I'll send young Johnny Pratt round about five o'clock to pick the shirts up!" Arnold made an energetic exit from the Clough's parlour to set further wheels of his plan in motion.

A quick word of explanation about Johnny Pratt: seventeen years old from a broken home, had minor brushes with the law from his early teens. As a would-be delinquent, a *"wide boy"* he is at a slight disadvantage. It's not all that easy for him to be a petty criminal, when everyone in the village, including Police Sergeant Wilkinson thinks the world of him. His forays into shoplifting hardly ever get reported and when they do the victims of his crime never press charges. They simply ask Arnold to deal with it in his own way, which he does, by making the lad work until he has earned enough to recompense the offended. That and a gentle kick up the arse is the only correctional treatment meted out.

There is a general understanding that the lad is at heart a "grand little fellow" and will grow out of his youthful misdemeanours. In any case, with his conscription papers due shortly the general opinion amongst those who care about him reason the Army will sort him out in no time at all. However hopeless Johnny may have been as a criminal, he did make a very fair stab at *looking* the part of a Spiv. With his enormous greasy quiff, side burns and

96

pencilled moustache, a 5/11d Greenwoods Trilby worn at the back of his head and floor length overcoat with numerous inside pockets to carry hoped-for Black Market goods. All this, together with a swagger and attitude enough to make James Cagney look demure, the lad fairly dripped sleaziness.

The only thing he lacked was the heart of a criminal instead of the heart of a nice but dozy young kid. It was the shady *look* and *manner* of the boy that was the crucially important ingredient in Arnold's plan

"Now then Johnny, take heed! Take these two shirts up to Townsends Textiles. Tell the secretary you must see Mr Townsend in person, say "it's to his own advantage... don't be put off - ASK FOR HIM IN PERSON and make sure you are seen by as many witnesses as possible.

Mantra like Johnny repeated his instructions. "No sweat! – *"...to his own advantage"* – *"...seen by as many witnesses as possible."*

"Tell him that an acquaintance of yours has managed to acquire these two shirts for him at a fiver apiece..."

"A *fiver!?* They're worth ten quid each if they're worth a penny!" Johnny piped in astonishment.

"I said a **fiver,** do you hear? It must be such a tempting offer the greedy bugger can't refuse." Arnold stressed, "Stir up a bit of commotion, have as many witnesses as you can. Have you got that? Right now get off with you."

....

The following morning Alderman Mrs Drusilla Townsend received an anonymous message in a registered envelope...

"...it is well known to us and proof is available to the writer and colleagues at the West Riding County Council Offices, that your husband was the recipient of certain 'labelled garments' from a character of known dubious activities..." Drusilla felt her knees go weak *"...Do you and/ or your husband know 'it is illegal' to have dealings with the Black Market...?"* Now she lost the colour in her cheeks, began to sweat and sank on to the settee, the rising perspiration neutralising her Marcel Wave. *"...However, due to your husband's high standing in the community and your own position on the Board of Magistrates the writer does not intend – 'at this time' to act upon this information, but advises extreme caution in any further dealings you or your husband may undertake.*

Mrs Townsend, being of a devious nature herself on seeing the sewn in Adela Gowns label on the two shirts had enough cunning to know she had been set up, enough guilt to know why but not enough of either to know by whom. However she certainly got the message that she must go her way and sin no more. Immediately she wrote a letter to resign her Honorary Chairmanship of the Sewing Circle, but not before she apologised – via the secretary – for her "hasty" behaviour in having Edgar Clough slung out. Edgar was welcomed back by the ladies with open arms. A terrible wrong had been righted. There was no more to be said on the subject. Justice had prevailed. That's about the end of this story, apart from a few loose ends... Shortly afterwards Johnny Pratt got his call up papers. The Drill Sergeant soon blew out of the water any signs of swagger or swank in the lad's demeanour. Aldershot Barracks ruthless military barber made short shrift of the quiff and sideburns, without them Johnny's pencilled moustache looked abandoned and somewhat barmy. So that went too, and with it all hopes of a life of crime.

Gossamer silks poured out from the House of Adela and once more began to adorn the maidens of Craggs Bottom. Gorgeous creations in various shades of pinks, blues, and other romantic hues continued to gladden the hearts of the glamour starved dancers as they Palais Glided around the mill canteen at the Saturday night hop. Edgar, of course went on to win first prize in the National Quilting Competition.

In the week coming up to Christmas for the prize giving, the packed Co-op Hall was heaving with excited women's guilds from all over the West Riding. For the presentation Edgar, now having so much more confidence in himself dearly wanted to wear one of his cut on the cross mid calf numbers in mauve silk.

"No Edgar, you will wear your Sunday suit, and that's the end of it!" Ada sensibly forbade her son permission to do so, Not only did she put her foot down forbidding him his own sartorial not to say gender choice, she insisted that he have the severest short back and sides to go with it.

As Edgar stepped forward to receive his certificate, the entire Town Council stood to applaud him for the prestige he had brought upon the Municipality. His Mam, full to brimming with pride led the ladies of the Sewing Circle (with one notable exception!) in the loudest and most heartfelt ovation. Edgar's heart was full to bursting. But to him, better than winning first prize for his quilt, better than the Certificate, better than the recognition, better than any thing. He caught sight of Police Sergeant Wilkinson beaming at him. He winked and with that one wink all the Christmases' Edgar had never really experienced hitherto, arrived in one glorious big lump.

AIN'T LOVE GRAND

Private Burgess (Buddy) Martin US Army, not yet twenty five, tall, blond, athletic with a dazzling smile and boyish blue eyes sparkling with an intensity that set him apart from all the other walking wounded who frequented the Feather's pub. Buddy was one of a number of casualties convalescing at what had been pre-war the local Cottage Hospital, extended now into a Military Recovery Unit covering acres of moor land on the outskirts of the village. Ask any girl in the village Buddy was a one hundred per cent, top drawer, rolled gold, mail order hunk of BEEFCAKE!

With almost manic energy Buddy ingratiated himself into the running of the pub. He made himself indispensable when the pub was at it's busiest and Eli the regular pot man was at his most inebriated. Buddy refilled shelves, lifted crates, washed and dried the glasses, even took Caesar the guard dog for his late night walk prior to Flossie Ingham, the hard-bitten landlady's call of *"Time gentlemen please."* That he should show Flossie any attention at all was baffling.

"I don't get it," Elenora said, on her regular Sunday morning call at Minnie's cottage, where she would get her weekly news on the doings around the village. "If he's such a gorgeous hunk as you say Min, how come a dish like that pays the slightest attention to a – pardon the understatement – slag like Flossie?"

"Don't ask me," Minnie laughed, "He's fascinated by her. Not in *that* way you understand. I suppose he's never seen anything like her in his life before. "No, Sally's the big draw."

"Ah, I see." Elenora answered, "For a minute there..."

"Well, poor love, might look like a Hollywood filum star but he's more than a bit naïve to think he might have a chance with Sally. No dear, like all the lads from the hospital Sally's the big attraction."

"Has this – what's his name – Burgess asked Sally out yet?"

"Everybody calls him Buddy. Not a day goes by when he doesn't ask her." Minnie replied, "Sally is not that easily impressed. Ah, but Miss Clapworthy, tha' hasn't seen him. He's bloody gorgeous! I tell thi', if I were forty years younger, I'd be in there. I'd teach him what it's for."

"He's that special then?" Elenora said chuckling at the exuberance of her friend's passionate reply.

"I could bite a lump out of him!" Minnie enthused; he's just like a blond version of Rudolph Vaselino!"

"Sally hasn't found herself a decent fellow yet then?" Elenora asked, "It must be two years since Billy was killed...?

"...It's over *two* year!" Minnie corrected, "I'm always reminding her that she could have her pick of any man around here, but she won't have it – blows cold when ever any of 'em asks her out." Minnie was warming to her inside knowledge of Sally's love life – or lack of it. "Ah, but did you know Miss Clapworthy, there's one lovely fellow watched over her religiously since Billy was killed! Without fail sees her safely home every night after the pub closes. He takes her little lad Brandon to the football, gives him all sorts of little treats. If his duties take him away from the immediate vicinity, he makes sure, his subordinate sees her home. If that isn't devotion I don't know what is. I'll bet you can't imagine who he is can you, eh? Go on, have a guess!" Revelling in her inside knowledge Minnie paused for effect as long as she could without bursting. *"...Sergeant Wilkinson!"* She revealed triumphantly.

"Arnold...?" Elenora said, "...but they're perfect for each other. What's the matter with the pair of them?"

"It's Arnold." Minnie answered, He's too backward in coming forward, too shy to ask her out. Thinks he's too old. She thinks he's just seeing her home out of a sense of duty. I'll tell thee summat though if he doesn't make a move soon some other fellow will snap her up."

Sally knew in her heart the gentle sergeant's affection for her was true and rock solid, but that knowledge had not yet reached her head. Nor would it until she felt able to throw off the layers of grief she still felt for her dead husband. Until such a time, there would be no sign of encouragement for any man, even Arnold.

The distance between *"The Feathers"*, where Sally works every evening and the little cottage she shares with her five year old son Brandon is less than a quarter of a mile distant, yet as Minnie so shrewdly observed, there was never a night passed when Arnold was not waiting to see her safely home.

"It's up to you Arnold" Minnie chastised, if I've told you once I've told you a dozen times – *make a damned move!* Don't be a wazzack. There's a queue a mile long for Sally's hand. Why do you think all them gorgeous Yankee lads fill the pub every night? Get in there!"

"She'll come round in good time Minnie." Arnold replied with a wry smile.

"Well you're not getting' no younger! No man can wait forever."

"I can." Arnold replied softly.

So it went on between the pair of them. Or more succinctly – so it **didn't** go on between them. Arnold would dutifully walk her home every night when he would talk of anything but the tender things he dearly wanted to say. Sally would walk along beside him with perfect ease, laugh sweetly whenever he made a joke, then at her door she would bid him a sweet but platonic "good-night", and he would lock his heart away until the next time.

When the blow came it came swiftly and devastatingly. One Friday night as they walked along Sally struggled to find the right words. When she did find them they came out far more glibly than she intended. Even off hand, and she regretted it.

"Don't bother picking me up tomorrow night after the pub closes Arnold," she said too casually, "I'm having the night off. Leah's minding Brandon. I'm going to a dance at the American barracks. They're providing transport."

"Oh right enough. "Arnold's voice was off hand and calm, diametrically opposed to the way he was feeling. Minnie's prediction was right. He should have made a move earlier. Now it was too late.

To compound his misery he had dismissed this monumental moment in his life with a casual *"Oh, right enough"*. Well it was *not* right enough. It was far from right enough. In fact the rising panic came to warn him that his life might never be right enough ever again.

That weekend was the lowest ebb in Arnold's entire life. He knew Sally had gone to the dance with all the other girls from the mill, and there was no mention of any one particular man involved. Still he felt – knew, things looked bad for him and his dream of a future with

Sally. In any case with so little to offer the message was clear – he was not necessary in her scheme of things. Where did he get off thinking he had any claim on her time in the first place?

Face it, he was much older than her – almost middle aged with few prospects of promotion. Receding hair! Come the end of the war he would be out of a job…and he was well aware that he was not termed a "flatfoot" for nothing he did actually have flat feet into the bargain.

The following Monday morning having had very little sleep over the weekend, plus all the aforementioned negatives rattling around inside his head he hardly noticed his straight talking old friend Minnie Clegg as she emerged from the Co-op shop with two loaded baskets of rations for the "*Feathers*"

"You might well look down in the mouth Arnold Wilkinson!" She admonished, in a tone as subtle as a clog iron."I've told thee time and time again to speak up and let Sally know how tha' feels. Now look what's happened"

"What! What's happened?" Arnold's heart momentarily stopped as his thoughts ran amuck imagining every possible disaster that might have happened ranging from road accident to rape and murder.

"Well, what did you expect?" Minnie let him have it straight from the shoulder. "She danced nearly every dance with that that Yankee sergeant, what's-his-name Jackson du Pree. Romantic name in't it? He walked her home afterwards an' all. You can't say I didn't warn you!"

"She has every right to let whoever she wants walk her home…" Arnold replied, trying to conceal the impossible weight of his sadness.   "…I don't own her you know Minnie, she has every right to go home with whoever she wants.

"Aye right," Minnie's patience was at an end, "...and tha' has every right to go and jump in't Mucky Beck you big lump, before I chuck you in for letting thy chances pass thi' by!" It was the nearest Minnie would ever come to kindly consolation, so he just smiled weakly and went about his business.

Never a bad loser Arnold carried on with his duties trying to put Sally out of his mind. But no matter how he tried he couldn't help dredging up all the negative reasons why she couldn't possibly have ever considered him as a suitor. After all, he told himself for the umpteenth time, he hadn't lost her really - he had never even won her in the first place. He was far too old for her. She was far too beautiful for him. He was far too dim. She was far too bright. Besides don't forget, he told himself - flat feet!

Such was Arnold's state of mind for the rest of that dreary Monday. Normally in the evening he would have checked the security with Bill Huggins the night watch man at Townsend's Textiles before strolling back towards the "Feathers" as it neared chucking out time, when he would hang around, officially to ensure the clientèle dispersed peacefully, but in reality it was to escort Sally home. Not this night. In his stead he sent his second in command Constable Barker to cover this task, whilst he wallowed in his misery back at the cop shop. He tried to concentrate on bringing the paper work up to date, but at the best of times his heart wasn't in office work and he fell once more to raking over the disastrous state of his heart. Roused from his musings by the telephone bell he was suddenly thrust back to consciousness with a cruel wallop.

"This is Craggs Bottom telephone h'exchange speaken..." It was Clara Oglethorp the elder by one hour of twins. The other twin Hazel, did the day shift at the tiny exchange, their official *"telephone"* voices indistinguishable one from the other. "...hurgint messidge for Sergeant Whilkinsen. Proceed h'immediately to the "Feathers" where there looks laik bein' a bit of bother to-naight. H'end of messidge!"

"Is that you Clara?" Arnold gently rebuked, "Why the 'ell don't you talk plain English. Cut to the quick Clara answered huffily,

"Hay'm h'enunciatin' the way Hay was taught to do,,,"

"You say there's a bit of bother at the "Feathers?" Arnold's concern rising alarmingly, knowing Constable Barker was not up to handling trouble, "...who gave you the message Clara?"

"Hay cawn't say, the pearson didn't leave a name. H'all Hay can say h'is, it was a female lady's voice."

Quick as a ferret on senna pods Arnold was out of the station and on his way to the "Feathers" before Clara had a chance to recite her official closer − "Thenk yew very match − h'end of messidge."

Relieved to find the *"Feathers"* customers all dispersed and the village deserted. Arnold found Constable Barker standing in Clitheroe's Pie Shop doorway yawning and waiting for the tiny blue safety light to go out in the pub doorway. This was the sign that Flossie had locked up for the night, when he could return to the warmth of the cosy sub station, sign off then go home to the comfort of his single bed.

"Nah then Archie, what's going on? It seems quiet enough, was there any bother at chucking out time?"

"...Quiet as a graveyard Sergeant."

"Right! Well, tha'd better get thi'sen back to the station," Arnold said, "I had a message that there was some bother on up here. "I wouldn't put it past Chief Superintendent Cartwright to send a false alarm like that to make sure we was on our toes then sneak round here to check that we had followed it up."

The very thought of Chief Superintendent Cartwright planning his downfall was enough to send Archie Barker into a muck sweat. "Right oh Sarge!" Seldom moving faster than a leisurely stroll Archie fairly leaped to obey.

"Calm down Archie. I didn't say it *was* from the C.O. I just said it *might have been.* Arnold shouted after the fast receding Constable. In spite of his heavy heart Arnold was forced to smile at the comic dread of his young assistant's fear of higher authority as he ran through the deserted street back to the cop shop.

"I'd better just check in case the phone call *did* come from the *"Feathers"* Arnold thought.

Flossie, annoyed to be disturbed whilst counting the day's takings screeched raucously at the beautiful Alsatian. "Get down Caesar. It's only Sergeant Wilkinson."

"I just thought I'd check. I had a message there was a disturbance..." Arnold said as his heart went into overdrive on catching sight of Sally donning her coat and headscarf.

"No Sergeant," Flossie replied in her usual brittle manner, "I didn't ring, did either of you two?"

"Not me." Sally answered, her lovely eyes looking straight into Arnold's, .

"What about you Minnie? Did you phone the Cop Shop?" Minnie didn't look up from the sink where she was finishing off the last of the nights washing up.

"Phone? Me?" Minnie fibbed. "You wouldn't catch me using one of them new fangled articles!" It did not escape Arnold's notice that she was beaming from ear to ear trying desperately hard to hide her guilty face from the other two women. "But since you are here young

Wilkinson you might make yourself useful and see this here lass gets home safely."

Once out side the pub Arnold turned to Sally with a wry smile. "You do realise we've been set up, don't you? Minnie the Matchmaker!"

"I'm a bit disappointed you needed "*setting up*" Sally replied with a mischievous smile that sent Arnold into meltdown. "I missed you when you didn't walk me home last night."

"Nay well, er..." Arnold faltered, "I thought that American GI Buddy Burgess or whatever his name is would be taking thee home...like he did the night before... after the dance at the barracks."

"Well, he wanted to," Sally replied. "But I told him not to bother; I went home on my own."

"He didn't try anything on did he? 'Cos if he did..."

"No, no." Sally answered, "Nothing like that. In fact he was the perfect gentleman."

"Well why didn't you let him walk you home?" Arnold couldn't let the subject drop.

"I don't know – maybe just the wrong person at the time. There's something about him I just can't fathom. Something about his eyes" Sally said as she linked her arm into Arnold's with he thought, more warmth than she had ever done before.

"What about his eyes? I understand from Minnie that all the Yankee's have gorgeous *"come to bed eyes."*

"They have!" Sally answered. Then without thinking she added, "But they're not your eyes...*like* your eyes I mean to say." She began to giggle, aware probably for the first time in their long acquaintanceship Arnold was the only man in front of whom she could make a slip like that and get away with it.

"Sally," Suddenly Arnold was anxious again, glad of the darkness covering his bashfulness. He looked straight ahead as they walked along, for if his gaze met hers he knew he would lose the ability to speak coherently. "I know you still have feelings for Billy, and always will have, and I respect that. I know I have nothing to offer you. I'm not even a proper bobby; I only have the job because there's a war on. I'm more than ten years older than you and I have fla..."

"...And you have flat feet, I know," she said affectionately. "Arnold don't go on,,,"

"Let me finish Sally..." He paused to find the right words, for he knew if he didn't find them now he never would. "I don't presume to have the right to say...but I live in the hope that one day I might have..."

"...I know Arnold," Suddenly hungry for the tenderness of Arnold's words. For the first time since Billy's death the pent up longing stabbed at her heart. "What kind of a fool would I be if I didn't see what a wonderful, sweet man you are? But I'm still not over Billy's death and don't know if I ever will be, it would be very wrong of me to keep you hanging.."

"I don't mind..."

"It's not fair on you..."

"I'll be the judge of that..."

"Supposing I never..."

She turned to look up at him through the near total darkness. There was enough light however for him to see her cheek wet with tears. He cupped her face tenderly in his hands, gently brushing away the tears with his thumbs.

"Never is a long time." He answered,

"But..."

"I can wait..."

"But Arno..."

"Forever, if you'll let me." And if he did live forever he would never know which of them initiated the kiss that followed. It was not a kiss that told him his wait was over. There was no happy ending in the kiss – not yet anyway. It was a kiss however that held promise. It was a kiss that meant hope and for now Arnold was more than content with that.

"Good night Arnold." Sally quickly turned and went indoors.

Arnold was no fool. He knew his life had just hit the high watermark. This new and exquisite feeling was important and blessedly welcome. His flat feet hardly touching the flagstones he blithely set off back to the sub-station. Through the sleeping village he floated seemingly two feet above the ground. In a state of romantic reverie he drifted past the Co-op, not the familiar everyday establishment he knew, for now the world had taken on a new and exquisite aura. The Co-op was now the Taj-Mahal, not hidden by the blackout but bathed in glorious Technicolour. He floated by the now fragrant palm bedecked public toilets. What had been only minutes earlier a cold wet March night was now swathed in moonlight and wasn't that a warm tropical sea breeze floating by? The string section of his imagined orchestra swelled reaching a romantic climax... Arnold stopped abruptly in his journey through wonderland feeling the need to remind himself this was not a Hollywood film set he found himself floating through..

"Get a grip Arnold Wilkinson, you daft bugger," he told himself. "This is Craggs Arse, not Santa Barbara Beach! There's no orchestra! You're losing the plot!" Then, without warning Cupid once more reasserted his hold. "Just hold on a minute, who says there isn't an orchestra? If I hear strings then I hear strings! And trumpets! And harps!

In a trice Police Sergeant Wilkinson re assumed his role as starry-eyed lover in his MGM fantasy. He smiled the most beguiling smile as if awaiting his bell note then in a voice as flat as his feet, began to sing ever so softly -"…*they wouldn't believe me, that from this great big world she's chosen me…*

………………………………..

FEATHERS FLOAT
WHILST PEARLS LIE LOW

Bill Huggins bustled cheerfully through the staff door ready to take over his shift as night watchman from his daytime counterpart Ernest Briggs.

"Time for you to get off Ernie," Bill said as he stacked the necessities that would see him through the lonely night until Ernie returned the following morning – a flask of cocoa and a box of sandwiches. "Your Bertha will be stood on the door step, watching out for thee coming. She'll have your tea waiting on the hob for you, you lucky man!"

"Aye. I would have been on my way before now," Ernie replied, "only I thought I'd better hang on to warn thee that his "Lordship" Mr Townsend is still in his office. His missus is having one her "at homes," one of her posh whist drives in aid of the refugees. So "him upstairs" is in no hurry to rush off home." Ernie mimed drinking from a glass, together with a drunken stagger conveying the warning that the boss, the "big man," was hitting the bottle.

"Ay, ay! Don't tell me…" Bill got the message.

"You guessed it – as a newt! He must have got through at least two of them there Black Market bottles of

White Horse. He's been at it since the middle of the morning. He'll be a while yet before he's fit to make a move for home.

Townsends Textiles owner, Mr Herbert Townsend had a number of fatal flaws – excess of booze, lack of moral fibre and a mean spirit. Not to mention a vile temper, and a total disregard for the well being of his workers. The list goes on. The workforce at the mill condensed these descriptions of the man into one short phrase – *"A right shithouse"*

"I'll get off home now Bill" Ernie said as he made for the door, "but watch the old bugger, he's been suppin' solid since ten o'clock this morning, and when I looked in at tea time he was still at it,"

"Right you are Ern!" I'll do me best to steer clear of him. Have a nice evening, see you in the morning!" Locking the door behind his friend, Bill went about his routine chores, tasks like checking the fire precautions were all in order and the lights were out, apart from the tiny blue emergency lights on each floor before returning to the little cubby hole with the two telephones – internal and National. All tickerty-boo! now, Bill had the deserted factory to himself. Apart from the big boss,

Some would have hated being alone in the vast empty building but Bill, a cheerful, good natured little fellow seemed perfectly suited to the post of night watchman. In spite of a few set backs, like a mean minded employer and rock bottom wages, he considered himself lucky to have such a cushy number. Especially since he was not from Craggs Bottom originally. There was no-one breathing down his neck for one thing, and the gassing he had received in the trenches had left his lungs in a bad way. He had to take it easy. Alone in the eight story mill at night, he was able to do just that.

Clocking on duties completed, he poured himself a mug of cocoa, switched on the wireless to listen to Alvar Liddell read the latest war news before settling down in the well worn wicker basket chair and his latest blood and thunder library book.

Shortly before ten o'clock the urgent ringing of the in-house telephone shattered the silence of the watchman's little room by the staff entrance. He reached out for the receiver and even before he got it to his ear he feared the worst.

"Come on! Come on!" Without preamble, the belligerent timbre of Mr Townsend's voice, heavy with liquor boded ill. "Where the bloody hell's the duty porter?"

"Duty porter speaking Mr Townsend", Bill answered pleasantly, remembering Ernie's warning.

"Well listen man, the bloody lift isn't working. **Both** bloody lifts aren't working. What the hell's going on?

""Oh! Sorry sir! That's right sir. The passenger lifts are switched off after the last shift on a Saturday." Trying to be helpful, Bill added, "but I left the emergency staircase lights on for you sir..." It was like the proverbial red rag to a drunken bull. Mr Townsend exploded.

"Dear Jesus...! Damn it all man, do you expect me to walk down eight bloody flights! What do you think I am...put me on to your immediate superior..."

"Can't do that sir, there's only me here!" Keeping his cool Bill remained matter of fact persevering to keep the old man as near sanity as possible. "But sir, of course you are right sir. What about the wool bale hoist? That's still operating? If you wouldn't mind walking down two flights to the sixth floor, that's as far as the hoist will reach, I'll bring it up to meet you."

"...The **hoist?** - That sodding cage thing? That's at the back of the building! Look here! Who the hell am I dealing with here? What's your name man?"

114

"It's Bill Huggins sir. Night watchman, I'm on my way up sir, meet you at the sixth floor. Unable to see any sense in prolonging the unpleasantness any longer, Bill hung up the phone.

The "old groaner", as the hoist was known by the staff, installed in the early part of the twentieth century and last renovated shortly after the Great War, was long past its efficient best. Slow and noisy with breakdowns almost a daily occurrence it would leave some unfortunate "bobbin ligger" - boy labourer, in tears. Or more likely nowadays, owing to the shortage of men, it would be a woman porter stranded between floors unable to escape until the maintenance men were called in.

The catalogue of breakdowns, mechanical and nervous was endless. The motor was operated not by pressing buttons but by pulling on opposing ropes – one for "up" and one for "down". It was a worryingly temperamental operation even for those used to its cantankerous moods. Unfortunately Bill Huggins was not one of them.

After three attempts he managed to coax some life into the old motor, then gently pulling on the "up" rope, just so far – not a fraction further, it began to inch its way heavenwards. After what seemed an eternity the broken winded workhorse of a lift bounced to a halt. Only vaguely in the vicinity of the sixth floor, but at least near enough to permit the diamond mesh rattrap like gates to open wide enough to allow Bill space enough to squeeze through and run up the final two flights of stairs. Arriving breathless and gasping asthmatically for breath he found the furious red faced, liquor bloated mill owner pacing the landing catatonic with rage.

"Where the hell have you been till now man...?" Herbert Townsend bellowed drunkenly, his face twisted with contempt. His show of anger only slightly dissipated somewhat by the sheer pleasantness of the little man he saw before him.

"Here we are sir, sorry it took so long." Bill remained calm and respectful as he closed the cage doors behind them. "Never mind, I'll have you downstairs in a couple of shakes." Once they were inside, Bill pulled gently on the "down" rope only to hear the Motor cough, splutter and fall silent, much to the disgust of his passenger whose ominous rumblings threatened to erupt again at any second. Bill had to repeat the operation three times before he made a successful connection with the motor. Finally the hoist wheezed into life, only to judder to an immediate halt once more.

"A work of art sir, trying to align these old gears" Bill offered by way of appeasement, "I suppose it's a thing the regular operators get used to." Bill threw an anxious glance over his shoulder at his brooding passenger who stood in the middle of the six by eight feet space the cage afforded. Impatiently seething and spoiling for a ruckus the inebriated man exploded

"Good God man! Will you get this bloody contraption **moving**?" The awaited tantrum arrived with a vengeance. "Are you altogether, completely sodding well useless?"

"I'm doing my best sir..."

"Get out of my way you bloody idiot, let me get at it..." Bill was hurled ferociously by the shoulder away from the controls, hitting the back wall of the lift, he watched with dismay as the big man tugged frantically, first on one rope and then on the other, making the ancient hoist jump violently down then up. Too much for the tired old motor! It gave up the ghost.

The final lurch upwards however took the hoist too far to allow the double gates to open. With the exception of about six inches at their feet, all that could be seen

116

through the diamond mesh of the gates was solid brick wall. They were trapped.

There was a moment of silence from the mill owner before he sprang to life again. Now he turned to vent his fury against this stupid underdog of a man who had stranded him in this dreadful Limbo. Growling like an animal before the kill, he pounced. Grabbing Bill by the lapels he began to shake him violently.

At the very instant he made his move, smoke from the burned out motor began to seep down the lift shaft to reach their nostrils. The effect this had on the big man was almost as alarming as had been his fury.

His ruddy face drained of colour, His eyes almost popped out with terror and an unearthly wail escaped him. Bill recognised this reaction. He had witnessed men cracking up twenty odd years earlier in the trenches of Flanders. It was a tragically too regular occurrence. But in this instance the smoke was an act of timely providence – it reversed their roles completely.

"Now then, now then," Bill's steady, calm approach had at least a temporary effect. "It's not as bad as it looks Mr Townsend. It's just that the motor has burnt out. The smoke will soon clear."

"But if the motor is dead, I'm stuck here! I can't get out! Supposing the fire isn't out, and it spreads? I could be burnt alive"

"No, no sir. You'll be alright." Bill's quiet strength was enough to reassure the other man, at least long enough to buy time. "Look sir, the smoke is already beginning to disperse." True enough, even as he spoke the smoke began to clear. "You see sir, its clearing. Now try to keep calm. I'll sound the alarm." Bill broke the glass panel and pressed the red button. Immediately in the distance six floors beneath them they heard the urgent clanging of the alarm bell

"There now," Bill said brightly, "you see sir, we'll soon be alright, and look the smoke's already almost gone."

Temporarily subdued the boss, like a frightened child looked pleadingly at Bill,. "Somebody will hear that bell won't they?"

"Of course they will sir, of course!" Bill averted his eyes. He got no pleasure seeing this unpleasant man disintegrate.

The good news was that the fire in the motor housing had died out, but the bad news, which Bill had no intentions of sharing - was the impossible odds of the alarm bell being heard by anybody but themselves. They were in for a long incarceration in the shabby, dead old hoist. The possibility of it plunging six floors was not his major concern. The unpredictable tantrums of his fellow captive posed a much greater danger.

From the opposite corner of their space Bill tried to assess the old man's condition. Under Bill's scrutiny his charge, for that is what the mill owner had become, stood shaking, his watery eyes darting first to the left then the right like a trapped animal, unaware of the wet patch at the front of his trousers.

Still, if the man's peed pants were the worst that might happen before this ordeal was over, that would suit Bill very nicely thank you! Unfortunately by the look of the agitation building up in Mr Townsend it might not be the end of Bill's trouble.

Going by the earlier flare up Bill tried to guess his chances in a one to one with his fellow prisoner. They didn't look good. The big man was almost twice his own weight, fit, strong, fuelled by at least two bottles of whisky and capable of doing a lot of harm. Slipping off his tie, Bill began working out a strategy – just in case...

In spite of the bizarre situation as it stood at present Bill was unable to throw off the niggling sensation of *déjà vu.* Vague images kept slipping into his mind of a similar situation having been played out in a previous life. Or was it a real memory he would rather forget? Whatever it was, the visions were vivid. Perhaps they were from that long ago battlefield of earlier times. He was getting flashes of himself trying to subdue a hysterical young officer whose antics were in danger attracting the attention of the enemy machine guns...

The sudden sound from above was like a rifle shot hurling Bill out of his reverie, returning him the present predicament with a jolt. Realising at once the noise he heard was the snapping of an overhead cable, followed by the screech of metal on metal as one side of the lift dropped alarmingly.

The sudden movement sent Bill careering across the floor, hitting his head hard on the opposite wall. He didn't have long to dwell on his injury however for with this new crisis Mr Townsend plunged into a renewed sate of high hysteria, skittering around the tiny confines like a cornered rat.

"It's alright!" Bill shouted above the unearthly squealing, "it's only dropped a little bit at one end. Nothing serious! You're going to be alright!" The mill owner swung around, his eyes wild, his voice shrill, cold fear cut through the alcohol making his words maniacal and aggressive. But for all that, He was articulate and measured.

"I'm **not** going to be alright you stupid little bastard. I'm going to be killed. Don't you know what that sound was?"

"It was one of the hawsers breaking." Bill answered calmly and honestly.

119

"…And you know what its purpose was, do you? It was probably the only thing preventing this shitty contraption from plummeting me six stories to my death! And it's all your fucking fault…!"

With the speed of the demons that possessed him the big man brought the back of his hand across Bill's jaw then grabbed him tightly by the lapels. Bill found himself nose to nose with a madman. Snorting like a bull in the ring, with his left hand the mill owner held Bill by his jacket whilst his right aimed heavy blows to Bill's jaw. No match for the strength of his opponent Bill knew he must put his only partly formed strategy into action.

With all the force he could muster he brought his knee up into Mr Townsend's unprotected wet crutch.

The effect was dramatic. Grasping his throbbing private parts Townsend doubled up gasping for breath. Then a well-aimed uppercut from Bill floored his crazed opponent. Swiftly and with deft handed efficiency Bill rolled the great hulk over on to his stomach. Using his necktie the diminutive night watchman tied the other man's hands behind his back. The blows to his jaw and the sheer strength needed to subdue the big man had aggravated Bill's asthma. This meant there was an added urgency to secure his boss so he may do no more damage. He knew he must act quickly before giving in to the inevitable bout of coughing that usually followed any such activity. Slipping the expensive silk tie from around the neck of his adversary Bill tied the man's feet to the diamond mesh grill of the hoist door.

Thankfully Bill's coughing fit was not as bad as he anticipated. He turned his attention back to the safely trussed up moaning figure. Crossing the now slanting floor, he heaved the old man up, propped him in a more comfortable position against the wall with his feet still tied securely to the bars of the gate. Thankful his captive boss didn't seem to realise he was tied both hands and feet. Bill tried again to reason with him.

"Now listen to me Mr Townsend." Bill was firm but gentle. "Can you understand me? I had to clock you one to stop you doing yourself, and me a mischief. But you'll be as right as rain after you've slept it off"

In a daze, his eyes gazing into space, jowls sagging and with saliva trickling freely from the corners of his gaping mouth Townsend's almost inaudible low pitched moan informed Bill how tenuous the big man's hold on reality was.

"Did you hear me Mr Townsend? Eh? You're going to be alright. Give us a nod if you heard me!" The sorry heap of humanity managed an almost non-existent nod, never the less this response to Bill's quiet authority was welcome.

"Now then, the hawser you heard snapping was only one of four holding this lift up. The chances are millions to one against any one of the remaining three breaking. On top of that there is still the Otis safety ratchet which is designed to hold twenty tons, let alone two old codgers like you and me!" Bill spoke convincingly and with confidence. The fact that his knowledge of "Otis ratchets and hawsers" was mostly guess work hardly mattered. The semi - fib had the desired effect

"Do you understand what I'm saying Mr Townsend?" The nod this time was more definite. "Now just try to be as relaxed as possible, it won't be long before they come to get us out." Bill rolled up his jacket and placed it behind the other man's head, then wiped the spittle from Townsend's chin before settling down for he long wait.

He knew of course, there was no chance of rescue before morning. Not early either, as the next day was Sunday and Ernie didn't arrive until nine thirty or ten o'clock. Mr Townsend mustn't know that of course. The most important thing was to keep the old man "sweet". Get him to talk. Open-up. Less isolated within his wretchedness.

"Mind you," Bill said brightly, as if the previous episode had never taken place. "These old hoists were built to last. There's no denying they've lost the knack nowadays. Throw away society! Built-in obsolescence! Eh, sir?" Bill tried not to sound too obvious in searching for a point of interest to get the old man to open up.

"...Nothings the same, is it?!" Bill went on, "...quality! Workmanship! Those were things that belonged to our generation...am I right, or am I right?"

Still the drunken man did not take the bait. Unmoved, he sat staring straight ahead.

"I mean to say, take a look at 'em today." Bill went on, "How can they be expected to come up with good work, they don't have the training you and me got, do they?

Still no answer was forthcoming.

."...I mean, nowadays," Bill kept at it, determined to get through, "How can they be expected to have the same attitude towards a good day's work as our generation had – eh? I ask you!" These bigoted clichés were not Bill's true opinions at all – he believed the present generation were no worse, no better than his had been. He was however one hundred per cent accurate in judging that the drooling capitalist he was trying to pacify would have a more reactionary outlook. Bill Huggins was right. He was rewarded by a slight but definite response, in the way of a half formed sneer. Encouraged, Bill ploughed on.

"I'll tell you what I think, Mr Townsend, and I'm sure you'll bear me out. – You wouldn't catch today's lot putting up with what we went through in 1914, would you? You would not!"

Mr Townsends eyes remained glazed and fixed at some point on the floor, but the sheer persistence of this voicing of the sentiments in which he was steeped and believed wholeheartedly, coaxed another, but this time more definite flicker of agreement. Bill seized upon it and pressed on with renewed enthusiasm.

"Can you, in all honesty, imagine today's armed forces putting up with what we had to endure in the trenches? Can you...?

"The Army...!" The voice was so tiny Mr Townsend hardly realise he had spoken, but speak he did, and Bingo! Bill had found the key to release the other man from his miserable isolation..

"Bet you could have shown them a thing or two, eh Mr Townsend?"

"...Buggers don't know they're born." The mill owner muttered in the smallest of voices. "...Don't know they're born! Different breed these days"

At last on a winner, Bill went for the home run.

"Did you serve in the Army sir?"

"Did I serve in the army? Huh! I should say so. I was one of the first to volunteer in 1914... served with BEF... France..."

Bull's eye! Bill had hit on the open sesame that released the floodgates. From then on there was no stopping the drunken ramblings. Bill, now more content he was in a less dangerous position, closed his eyes, only half listening to the drawling speech of his half mad captive.

"...Peace by Chrizzmas..." Mr Townsend slurred, happy now in his sozzled mind that he "had the floor" he launched into his oft repeated reactionary diatribe that had probably bored generations of unfortunate Rotary members. "...Sir John French promizzed. Peace by Chrizzmas! I sez to him...I told him...there was no quesh'n that Kaiser Willy and the whole bloorry Gerry war machine realised... *knew* frrr-aa fact they were up the prover-bal creek without the prover-bal- fuck'n -paddle..."

....

Bill awoke with a start wondering how long he'd been asleep. He looked at his watch it was ten past four. The night was passing nicely. His cellmate was still droning on, not quite in the same drunken monotone as earlier, but talking with a little more coherence. Happily either unaware or perhaps past caring he was still bound hand and foot. Judging it would be wise to leave him Bill closed his eyes again, only half listening to the other man's bigoted ramblings.   The night was passing, that was the main thing.

"...Not just the officers, some of the men too... heroes, the bloody lot of us" On and on droned the biased, self promoting monologue. "Probably the most decorated battalion in the British Army! Deservedly too! Like one little fellow in my unit, crawled back into enemy lines time after time to drag the wounded back to safety, and bear in mind he was under constant fire from the blasted German machine gun nest..."

Bill was suddenly starkly alert! The story being told by the drunken man related directly to his previous feeling of déjà vu.

",,, not a big fellow but he was fearless. He must have gone back half a dozen times to bring someone else out. Mentioned in Dispatches I saw to that!"

"In your Unit sir, where was that again?"   Bill asked quietly

"Ypres, you fool! Where else?" Mr Townsend seemed annoyed at the interruption. He was on a roll now and eager to resume his narrative.

"Brave little bugger. Naturally I ordered him to attend to the wounded, other ranks first.

"I was the last to be evacuated from the bomb crater." .

He knew there was something familiar about Mr Townsend which he hadn't been able to pin down. Now here in this broken old hoist, in this broken old man, he recognised the boy.

Bill stared incredulously as all the facts fell into place. Although Mr Townsend's warped version of events were enough to prompt Bill's memory, they were also enough to remind him of the truth of that fateful day they shared in that shell crater in No Man's Land.

"...Never forget him," Mr Townsend picked up his story once again, "...nondescript sort of a fellow, labourer I suppose in Civvies Street. I remember vividly, he had jokey, lower order sort of name, like the servants used to have in those drawing room plays. Now, let's see... Huggett! That's it! Charlie Huggett! His name was in all the papers at the time

"Huggins!" Bill corrected with a quiet irony. "Bill Huggins."

"Eh? Hold your tongue man, who asked your opinion?" Townsend's train of thought had once again been violated. His temper flared momentarily before he picked up on this oft told version, riddled with well polished anecdotes, repeated ad nauseam for the benefit of fellow members of some expensive "Club"

Listening intently now to this travesty, Bill was forced to face up to the real story he had tried so hard to forget. There were no "Boy's Own" heroics in his memory of the incident. There was only sadness, loss, humility, gratitude plus a lasting conviction that some other greater power had taken care of them on that long-ago day in the mud of Flanders.

Cut off by the German machine gun post, Bill Huggins, the only able bodied man present in that shell hole knew he must get his mates out of there before the heavy artillery started up again, as it surely would. Scrambling on his hands and knees Bill did a quick body count at the same time trying to make the wounded as comfortable as possible. Apart from himself there were two young boys both badly wounded, and Sergeant Holloway who although unable to walk, having been hit in the shoulder and leg was still however very much in charge and concerned about his men.

"Right now Bill," although unable to move it was impossible to realise that Sergeant Bert Holloway was in any other way injured, "I'd go me self, but you're younger and lither than me so I want you to run and tell the mad buggers at head quarters. Tell them there's what's left of our division in this shit hole, tell the barmy sods to hold their fire ..."

"Right, Bert! Bill hoisted one of the young boys on to his shoulder, "No point in going empty handed is there Serge?" The second he got out of the hole with the boy on his back the machine gun started again. Sergeant Holloway knew that Bill couldn't possibly survive, but miracles happen and within what seemed like no time at all Bill came slithering down the side of the crater again.

"What the bloody hell are you doing back here?" the amazed sergeant asked, "did you manage to get the lad back to our lines, and most importantly did you tell them to hold their fire.

"...Did all of that Serge...!"

"Well what in God's name are you doing back here?"

"I came back for you two. I'm not leaving you here it's your turn to buy the drinks!" The friendly banter was cut short by the entry of yet another character seeking shelter from the gunfire. Down the side of the muddy incline of their dubious shelter came slithering a young British Officer, flailing around with the most severe bout of hysterics Sergeant Holloway had ever seen.

"He's lost his marbles Bill. Try to get him to keep his head down, if he's seen above the parapet he'll draw their fire. Try to hold him down."

Bill struggled with the young officer whose arms and legs were lashing around dangerously. Managing at last, after a tussle he could well have done without Bill managed to subdue the young man and bring him down next to the wounded sergeant, who without further ado administered a sharp but effective tap with his rifle butt to the back of the officer's head, rendering him unconscious and therefore harmless.

"That should keep him quiet long enough for you to get out again"

"No Serge, you've enough on your hands. I'll take him with me. See you serge!" Again Bill climbed out of the muddy pit with the young Lieutenant on his back. Again the machine gun played the deadly accompaniment as Bill ran for the Allied trenches.

Burt Holloway gasped in total admiration and wonder as Bill came sliding back into the hole for a third time. Neither Bill nor the Sergeant could find words for the sheer miracle that had allowed Bill to escape certain death for a second time. As he hoisted the last of the young wounded boys on to his back he merely turned and winked to the sergeant and left. Alone now in the crater Sergeant Holloway didn't dare hope that Bill's luck would extend to yet another trip back to the Allied Trenches. Yet in that parting wink of the eye from Bill, there was a sign, something holy, otherworldly.

. In the face of incredible odds Sergeant Holloway kept faith. Bill ran the gauntlet for the fourth time.

Exhausted now, stumbling clumsily he went down on his knees a few times but each time with the bullets whizzing by he managed to get back on his feet, to complete the miracle. Sgt. Holloway. the last of the wounded men was returned to comparative safety. The machine gun went silent and there was a sound of cheering coming from the German lines.

....

"Bill! Bill! Can you hear me? Are you alright? Ernie's voice carried up the lift shaft.

"Yes we're fine Ernie, nice to hear your voice!"

"Hang on! We'll have you down in no time at all. Hang on!" Within five minutes the hoist was being lowered gingerly inch by inch, to the nearest exit and finally the two men were released from their prison. Ernie, Police Sergeant Wilkinson, Constable Barker greeted them with concerned and anxious expressions on their faces. Mr Townsend ignored their attentions and without acknowledging either his fellow captive or the elated group celebrating the successful rescue. The mill owner walked away from the madness of the previous night into the normality of the bright Sunday morning.

"Do you think he'll be alright, Mr Huggins?" Constable Barker asked,

"He'll be alright son", Bill answered, "It was a bit of an ordeal for him. Bit of a shock you understand?"

"Bit of an ordeal for you too!" Ernie put in with genuine concern. "You must be knackered. You make sure you take a day or two off work to get over it!"

"Can't do that Ernie, got to come in tonight. I didn't get a chance to finish my library book, and it's due back on Monday." jokingly replied ex 241609 Private William Higgins V.C.

....

THE KEEPER OF THE FLAME

It was common knowledge in the village that Ambler Thorn or Ambler Manor as it has been known from antiquity was *"infested"*, *"alive"*, *"running wick"* with ghosts of every description.

But since the old building, so often rumoured as being Emily Bronte's model for her classic, *"Wuthering Heights"* was now the home and workplace of Elenora Clapworthy. Primarily a Veterinary Surgeon also a leading Pedigree Alsatian breeder, leader of the hottest little Jazz band in Yorkshire,not to mention occasionally sitting on the Board of Magistrates. It was felt that no traditional, regular ghost could possibly function in such lively and fun filled atmosphere.

Young Mickie Ryan though, lived in the new housing estate and the ancient pile's reputation hadn't yet reached his ears. To him on this winter afternoon as the meagre light was losing its grip on the day, it looked decidedly spooky. Catching the first gloomy sight of the heavy slate roof and thick granite walls with its deep set bubble glass window panes he could well imagine, especially having so recently seen the movie where Cathie Earnshaw (Merle Oberon) was seen calling for her Heathcliff (Laurence Olivier) through just such a window. Ambler Manor was definitely a scary aspect.

He hesitated as he dragged his bogey-cart, an orange box mounted on a set of old pram wheels, from which he hawked his bundles of firewood. The wind whistling noisily around the gable end of the building tugging at his shabby coat and lifting the flaps of his imitation flying helmet. Should he heed the warning of the wind and make a dash for it whilst he was still able? Then he remembered he hadn't made more than a bob all day. No, sod the ghosts! He needed a sale. Again he hesitated as he heard what sounded like the snuffling of a wolf inside one of the out-buildings – he had no doubt this was the case, after all Sherlock Holmes (Basil Rathbone) came to exactly the came conclusion in *"Hound of the Baskervilles"*, it could only be a wolf in such a setting. Should he turn back before it was too late? But by this time he had passed through the gate into the circular driveway where carriages would have pulled up, no doubt with a headless driver on the reins. For a third time he stopped only a couple of yards from the forbidding front door remembering his own appearance was hardly likely to make any customer, either alive or of the spirit world warm to him. He was more than grubby and he knew it.

In fact he was downright filthy! But damn it all, scrounging wood and chopping it up is a mucky job! There was no response to his first timid attempt on the heavy knocker. Steeling himself to try once more he lifted the striker– a sneering cast iron lion's head - reminding him that his every move was tempting all the ghosts who lay in wait ready to pounce. He slammed the knocker down with more than reasonable force, immediately regretting the reverberating cacophony he had set loose, sending overlapping echoes bouncing throughout the interior of the big old house. The chaos in the kennels, together with the angry barking of another hell hound on the other side of this very door almost sent him into a panic. Only his steely determination to improve his miserable sales record empowered him to resist the desire to turn and run away.

At last he heard footsteps from deep inside. They were coming nearer. Eventually the heavy oak door creaked opened revealing not the hound of hell he feared, or the stony faced housekeeper as played by Judith Anderson in *"Rebecca."* His heart returned from his mouth to it's rightful place when he saw it was none other than lovely old Dora Armitage, one of his regular customers who lived in one of the cottages in Stephenson's Fold. In his self inflicted terrorized state he'd forgotten that Mrs. Armitage worked as kennel maid cum housekeeper to the famous Elenora Clapworthy

"Mick love, is that you?" she queried, and then to the sloppy looking mongrel who had previously made such a frightening noise, who now rather than attacking the caller was being embarrassingly affectionate. "Get down Heinz! Its nobbut Mickie Ryan! Was that you Mick, trying to bang the door down?"

"Sorry Mrs. Armitage, I didn't mean to knock so loud."

"It's alright doy. Not your fault that damned knocker has a will of its own. "Oh Love I'm sorry to have to disappoint you but tha' wasting thee time here lad, hawking kindling! But you better come in to't kitchen, tha' looks frozen to thi' marrers." She bustled the boy into the kitchen where she bade him sit up to the stove whilst she made him a cup of cocoa and gave him a thick slice of bread and dripping.

"Why do you say I'm wasting me time trying to sell firewood here, Mrs. Armitage?" Mick asked, "Have they got a gas poker or summat?"

"Didn't you know? There's no use for kindling wood here, the fire in Ambler Thorn's main fireplace has never gone out for over a hundred years!"

"A hundred years?" Mick repeated in disbelief.

"Aye lad, it's still alight. Have you never heard the legend?" Mrs. Armitage was pleased to watch people's reaction when she repeated the legend of the *"fire that never went out."* She felt It gave her a certain gravity. "Owing to fuel rationing, it's no more than a few hot ashes, but there's still a tiny bit of life in it. They do say..." she adopted a reverent, mysterious voice, "...if ever these embers are allowed to perish anyone who has ever warmed their arse agen' it would never be warm again for as long as they live. Because then lad, the *"Lady in Grey"* would depart forever!" In spite of the awesome surroundings Mick stifled a smile at Dora's earnest histrionics. He came back to earth with a jolt. Having only a few moments earlier banished from his imagination any possibility of the supernatural, suddenly from the kitchen door directly behind where he was sitting came a third voice. He leaped from his seat with a yelp.

"You didn't tell me we were having company Dorothy..." Then the voice addressed Mick. "...Oh, sorry honey, I didn't mean to make you jump." Although he'd never met her Mick realized this was no ghost but was the fabled Elenora Clapworthy herself, in person. After the first glance he realized she was not at all frightening as expected. In fact she was very nice... old... very old by his reckoning, at least forty, but still good looking and attractive. More than that, there was a magnetism he found irresistible. He learned later this was the effect she had on most people. He was instantly at ease.

"Oh, Miss Clapworthy," Dorothy said, "this is Mickie Ryan, I've just made us both a cup of cocoa. Can I make thee one?"

132

"Love one." Elenora joined them at the enormous pine table. "Your fame precedes you young man!" She said, treating the boy to a beguiling smile. "Are you the same Mick Ryan who looked after his Mum when she had pneumonia?" Mick looked surprised, "and takes care of his little brothers..." Mick thought perhaps he had been wrong to dismiss his earlier pooh-poo-ing of there being no supernatural forces at work in this magical old house, this lady knew everything about him! And she'd never even met him until a minute earlier! "...and correct me if I'm wrong..." Elenora went on, her blue eyes twinkling mischievously, "...but I understand you're the young man who tamed Big Nellie Fawcett a couple of years ago? Noticing the boy's genuine bewilderment, Elenora decided to let him off the hook.

"No son, I'm not a mind reader" she laughed, "Mr. Walsh and Dora here are always singing your praises. It's an honour to meet you in person" Slightly embarrassed Mick smiled modestly. "Same here." he answered with a shy smile.

"Mick came to see if we wanted any kindling," Dora said, "I told him, it was like coals to Newcastle at this house, seeing as how the fire never went out."

"Hold on Dora," Elenora replied, "Its one thing never allowing the damn thing to die out, it's quite another finding the fuel to keep it alight. We'll take all you have son, if you can spare it." Mick couldn't believe his luck.

"Now...!" Elenora exclaimed with a burst of enthusiasm, "...how's this for a proposition Mick? Will you be good enough to stack the wood in the lean to? Work out how much we owe you. Then come and have a bite to eat with us – that's if we have any rations left. Have we Dora?"

"Well, I made us a *"Hunt Pie"* Dora said, "Got the recipe from *"Home Front"* It say's it's enough for six, so it should be enough for three of us."

"What's in it? Elenora asked.

"There's Lentils! Onions! Taters! Beans! Taters! Herbs! Did 'Ah mention taters? – "Oh, there's also four ounces of skirting!"

"…Four ounces of skirting! Such luxury!" Elenora laughed, "…You can see how it got the name "Hunt Pie" can't you Mick?"

"Yeah! You have to hunt for the meat!" The kid answered with a cheeky smile.

Sharing her meal with this bright youngster delighted the lady of the house enormously. In her role as a *"sometime magistrate"* she had become aware of the neglect of some of these kids from the poorer quarters, due to the call up of often both parents – the father to the Armed Forces, the mother to essential war work. Elenora knew via one of her major source of tittle-tattle - Mr. Walsh the local Air Raid Warden, that Mick, with father away in the Eighth Army and mother's ill health he was the one who held the family together.

She also knew one of the least workable directives from the Department of Education in the early stages of this war, was to order the closure of all school buildings within a two mile radius of the city centre in case of daylight raids. This seemed to her most ill considered. What she now learned from Mick - pupils from these inner areas, had to trek, often many weary miles, daily to share floor space in schools outside the so-called danger regions. With sometimes three classes in one room this soon became an impossible situation for both pupil and teacher. Chaos ensued. The solution was to close down all schools until further notice.

"Imagine the heartbreak amongst you kids!" Elenora said in mock sorrow. Mick recognized the irony of any kid being forced to stay away from school. His grin lit up the room.

"So what do you do with yourselves all day Mick?" Elenora asked.

"Run wild, over the moors and that...when I'm not selling firewood."

"Don't you miss school, just a little bit?"

"Not much," Mick answered, "maybe I miss painting and reading and music and history, but I don't miss getting caned by Mr. Dykes – Oh, and maths I don't miss maths, not one bit."

"That's a pretty comprehensive answer." Elenora smiled at his spontaneity. "What I can't understand," Mick said, having given the matter a little thought during the wood stacking, "if you want to get rid of the ghost why do you keep the fire going?"

"Get rid of Lulu!?" Elenora said in semi-mock shock, "we don't want to get rid of her! She lives here! That is, correction - she *haunts* here. It's her home too. Are you afraid of ghosts Mick?"

"There's no such thing." Mick answered with the assurance of someone who's not at all sure, then quickly added for fear he had hurt the lady's feelings."You don't believe in 'em, do you?"

"Well I've never seen one. Not even Lulu. I can't speak for Mrs Armitage though she's known this place longer than I have, eh Dora?"

"That's summat I don't discuss lightly." Dora said with only the barest hint of a smile.

"Let's just say this," Elenora said, "if Lulu does exist, she deserves a nice warm fire, don't you think Mick?"

"Yeah, I don't see why not." Then, his mind still on the wonder of the ancient flame, "what does a hundred year old fire look like?"

"At the moment, run down and decidedly old and grey," Elenora said, "But when we stoke up and get a bit of a roar going it works wonders and the old ashes don't look a day over ninety nine. Come through and I'll show you."

She led him from the kitchen, through the hall with the fine oak open staircase, their footsteps ringing on the flagstone floor and into the main split level reception room. Mick, like all first time visitors to Ambler Thorn was amazed at how so large a room on two levels, remained cosy and inviting. In his eagerness to see for himself, he made a beeline for the lower part of the room where the enormous inglenook fireplace dominated. Delighted to see stone benches set *inside* the walls of the open chimney, he went straight to examine the small heap of ashes with the almost non-existent live embers at its core, although they looked no different to ordinary mortal embers still they did not disappoint Mick's youthful imagination..

"Is that really over a hundred years old?" he asked with wide-eyed incredulity.

"It sure is!" Elenora replied smiling at his enthusiasm

"Wow!" Mick gasped, almost speechless with wonder, not just at the fire's great age but at the casual splendour of the room itself.

The deep, comfortable armchairs and sofas arranged around the vast Persian carpet with the large oak occasional table at its centre, a general dumping ground for sheet music, books, drinks trays, gramophone records, pens, pads, bric-a-brac, typewriter –all the tools of a busy professional. The room abounded with style, yet such was its welcoming aura there was nothing in the least intimidating for the kid from the estate. He was fascinated. Exploring the higher level of the room Mick was eager to take in the second most dominant feature after the fireplace, a full sized grand piano! Standing majestically in spite of the fact that little attempt had been made to impose tidiness in this area either. Amongst the happy clutter on the closed lid of the Steinway were silver photo frames a beautiful Fortuny Glass reading lamp, with yet more sheet music and gramophone records. Behind the piano stood an ancient jardinière holding a giant sized multi coloured Clarice Cliff vase, with an unstudied but tasteful arrangement of grasses, dried branches, berries and bulrushes. It was obvious however that in spite of the clutter the beautiful Steinway was far more than ornamental. Sharing the upper level of the room were music stands, a full drum kit, complete with a row of Jazz sculls. Band parts were strewn everywhere. Gingerly picking up a copy of sheet music with a photograph of Fred Astaire and Ginger Rogers on the cover, with as much reverence as if it were the *Mapa Mundi* Mick read aloud the name of the composer.

"Cole Porter!" he breathed in awe.

"You know of Cole Porter then Mick?" Elenora asked.

"Oh yes Miss," he answered innocently, "I know he writes some of the best songs in the world." He continued to leaf through the pile of manuscripts occasionally pausing to gasp in wonder when he came across yet another of his "most favourite" composers.

"Can you read music Mick?" Elenora asked.

"A little bit. I can read the top line, but it takes me a bit longer to read the bottom. But I have a piano! I bought one with me own money from the second hand shop for two pounds ten shillings!" He said proudly. "It needs tuning though."

"Do you have lessons?"

"No," Mick answered, without the slightest hint of self pity, me Mam say's we can't run to it."

It took Elenora no time at all to recognize the potential of this bright kid. She also recognized the dull future to which his present circumstances were leading him. She decided there and then she was having none of it.

"Mick, how would you like to help Dorothy and me in the kennels? Of course I'll pay you the going rate – and I'll teach you to play the Joanna. What do you say? - Better than humping firewood - right?" The look on the boy's face said it all. "O.K., that's settled then. All that remains is to get your Mam's permission, then you can start whenever you like."

Life took on a new meaning for Mickie Ryan. He loved his job in the kennels: his natural work ethic, his industry and aptitude with the animals, his total lack of queasiness preparing the offal for their feed pleased and delighted Dora. His talent for handling the temperamental coke fired boiler that heated the house, kennels and surgery soon made him an indispensable member of the household. But far above all else, his time spent in the big music room with Elenora at the Steinway teaching, encouraging, willing him forward opened a window on a life he never dreamed would be within his reach. The thing that thrilled his benefactress most of all was his boundless enthusiasm and progress with his music. Wisely his studies were not restricted to the piano. He was given free access to try guitar, banjulele and the more complicated banjo, even encouraged to bang away on the drums. Both teacher and pupil appeared to be merely having fun during these seemingly unstructured lessons, as indeed they were. But for all the laughter and fun his rapidly expanding expertise grew by the day and seemed to come mostly by example, but learn he certainly did, and furiously fast.

"Mick dear heart," suddenly serious after an energetic session with her playing piano and him on the drums on some early New Orleans jazz numbers, Elenora said casually, "I think its time for you to sit in with the *"Hot Shots"*. Now you know we rehearse every Saturday Night when we don't have a gig on?" Mick tried, but his soaring elation made it hard to find a voice. "Right? Well," she went on, "There'll be me on piano, Ossie Cartwright on bass, Charlie Bassett on tenor sax, and I want you to have a go on the dustbins - drums. I've noticed you whilst you've been playing, not just with me, but along with those Benny Goodman records and I know you'll be terrific..." Then as if it were an unimportant throwaway line, she added, "...by the way, you'll be playing with us and the full complement when we do the *"Worker's Playtime"* for the BBC."

If he was on cloud nine before this announcement, now he was positively in outer space. "Me! Mick Ryan to appear with the *"Hot Shots"* on *"Worker's Playtime!"* on the BBC! ON THE WIRELESS!"

"That's not all. Here's the best bit," Elenora said, "If you work like a maniac between now and the broadcast, you get to do a three minute solo spot on the piano! How about that for a gold plated offer Mr. Ryan?

Apart from Adolph Hitler, accidentally cutting his throat whilst shaving and a shipment of bananas getting through to Craggs Bottom Co-op how could life possibly be get any better for Mick? (a) He was legally still unable to attend school because of the forced lay off, (b) doing a job he loved, in the kennels, (c) Already the official drummer with *"The Hot Shots"* and (d) soon to be a solo pianist on the **WIRELESS!** Things couldn't get any better could they? No, but they could get a lot worse. And they did!

On that black Monday morning before the broadcast, her eyes red from crying, Dora was waiting on the doorstep anxious to share the devastating news with Mick as he arrived to tend to the dogs in the kennels. News so awful she hardly knew where to begin.

"Oh, Mickie, we're in a lot o' bother lad" she sobbed; "some bugger has reported Miss Clapworthy to the police for driving her car on unofficial business…"

"But she never has done that, has she? In any case Sergeant Wilkinson would never charge Miss Clapworthy…"

"Whoever reported her knew *that…*" Dora continued, her fear increasing by the telling, "they've reported her to the Bradford police station and because she's on essential work, they're sending a fellow from the Ministry here to interview her."

"So what?" Mickie said, "That won't worry Miss Clapworthy. She's done nothing wrong"

"Well doy, she did drive you all to that concert for the walking wounded at the Infirmary last week," visions of her dearest friend behind bars, sent her voice quivering with mounting hysteria, "and that counts as unessential use of petrol."

"Yeah but don't forget," Mick said as soothingly as he knew how, "on the way we called at Joe Hoyle's smallholding to check on his pigs' for swine fever! That's official use of petrol isn't it?"

"Nay love, they're that keen on petrol rationing at the moment, they are looking for folk to make examples of – folk prominent in the community. Even in London that gorgeous Ivor Novello got twelve months, and he wasn't even driving his car at the time! He'd lent it to a friend"

"But what about the..." Mick began, he was about to say "the Broadcast" but stopped himself just in time knowing it would have sounded selfish to worry about his debut with things of such import about to descend upon them.

"Any road love, they've just been on the phone to tell us they're sending' an official fellow, a Mr. Pye, in the morning to interrogate her, and if he isn't satisfied with her explanation she'll be charged! Oh my God..." The tears now in full flood Dora was in breakdown mode. The only thing that seemed to slightly alleviate Dora's distress in this ordeal was Miss Clapworthy's own attitude to the crisis. "Do you know Mickie; she didn't turn a hair when they told her she was a suspect! In fact she laughed like she'd been told a joke"! The following morning Dora was still more red eyed, frazzled and on edge as she and Mick peeped from behind the curtain as the stern looking official trod purposefully up to the front door.

"Thee let him in Mick..." Dora whispered paralysed with terror, "...ah'sll be bound to break down if I have to face him.

"Maybe he'll be a nice man, Mrs. Armitage," Mick said a vain attempt to comfort the old lady, "but he wasn't a nice man. He was as un-nice as could be. Brushing Mick aside arrogantly he stepped tight lipped into the hall. His soiled wing collar, pin striped suit smelling strongly of stale tobacco, frayed edged bowler hat, furled umbrella – to Dora as she peeped around the kitchen door, everything about Mr Pye was un-nice. Even the man's tortoise shell fountain pen seemed designed to intimidate. If the vile man had his way, both she and the young drummer boy knew their beloved Elenora would be languishing in clink and Mick's own big moment on the wireless gone forever.

Under strict instructions from Dora to remain scrupulously polite, but with a heavy heart Mick showed the inquisitor into the large living room where Elenora stood in front of the inglenook fireplace regally exuding unshakable confidence.

In his heart Mick knew his beloved mistress could chew this little runt Mr Pye to pulp if the spirit so took her. But the boy also feared the little runt Mr Pye had the trump card.

"Thank you Mick," Elenora said, "If you wouldn't mind waiting in the kitchen to answer the phone in case there are any emergency calls...there's a sweetheart! This shouldn't take long. Close the door behind you dear." Elenora made it clear by tone of voice, body language demeanour and sheer intellectual prowess that she had every intention of being totally in control of this confrontation. As he left the room, one glance and Mick knew he would remember forever the look of unshakeable authority on the face of the great lady as she directed the full power of her awesome attention on her miserable persecutor.

"Now... Mr Pry is it?

"Pye Madam, Pye!

"Of course it is! Please sit down. No, not there, over here if you please"

Even before his prepared opening accusation, the man from the Ministry had lost the initiative. Defeat was already spreading over his mean features, his tight lips beginning to quiver as he tried to assert his authority.

From behind the stout living room door Dora and Mick strained to hear the conversation between the two contenders - to no avail. Fearing the odds were stacked against his "best friend in the entire world" the boy joined Dora in her prayer for Divine intervention.

Hardly Divine, but certainly intervention came barely ten minutes into the interview. Gertie Hoyle's distraught voice came screaming over the telephone pleading for Elenora come at once to aid the birth of a calf with its head and one hoof visible but the rest of its body well and truly stuck. After first knocking timidly, Mick put his head around the door to convey the telephone message to his mentor, who at that moment was delivering the body blow, in the form of a number of sworn affidavits from more than a dozen high ranking notaries. Mr. Pye knew he was up the proverbial creek when he saw included amongst these papers one from Chief Constable Oswald Cartwright of the West Riding Constabulary, who incidentally, being the big bass player with the *"Hot Shots"* was present in the car with her the night she was supposedly wasting petrol.

"Thank you Mick" she said gently, then her expression turning icily cold again as she turned back to the ashen faced official, who looked as if he had been dragged through hell. "I must leave you now for a while Mr. Pry, I have **important** work to attend to. If you would be so good as to wait until I return, I have one or two more things I need to say to you." Elenora briskly left Mr. Pye alone in the room, closing the door behind her, not a second too soon as the laugh she had been concealing broke loose, loud and victorious. On her way out to attend the distressed cow she gave a quick warm hug to her still highly distressed housekeeper.

"Cheer up Dora," She said blithely, "the dreary little sod hasn't a leg to stand on. I've given him a bit of a verbal battering Mick, make him a cup of tea, and tell him I'll be back shortly." With no more ado she was zooming off in her car to attend the confinement of her bovine patient.

143

Mick, not at all as confident as Elenora, entered with the tea tray knowing the little man from the Ministry had had gone through one hell of roasting at the hands of his intended victim. The young boy approached with polite cautiousness. Mr Pye was sitting, staring straight ahead, in a state of deep shock his eyes almost popping from his head.

"Sir," Mick ventured nervously, "There's a cup of tea for you."

Mr Pye made no reply.

"Sir...?" Mick tried again, "...cup of tea sir...?" it was if the man was looking straight through him. At last the troubled eyes flickered and focused, not on Mick but beyond him – into the far corner of the inglenook fireplace. In one bound the officious little pen pusher leapt to his feet and fled the room as if the hounds of Hell were at his heels.

On the way through the kitchen he found his voice. Gone was the arrogance he had on arrival. Now totally defeated, but determinedly coherent he shouted to anyone who might hear.

"Tell Miss Clapworthy there is no case to answer. This is the last you'll hear from me or anyone else from my office. Not for a million pounds would you get me to follow this up..." Dora and Mick stood in the doorway and watched delightedly as the man ran through the muddy rut in the drive and off into the distance as fast as his Freeman, Hardy and Willis clad feet could carry him.

"Honest Miss Clapworthy,"Mick explained on her return "...his eyes were wide and terrified but he wasn't looking at me, he seemed to be looking through me – into the fireplace..." Realization hit the three friends at the same time. In unison they exploded with one word –

"...LULU!"

Of course Mick didn't believe in ghosts did he? He knew – thought he knew – in his heart of hearts that it was Miss Clapworthy's skill in presenting the *"relevant mitigating evidence"* that had put the wind up the little jerk and made him take flight, not any ghostly visitation he had received during the time he was alone facing the fireplace. Still the logical answer didn't mean he shouldn't put just that little extra wood on the fire that evening by way of reward to his "most favourite ghost in all the world"

Elenora smiled at the boy's kindly gesture as they seated themselves at their respective instruments – He on drums, she on piano.

"…Ever heard this number Mick?" She began to play a raunchy bar room vamp by way of introduction then started to *ad lib* the words –

> *"You can jilt Pearl she's a darn nice girl,*
> *But don't cross Lulu,*
> *Mr Pry got one in the eye*
> *'Cos he crossed Lulu,*
> *Lulu's one of those spectres -*
> *Hate's gasoline inspectors.*
> *So whatever you do – do, don't cross Lulu*
> *Lulu's here to stay"*

....

SPARE A CRUST

There were other air raids far more damaging, but whenever the locals referred to the "big raid" on Craggs Bottom they meant the raid that consisted of one solitary bomb.

This maverick five hundred pounder was jettisoned by an off course Luftwaffe bomber, on a home run after a major raid on Manchester. The consequences of the wayward bomb made such an indelible impression on the quiet Yorkshire village in a way that would be recounted with the same awesome wonder given to an Arthurian legend.

Not that the explosion dented the Allied War Effort in the slightest, for there were no industries in the village able to claim even semi-essential category. The only factory was Townsends Textiles, which although exclusively on khaki and air force blue coarse worsted, could hardly be rated as a threat to the Third Reich. It was _where_ the bomb struck and _what_ it struck that gave birth to the story.

No one was killed or even injured. That in itself was something of a minor miracle as, since the early days of the "phoney war" when everyone dutifully obeyed the air raid sirens and took to their Anderson shelter, lethargy had set in. Too many alarms were false. Too many hours of sleep were wasted crossing back gardens to no avail. One by one, the entire village population - with the exception of a few families like the Clitheroe family, ignored the sirens and remained abed.

There had been a Clitheroe's Pea and Pie shop on the site longer than anyone could remember. It only reached cult status when Ellis Clitheroe's father, Lord Raglan Clitheroe (b, 1885. the year of the Charge of the Light Brigade -hence his ridiculous given name decided to *"spend a bob or two elevatin' our grand family business into't Twentieth Century!"* Once the furore of his namesake's exploits in the Crimea had gone from hero worship to being one of the masters of the most notorious military cock-ups in history, "Rags" Clitheroe, as he chose to be known boasted that he – *"Niver did owt be halves. If 'ah do owt ah' do it reight or not at all".* True to his cliché he equipped himself with trade magazines and catalogues filled from cover to cover with the very latest décor and labour saving restaurant fittings. Favouring the Pre Raphaelite Brotherhood Movement with its exciting new approach he ordered the walls to be tiled with the latest Arts and Crafts movement pattern. New fangled electric light bulbs sent prisms of brazen cheerfulness through cut glass shades into every corner. A massive slab of dazzling white marble replaced the old oilcloth covered counter. Thirty elegant matching marble-topped tables with fancy wrought iron legs in the latest Art Nouveau style, were installed instead of the old scrubbed pine top tables. *For the comfort of me sittin' down clientele"* - individual chairs sat elegantly on the black and white *"chess board"* tiled floor. To soften the clinical look, Rags placed potted palms strategically in all the alcoves. The effect was stunning. He even considered re-naming the smart new establishment "Clitheroe's Pea and Pie *Salon"*, but thought better of it. However, he did think he ought to have some object, some symbol, a signature motif that would tell the world his was more than a run of the mill Pea and Pie Shop that his was a unique and very special establishment. He thought long and hard, even delayed the grand opening as he searched late into the night through trade magazines and interior decorators leaflets. His research paid off! In a moment of *"eureka"* proportions he discovered his *"piece de resistance"* in the latest catalogue for the "1904 Great Exposition of St. Louis. Missouri." It would become not only his trademark it would be his Talisman, his crowning glory!

The centrepiece of his window display! For it was not just any ordinary theatrical prop. It was inspired.

An enormous pie crust made from toughened plaster – over two yards in diameter – the most lifelike crust which defied the closest scrutiny. Totally convincing fake pastry plaits ran from the outer edge to meet at the peak where a hole in the crowning rosette, beautifully glazed and golden, emitted a vapour so potent, so intoxicatingly appetising it turned the strongest willed man into a Bisto Kid.

Rags' efforts paid off. Takings went through the roof. Business had always been pretty good because Clitheroe's always turned out an excellent product but now it was phenomenal. At week-ends and wakes week's hikers and cycling clubs from all around the West Riding could be seen trudging up Grantham Hill. Once past the famous granite outcrop that gave Craggs Bottom its name they would catch a whiff of the intoxicating aroma of home made meat and potato pie and all they had to do was follow their noses. Like pilgrims, on a visit to a holy shrine they followed the divine tang that led them directly to Rags' Pie Shop where they would willingly wait, often for more than an hour, to get a seat. Whilst they waited they were able to gaze open mouthed in wonder through the window at the magnificent pie and speculate whether it was real or just for show. Consistently they came to the conclusion that with such a wonderfully appetising aroma it could only be real. It would not be an exaggeration to say that Clitheroe's Pie put Craggs Bottom on the map. Fame for the beautiful pie spread, fuelled by speculation as to what the ingredients could be that gave the pie such a heavenly aroma. Rags learned to manipulate the press, and invented the legend that he had been offered large amounts if he would only disclose the secret. The fact that it was no more and no less than the same old recipe most wives made every Sunday to pour over their Yorkshire puddings did nothing to lessen its mystique.

For a good few years every thing in Lord Raglan Clitheroe's charmed world was perfection. But then disaster struck. Directly opposite his Pie shop on that piece of land between the Liberal Club and the Co-op Emporium the Council decided to build, would you credit it? Of all things a public convenience! Rags was almost catatonic with disgust on many counts. First at the choice of, not a library, or a museum or some other more appropriate structure to celebrate the coronation of George the Fifth – but of all things a pissoir! Secondly, the project was instigated by Rags' nemesis that bloated jumped up Alderman Uriah Butterworth! Hardly had the mortar time to set before the edifice took on the soubriquet of *"Uriah's Urinal"*- most undignified! Unspeakable! Thirdly, and most importantly Rags feared the smell would rival, nay obliterate his own delicious aroma coming from the pie. His livelihood, his very legend was at stake!

"That damned obscenity!" he fumed at least twice a day, "directly in the eye line of me paying customers! Right there! Un-a-bloody-voidable and the smell? Can you credit it?

There had been no attempt for the sake of delicacy to disguise the imposing structure. On the contrary, unashamedly it advertised its use over the entrance in ostentatious wrought iron lettering, in the style of the Paris Metro. There was also, but this time in stout British engraving a brass plaque placed prominently praising the Council and especially Alderman Butterworth.

Once inside this brutal construction (the entry marked Gentlemen) each of the twelve individual stalls in stout glazed pottery bore the legend – at eye level when in use, therefore compulsive reading – *"Watt's Hygena. By appointment to Her Majesty Queen Victoria"* It did puzzle some readers as to what earthly use the dear old Queen might have had for such a commodity. Only a few low-minded clients guffawed out loud. The entire roof was of varying shades of green leaded lights, the effect combined with the waving seaweed pattern on the wall tiles, plus the highly polished brass fittings was that of being fathoms beneath the sea, which is exactly where Rags wished it were. Although there rarely was any smell, certainly not enough to rival the pie's glorious aroma and it never harmed the shops takings one iota. Yet that stout convenience remained Rags' *bête noire* for the rest of his life. He could never get over what he considered a obscenity of the lowest order. Rags died a few years later and unforgiving man.

Ellis Clitheroe, Rags' only son inherited the business. He also inherited his father's loathing of Uriah's Urinal. Apart from this, life went on happily for the next twenty odd years or so. Trade never slackened and even when rationing kicked in and Woolton Pie and mushy peas replaced the famous meat and potato pie, the gorgeous bouquet remained the same to entice customers into the still attractive café. Until that is, the night of "The Big Raid"

No one in the village remembers hearing either the drone of the enemy bomber, nor the warning screech as the bomb sped earthwards. Thanks Be to God, Ellis, his wife Norah and their sizable brood were one of the few families safely ensconced in the Anderson shelter. The five hundred pound explosive penetrated the roof and struck the kitchen floor before it detonated.

One almighty bang and Clitheroe's Pie and Pea Shop was no more. The explosion blew everything outwards and upwards.

First into orbit in the most spectacular manner was the plaster pie crust. Now separated from its base the conical plaster crust took on a determined life force of its own. The heavy plate glass window was as ineffective as a gossamer christening veil against the fury of the crust's destructive mission. Like Ate come hot from Hell, spinning and screeching like a furious wraith it went for its next victim. Without pause or pity the overhead tram cables never knew what hit them. In a flash the tram shelter on the opposite side of the road was no more. Still not satisfied it continued on its relentless trajectory - towards Uriah's Urinal.

The green leaded lights of the glass roof stood no chance, not one pane was spared. Once inside the building, like a malevolent whirling Dervish, Lord Raglan's crust ricocheted from wall to wall, shattering the tiles to dust and cutting through the polished copper pipes releasing torrents of water in all directions. At last having completed its mission of revenge on the urinals the still intact crust finally began to lose its impetus.

In its dying throes it began a slow spiral, rolled a little way over the debris it had created. At long last Its awesome momentum finally spent, like a spun coin winding down it came to rest in the stall next to where

Harry Petty, the village drunk had been unloading fourteen pints of processed mild and bitter.

The trauma of witnessing Armageddon first hand drained him of his normally ruddy complexion, instantly cured his constipation and sobered him enough to vow never to touch another drop so long as he lived. A pledge he religiously kept until next day's opening time at the "Feathers"

The following morning Ellis Clitheroe viewed the devastation in a state of deep shock. He sat amongst the rubble and silently wept. Everything was gone, his tables, his chairs, his beautiful white marble counter. Worst of all there was not the slightest trace of his beautiful plaster pie. The very symbol of Clitheroe's Pea and Pie Shop's long established success – gone! Gone without a trace! Ellis heart broke in two. He took to his bed to await the end.

Norah Clitheroe however, was made of sterner stuff. By nine o'clock that morning, with the help of Police Sergeant Wilkinson, Mr Walsh the Air Raid Warden and of course her five sons she began the clear-up operation. The Civil Defence people were alerted and a Nissan Hut was on its way. Within one day a number of oil stoves had been requisitioned and the makeshift café was turning out steaming portions of Cornish pasties and mushy peas for "take away customers."

Within a week "sitting down" customers were enjoying their meals beneath a hastily written banner shamelessly borrowing Her Majesty's quotation which announced defiantly – "NOW WE CAN LOOK THE EAST END IN THE EYE!! LIKE THE WINDMILL THEATRE **WE** NEVER CLOSED!

In spite of Norah's magnificent show of northern grit, Ellis slid further into a decline. He would try to show willing, but he was a beaten man. Norah and the kids kept

152

the business ticking over, but it was clear Ellis had thrown in the towel. Inconsolable at the loss of his pie, his talisman, he lay abed awaiting the end and there was nothing anyone could do about it.

It was round about this period Sergeant Wilkinson had occasion to restrain Harry Petty for singing "*Jerusalem*" at the top of his voice at one o'clock in the morning on Main Street. There was nothing unusual in this; Harry was put in the cells at least once a week. He was never charged. Sergeant Wilkinson was as soft as warm butter. He hadn't the heart to charge a battery, least of all lovable old Harry. This night however, Harry was not troublesome enough to warrant the cell. All that was necessary was to see him safely home and, as he lived alone, make sure he didn't collapse on the cold kitchen flagstones.

"Now behave thi'sen Harry and drink this pot of tea. You raise enough Bedlam to awaken the dead." Arnold said, once he had Harry safely in his little house, "now sup up thi tea and get off to bed!"

"I know summat tha' doesn't know, Ar-old Winkindon…" Becoming conspiratorial the way drunken men do when they feel they have a friendly ear, Harry slurred, "…The Gerry's have a secret weapon!"

"Is that right?" Arnold replied, humouring the old man.

"Tha' doesn't believe me, does ta', Arlon Winkinson?" Harry persisted. Then dropping his voice lest the German Intelligence should hear, he thrust his face into Arnold's, "…remember the neet of the big raid? That wasn't a 'nordinary bomb, that were summat else! I saw it wi' me own eyes!"

"Lord love us Harry, thy breath is enough to fell a beast." Arnold said shrinking back.

"But I'm telling thee Arlon. I saw it take the glass roof off the khasi! The Chrystal Palace! Uriah's Urinal! I saw it wi' me own eyes!"

"Get away with you," Arnold said, "secret weapon my arse! That wa' the blast from the bomb that hit the Pie shop. Come on now get off to bed..."

"But I'm tellin' thee...look, if tha' doesn't believe me..." Harry leaped to his feet, and in a flash brought from behind the scullery door, a six foot in diameter cone shaped object. "...nah then!" he drawled triumphantly, "...if that isn't the most dia-lobical secret weapon ever invented I'll be..."

"Good God Harry! Doesn't ta' know what this is?" Arnold bawled, **"its Clitheroe's Pie Crust!"**

First thing the following morning, for the first time since his breakdown, Ellis Clitheroe sat up in bed and ran his hands lovingly over the contours of the plaster crust. Miraculously, apart from a scratch or two it was perfect. Ellis' eye's filled up, but now they were no longer tears of despair, they were tears of hope and resolve.

....

SISTER HANNAH,
CARRY THE BANNER

Every generation of kids seem to come up with their own special song, rhyme or monologue that sets in their memories the style of the period in stone.

"I've Got Sixpence" – *"The Quartermasters Store"* - *"Rolling Home, By the light of the Silvery Moon"* Songs which will immediately transport whoever lived in that time back again in a flash. Simple songs to which they can add naughty stanza's or extra risqué verses until it becomes their own personal mantra. Sometimes these illicit versions even get taken up by the adult population. Then quite suddenly the craze reaches a saturation peak dies a natural death is discarded but is never forgotten.

Just such a phenomenon was **"Sister Hannah, Carry the Banner"** perhaps more like a chant than a song but as universally and aggravatingly popular. Perhaps its strength was in it being a duologue - a statement demanding an answer that made it so irresistibly funny. This is how it went: -

Stern deep bass voice:
"Sister Hannah! Carry the Banner!"
Timid falsetto voice:
"But I carried the banner last week!"
Stern deep voice:
"If I say so you'll carry the banner every week!"

155

…And so on with increasingly daring additions.

The chant grew in popularity - almost to the point of obsession with some of the louts who gathered outside the "Feathers" every Friday night. When the Salvation Army band would play before going inside the pub to sell their copies of the *"War Cry"* These louts, knew full well that Major Raistrict, who's Christian name was Hannah but that it was also her duty to carry the Banner.

Oh, brother they showed no mercy!

Their chanting, hilarious though it was, upset Major Hannah to such an extent that she found it increasing hard to function. She would burst into tears then retire to the safety of the Citadel to nurse her embarrassment and lick her wounds. Consequently the sales of the weekly newspaper, "The War Cry" dropped dramatically since it was mostly Hannah's efforts persuading the regulars in the taproom to part with their two twopence's for a copy, which they immediately discarded.

Where ever she went in the village the chant would follow her to the point when she felt she could scream. She tried, but it was impossible to ignore it. Hannah knew in her heart of hearts that it was no more than a bit of harmless fun, and that it would be wiser to laugh it off rather than take it to heart. At other times in her life she would have done exactly that, but lately she had been feeling vulnerable and old. She had reached a watershed in her life telling herself she must not allow the ridiculous chant to interfere with her duty to God, equating the Banner with the Cross she had to carry.

But the Cross became harder to bear with each passing year for Hannah. She was one of the generation of women deprived of any hope of finding a marriage partner due to the mindless slaughter in the fields of Flanders that almost obliterated the cream of the Nation's youth. Never one to fool herself, Hannah knew that physical beauty was a gift God bestowed in his infinite wisdom on others – not on her. The fact had to be faced "I'm an old maid," she told herself, "and old maids are a joke aren't they?" Now because of that silly chant she felt more unlovely and increasingly isolated without she thought, a living soul to look upon her as a person and not an object of ridicule.

How wrong she was! Un-noticed by her as she marched along, only a few short paces in her wake, entwined in the complicated coils of his Sousaphone, Fred Jarrett positively um-pah-pah-ed with passion and ached with unrequited love for her. Not that he'd ever attempted to requite himself. He just didn't know how to. He was not worldly, hopeless at social skills and painfully bashful into the bargain. Confirmation of his inferiority came home to him most forcefully in 1914 when he was turned down for military service on medical grounds and dismissed unceremoniously by the recruiting sergeant as *"a miserable specimen of English manhood if ever there was one. Get out 'o me sight"* The insult went deep. After that what little hope he had of any romantic future with anyone, least of all Hannah Raistrict was gone for good. From that moment on all that was left to him was to worship her from afar.

But not all that much afar – for not only did he share his Sundays and Fridays, following behind her as she marched along, he enjoyed even closer proximity during the week. Either by sub-conscious design or heaven sent accident together they jointly managed the Elysian Palace Picture house; Fred, multi-tasking as commissionaire, boiler man, cleaner and dogsbody.

Hannah, the brains of the outfit, was chief cashier, wages clerk and business manager.

Then there was gorgeous Brenda Chandler, *"evenings only"* usherette. A little bit too "forward" for Hannah's liking but she was popular with the clientele and whenever she was on duty the War-time-home-made ice lollies sold like wildfire.

Up in the projection hole,gentle unassuming Percy Dolby together with his son Kenny, was chief and apprentice projectionists in that order. Thus completing the entire workforce of the little cinema. Between the five of them the dull building that had been converted at the turn of the century from a light engineering shed into a palace of dreams chugged along nicely.

Believing *"moving pictures"* to be nothing more than a passing fancy with little chance of them ever catching on.The then proprietor spent as little money as possible on the decorations. Neither inside nor outside had the building enjoyed a lick of paint since. Yet the smoke filled little cinema was cosy and warm most of the time and everyone who bought a ticket, whether on the front bench or the double *"lovers seat"* on the back row felt comfortable and at home. To any outsider the lack lustre Elysian Palace Picturedrome or *"Lizzy"* as it was affectionately known had little to commend it. But the locals, also of late, the troops stationed in the local Barracks and the walking wounded from the Military Hospital loved the little *"flea pit"* with a passion as confirmed by the size of the attendances. Nearly always full houses on a twice-nightly two matinees per week basis!

"Pretty good returns Miss Raistrict for a rat-hole like the *"Lizzie.""* As the absentee owner Mr Boyce said on one of his rare phone conversations with Hannah, when she had the temerity to ask for the roof to be mended. For when it rained the customers directly under the leaking roof, more in order to draw attention to the deluge than to remain dry had taken to sitting under an open umbrella during the screening. "No, Miss Raistrict, not bad returns! Not bad at all." But he never did anything about the leaky roof.

Another thing Mr Boyce was aware of but never mentioned was that many of the supporting films shown at the *"Lizzie"* were second-rate potboilers from Hollywood's *"poverty row"* - or even worse Islington's poverty row. Some like the excruciatingly tedious Edgar Lustgarten crime howlers, so desperately bad the audience would erupt into uproarious and prolonged laughter as the on-screen deaths mounted and the film staggered to an embarrassing close in a moralising speech delivered by Mr Lustgarten in person.

The *"Lizzie's"* programming did however have one saving grace. The distributors allowed the showing of one major studio – Twentieth Century Fox's – latest, glorious Technicolor musical films. Not only was the lush warmth of the colour a temporary release from the usual greyness the war weary populace endured on the Home Front. These twice weekly glimpses of Paradise also had the beautiful stars like Alice Faye, Betty Grable, Carmen Miranda and a host of other glamorous talents under contract.

Also as an added boost to the evening's delights and particularly the men's libido's, there was the gorgeous Brenda Chandler, that cheeky, blowzy, bold, over made-up usherette. Incorrigibly flirtatious, with a skirt short enough to reveal a pair of legs to rival even the great Miss Grable's. Brenda would totter up and down the centre aisle on impossibly high heels as the audience entered and before the programme began. This duty was ostensibly to keep the more rowdy youths quiet and in their seats, but everyone knew it was to flirt, spread joy and raise the spirits of all the men in the audience. That was Brenda's speciality. A perfect curtain raiser!

Eventually Hannah would put up the *"house full"* notice, Percy would tip the switch to play the cacophonous fanfare to demand everyone's full attention for the all-important verbal Air Raid Warning speech. Only then would the good-natured house settle down. This night was to be different.

The law demanded that any announcements regarding safety during air raids be made in front of the screen by Hannah. Of course by rights it should have been Fred, but Fred being far too shy to speak in public was more than glad to leave it to Hannah. It was on this occasion the *"Hannah, Carry the Banner"* phenomenon came to a head.

She mounted the steps at the side of the stage to face the full house, cleared her throat and began,

"In the event of an air raid warning from Sergeant Wilkinson," Hannah's tone implied that she did not expect anyone to heed the warning, hardly anyone ever did, but rules were rules and she delivered the speech in her best announcers voice "Naturally we shall continue with the performance, but those wishing to leave may do so calmly and without panic by the front of house exit..." With perfect timing the single powerful male voice from the sixpenny seats rang out rudely interupting her...

"SISTER   HANNAH,   CARRY   THE BANNER!" The house exploded in laughter. Hannah stood transfixed. Embarrassed and humiliated she began to tremble not knowing what to do. Then in utter disarray she ran wildly for the safety of the office.

Fred, who had witnessed the scene from the back of the stalls, went after her. He had never seen her so distressed before and he was profoundly shaken. More than anything he wanted to comfort her. Take her in his arms and hold her until the hurt went away. Of course he did no such thing. He just burst into the office and stood there awkwardly shifting from one foot to the other.

"Have you come to gloat as well? Have you come to join the rest of the rabble who seemed get such pleasure making fun of me and me religion?"

But Fred wasn't laughing, he wasn't gloating he was just standing there with his mouth open. In the end his dithering presence drove Hannah to do something very much against her nature. She slapped him across the face with all the strength and venom she could muster.

"Get out you useless man! Leave me alone!" She yelled, pushing him bodily out of the office and slamming the door on him. Then giving way to the dam within her she cried as she had not done since she was a little girl. Her tears were not so much because of the humiliation she had just undergone that was merely the trigger. In her heart she knew the tears that flowed so profusly were the tears of mourning over a life she felt was unfulfilled.

All this happened on the Monday evening. The next day Fred went about his work on automatic pilot. He could think of nothing other than how much Hannah must loath him to have given him such a whack across his chops. His guilt compounded by reminding himself that had he been man enough to make the public announcement in the first place, Hannah would not have been subjected to that public shaming. He dearly wanted to plead his case, to apologise, to beg forgiveness. But right up until the time she opened the box office for the early performance, she kept her eyes averted whenever he came near.

The first house on the Tuesday was uneventful – no chanting. Fred dared to hope that if this kept up, maybe things would return to normal. "Things have to! I can't function much longer out side her good books, with me in this present state of limbo."

His hopes for a ceasefire were dashed however as the stalls filled for the second house. Hannah also thought there might have been a truce and the chanting over and done. Both their hopes were to be dashed. As she was about to close the hatch on the box office prior to making her Air Raid Precaution speech it started up, only now the chanters had been working on their routine and had formed a sort of Greek chorus. Bass lecherous male voices v. Sweet innocent maiden voices: -

SISTER HANNAH, CARRY THE BANNER!
BUT KIND SIR, I'M ONLY THIRTEEN
THIS IS NO TIME TO BE SUPERSTITIOUS –
THE BANNER - HANNAH!

At this point the spontaneity dried up and the entire house fell into helpless anarchic laughter. There was no such merriment in the box office. In a return of the humiliating horrors of the night before, Hannah hastily cashed up, locked the takings in the safe, threw on her coat and ran out of the building almost knocking Fred over in her haste. Struck dumb, Fred could only watch as she ran off in a fresh burst of tears. After the last member of the audience, plus Percy, Kenny, and Brenda had left the cinema that night Fred was left alone to lock up, nothing new there, he had followed the same routine for many years. Only this night was different. Never had he felt so desperately alone as he walked in numbing misery to his lonely two roomed back to back on Haycliff Street. Only to find there was no escape from his desolation in sleep, for even sleep had deserted him. He tossed and turned the entire night his wretchedness compounded when Hannah didn't turn up for work on the Wednesday morning.

Her older sister Olive, who took over once each week to allow Hannah time off to lead the Salvation Army in their weekly parade around the village culminating outside the Feathers when she would summon up the courage to enter the tap room and bravely offer to sell The "War Cry".

Olive, unlike her sister Hannah was a blunt unsmiling woman. "Our Hannah won't be coming in. she's in a terrible state." She said nothing to ease Fred's pain. "She's of a nervous disposition is our Hannah. I've no idea when she'll be back, if ever!"

Was it possible that Fred could sink any lower? Only his instinctive work ethic kept him alive and functioning. He knew he should do something, but what? Hannah had made it abundantly clear by the slap across his face that she didn't want anything from him, not even contact at work, least of all his affection. The sorry state of affairs carried on throughout the day, through two interminable shows and another sleepless night of hell. When Hannah didn't show up for work on the Thursday morning he knew something must be done, and he must do it. The trouble was he was not very good at making ordinary run of the mill decisions, let alone life altering ones!

From what source came the blinding realisation he had no idea, but like a sixty watt Osram light bulb being switched on everything became clear. All these years he had only considered how much *he needed* her but now miraculously he realised how much *she* needed *him*. Dense though was, he did know that he had received a wonderous answer to his prayer and the beginnings of a plan was forming to put paid to the hateful chanting that so plagued her.

Like a man possessed he dropped what he was doing and raced with supercharged energy to the office.

"Can you hold the fort for an hour or so Olive?" It was a rhetorical question, the vigour in Fred's voice told Olive she had better concede, or else...! "I'll be back in time for the matinee."

There was also a new and welcome determination in his step as he strode out past the schoolyard towards Miss Raistrict's cottage. Without hesitation he rapped confidently on the door.

"Now then Hannah Raistrict," Fred began forcefully once inside the kitchen, "I owe thee an apology for not being man enough in the past to do all the jobs I should have done, like making the announcements, and **demanding** that Mr Boyce mended the roof. Well lass them days is past! I have an announcement, well more of a proposal I intend to make in the very near future..."

"Oh, Fred, I never really blamed...I should never have taken it out on thee..."

"Don't stop me now lass, I might never get going again," his confident delivery surprising both of them, especially himself. Hannah was deeply impressed.

"I have summat I have to say to thee," He continued earnestly "but not until we've gotten this *"Hannah carry the banner"* business sorted out, I want you to come back to the Lizzy. It isn't the same without you. You are needed. I need you. You have to come back."

She was looking at him with new eyes. Hardly knowing how to address this total stranger she'd known all her life. Not an unattractive stranger at that.

"Of course you're right." She said at last, "I'll just get me coat..."

"No, not today" He said, with his new authoritative tone of voice. "Take the rest of today off. But tomorrow, Friday I have a plan that's going to put this whole barmy

"Hannah, carry the Banner" business into its proper perspective!" *Perspective...?!* He'd never used such long words in all his life! The realisation he was able to call on such a vocabulary fairly made him reel. "Now then Hannah, this is what I want you to do. Sit thee down and take heed..."

The rest of Thursday Fred spent every spare minute he had either in a secret huddle with young Kenny Dolby the apprentice projectionist. Or on the phone to Mr Corbett the musical director of the Salvation Army band or scribbling away avidly at something he was composing...Composing? Fred? Believe it!

"Now then Kenny lad," Fred began conspiratorially. "I know you're a dab hand at making glass advertising slides, well I want you to make me a song sheet slide, tha' knows, like them ones on the *"follow the bouncing ball "* sing along shorts we sometimes show."

"No bother Mr Jarrott," Kenny chirped, excited to be part of this intriguing plan, "considerate it done!"

"You're a grand lad Kenny," Fred was more alive than he had ever been in his life. "Now these are the special words to the song I want you to put on the slide." He surreptitiously handed a folded piece of foolscap to the boy, tapping the side of his nose to indicate that it was strictly between the two of them.

One final word of instruction to Brenda and Fred's grand plan was completed.

"Right now Brenda, I want you to point out the words if you will as only you can. I want you, looking you're most glamorous!" Fred instructing Brenda in seduction was like teaching Granny how to beat air into the Yorkshire pudding batter, but he was on a roll and enervated to the point of exploding.

"High heels, lipstick and all that *"vamp"* stuff, just get their attention."

"Leave it to me Fred," Brenda said huskily, like Mae West with a North Country accent, "Trust me I'll take no prisoners, I'll show 'em no mercy big boy!"

The moment Fred had worked so hard to bring about came at last. The slides advertising the local traders were being shown prior to the last house on the Friday night. The full house was as lively as ever. In the tiny foyer at the back of the auditorium Fred and Mr Corbett the musical director had assembled the entire Sally Army Band. Calm and brave in her uniform and bonnet, banner unfurled, Hannah stood awaiting her cue. There was a new extra feistiness about her this night, and it was exciting and attractive.

As expected the chanting began…
B.L.M.V
HANNAH, CARRY THE BANNER!
S.I.M.V
BUT I WANT TO GO TO THE PICTURES!
B.L.M.V
THERE ARE PICTURES ON THE BANNER!
S.I.M.V
BUT I MEAN MOVING PICTURES
B.L.M.V
MOVE THE BLOODY BANNER!!!

At the height of the laughter Fred gave the cue. The band struck up full blast. At the same time Kenny projected the slide showing the new words. Brenda, vamping seductively like a seasoned Coney Island chantusse stepped onto the stage with a billiard cue to point out the words. Then Hannah, the star of the evening stepped through the door at the back of the auditorium, banner held proudly aloft, leading the twenty or so musicians down the centre aisle blasting out the tune Fred had so laboured over. On they marched to the front of the screen where they formed a tableau facing the surprised audience. To a man the delighted packed house cottoned on immediately. Brenda pointed out the lyrics and they began with a lusty willingness to sing the new words. It was the most thrilling moment in the history of the Elysian Palace as Hannah Raistrict led the chorus.

YOU WERE DRIVING ME BARMY.
BUT THE SALVATION ARMY
WON'T BE BEAT THAT EASY
WATCH ME PUT UP A FIGHT
IN FEARLESS MANNER,
I'LL CARRY ME BANNER
i'LL GIVE AS GOOD AS I GET
AND FIGHT YOU WITH ALL OF ME MIGHT

"Come on everybody! Join in! Lets hear you! Sing out, all together now. Don't be shy! You were never shy before! Come on sing out, with feeling!"

MY NAME IS HANNAH,
I'LL CARRY MY BANNER
I'LL TAKE THE WORD OF JESUS
INTO THE JAWS OF HELL
IN FEARLESS MANNER,
I'LL CARRY MY BANNER
I'LL LET THE DEVIL KNOW
THAT THIS IS HIS FUNERAL KNELL...

How many times they repeated the chorus that night, no-one could ever remember. It would be a long time however before Craggs Bottom ever forgot the rush of adrenaline as the audience rose ecstatically to its feet to pay homage to the sheer guts displayed by Hannah Raistrict that night.

As the new confident Fred walked Hannah home after everyone had finally gone he proudly acknowledged his wildly ambitious plan had worked.

"I think we can safely say that damned chant has lost any heat it had. I don't think it'll bother you no more lass."

"Shame in a way," Hannah replied, glowing with all kinds of happy feelings, "For the first time tonight I realised it was really very funny, in parts."

"Aye, and another thing," Fred chuckled, "do you know lass, we sold more "War Cries" tonight than we've sold in years.

"Did we? Isn't that champion!" Hannah said delightedly. They fell into an easy silence as they walked along in the moonlight. Hannah linked her arm cosily in his as if they had always enjoyed such intimate closeness. After a timeless pause with some gravity she said,

"Now Fred Jarrott, what's this 'ere proposal you have for me?"

....

57 VARIETIES

"Come on Heinz, there's a good dog!" Elenora tried for a full ten minutes to coax her beloved mongrel to venture from the warmth of the kitchen into the strange, white new world of winter. "Trust me Heinz it's wonderful once you take the first step."

Not as robust and patently not as confident as his mistress, certainly not at all sure whether he should risk leaving the familiarity of Ambler Thorn for this alien planet that had descended overnight. Even though the one he adored was already making snowballs and having fun, still he hesitated on the known side of the threshold.

Heinz was like no other dog Elenora had come across, and as a Veterinarian Surgeon she had come across many. Heinz was a strange mixture of indefinable breeds, hence his name – "Heinz 57 Varieties". With a long heavy body, short bowlegs, a tail docked to a sturdy stub. At the opposite end of his body was the most incongruous delicate head, with big trusting eyes that could melt a bar of pig iron. There was no way on earth he could ever be described as graceful of form. Heinz may have been a born comic but he was also heartbreakingly loyal to his mistress who he loved more than life itself. This is why he was in his present state of indecision.

"Come on Heinz, don't be fright you've seen snow before you dozy bugger." Elenora's beautifully modulated

170

Standard English in tandem with her adopted North Country turn of phrase, so incongruous on this West Riding mountain side never failed to raise a smile from the locals. She made a soft snowball and gently threw it to the reluctant animal in an effort to draw him away from the safety of the doorway.

"It's only snow baby, it won't hurt you," she cajoled, "would I lie to you?" Grunting with studied effort Heinz finally summoned the courage to risk a balletic leap into the air, as high as his little legs would propel him - all of two inches. He plopped, belly first into the snow with all the elegance of a combined harvester on Pointe. As promised, this snow stuff was pure fun, releasing a playful energy in both dog and mistress. High spirits belied their respective maturity; for both were well past the first, nay second flush of youth.

Trudging upwards through the thick snow towards Craggs Bottom, the village which sat defiantly on top of the mountain in what was locally purported to be the *"Highest inhabited point in England"* pausing for a breather, as they usually did on the famous crag itself, This gigantic granite rock shelf, swept clean of the snow by the keen overnight wind stood out bleak and dramatic against the bright winter morning. This celebrated spot always reminded Elenora of a painting by one of the Pre-Raphaelite Brotherhood, or was it a Landseer? What did it matter, someone should have immortalised it on canvas, and to her knowledge no one had.

Elenora flopped inelegantly onto the rock surface for "breather" mostly for Heinz's sake. The pair followed the same routine almost every Sunday morning on their way to collect Caesar the beautiful Alsatian guard dog from *"The Feathers"*, then on to Minnie Clegg's welcoming kitchen for a brew of tea so strong, *"you could ride a donkey on it"* before setting off across the moors towards Haworth.

Heinz in particular welcomed the break in their journey, and resting his head in her lap, looked up at her with such love one could almost hear violins playing.

"Morning Miss Clapworthy" Police Sergeant Wilkinson kicked the snow from his boots as he walked along the rock to join them, his trademark smile lighting up his face. "You're up and about early aren't you?"

"…Might say the same about you Arnold.   I thought you liked a lie in on a Sunday morning?"

"…do as a rule," he answered, "but…

"…Don't tell me, you're off to shovel snow for the old folks In Stephenson's Fold?"

"Right you are, first time!"   Arnold replied with a grin. Then noticing Heinz snuggle possessively even closer to his mistress, "by gum, Miss Clapworthy, can this be the same little runt you rescued from that sleaze bag Sidney Slickey?"

"He certainly is!" Elenora replied, then addressing the dog, "Give Sergeant Wilkinson a paw Heinz." Heinz duly obeyed, following the principle that any friend of his mistress's was a friend of his, so long as they understood he had prior claim on her affections. The big policeman crouched in order to pet the dog, remembering the same animal of a few years before when he had to call on Miss Clapworthy in her official capacity as veterinary surgeon.

A tip off had alerted him to the pitiful plight of a mongrel locked, starving and neglected in the tool shed at the back of Sidney Slickey's butchers shop. "So this is that funny looking little bag of bones you transformed into this, well, let's be honest, funny looking big bag of bones."

"Don't be rotten Arnold." Elenora smiled, perfectly accustomed to having to defend her dog's weird appearance. "He's beautiful, aren't you Heinz?"

172

"If you say so, Miss Clapworthy, who am I to argue …!" Arnold was, as everyone knew "*a champion fellow… a grand lad… one of a kind…*" famous in the village for his easy-going and often unconventional methods of law keeping. Arnold would do almost anything to avoid writing out a charge sheet. Indeed he had been brought before Chief Superintendent Oswald Cartwright for just such "*dereliction of duty*" on a number of occasions. Arnold believed that real criminals were rare, and the offences committed in his manor were minor and hardly ever worthy of sending someone to clink. Slickey was the exception. It was the dreadful condition of the little mutt that, under Elenora's care, grew up to become Heinz that tipped the scales for Arnold. He gladly charged the owner. Without a trace of remorse Arnold made as strong a case as he could against "Slimy" Slickey. Arnold and Miss Clapworthy even had celebratory half pint when the defendant was found guilty and fined as heavily as the law would allow.

In the early days of the war the village sported two known "*Social Parasites and Itinerant Vagrants*" or in the war-time parlance – SPIVS. If young Johnny Pratt the other acknowledged SPIV in the village *played* the part of a "*jack the lad*" and convincingly *looked* the part of a petty miscreant - a "*wide boy*" at least the kid had done it with a certain amount of humour and style, and absolutely no malice whatsoever.

Slimy Slickey, on the other hand was void of charm, scruples or decency. Short and skinny, his sunken cheek bones and sallow complexion was matched by dirty and nicotine stained fingers. His lank thinning hair matted with cheap smelling brilliantine and combed straight back creating a permanent greasy stain on his grubby shirt collar. His imitation camel hair-ankle-length overcoat, pencilled moustaches and wide brimmed Trilby hat completed the archetypal small town crook.

Naturally this is not how he saw himself. On the contrary, he imagined himself ten steps ahead of the game. His studied lop-sided grin and self satisfied swagger informed the world that here was a sophisticated masher, a ladies man, handsome and urbane. He believed himself to be a sex symbol with at least twice the charisma of Errol Flynn.

Sergeant Wilkinson, himself no stranger to bending the law in the name of justice if circumstances called for it, knew better then to underestimate Slimy Slickey. Arnold knew that if it served the little crook's dubious purposes he would not think twice about "*shopping*" the many ordinary (semi) innocent villagers who had at times, availed themselves of his services. With regard to this very subject, Sergeant Wilkinson had received a message to call in at Ambler Heights – whilst Miss Clapworthy was out.

"I'm just going to call in at your place if that's alright," Arnold said, "I want to have a quick word with your kennel maid Dorothy Armitage."

"Why, what's she done?" Elenora asked as she arose to continue on her way up to the village, "Nicked the Crown Jewels?"

"Worse than that, she never called in at the cop shop with one of her scones last Friday"

"That is serious!" Elenora answered as she moved off, "Come on Heinz!"

A desperately worried frown replaced Dorothy Armitage's usual cheerful greeting as she let Arnold into the spacious kitchen of the old Manor House. "I'm glad you could come while she was out. I don't want Miss Clapworthy worried. It's not her fault, it's mine!"

"It's alright, I just passed her on the crag, and she won't be back for a bit. Now then, what's thy fault?

"Oh, Arnold lad, I'm that worried…"

"Stop witterin' Dora and tell me what tha's done…"

"Well, tha' knows we're registered for our personal meat rations with Sidney Slickey…" Dorothy faltered in her well-rehearsed confession. "Oh, Arnold I've done a very silly thing. I've broke the law!"

"Thee Dora," Arnold replied gently, "Broke the law! *Thee* Dora? You're not capable of breaking wind without showing your guilt. What have you done?"

"Well, six months since…" Dora paused so deeply worried she found it impossible to hold back the tears. Taking a deep breath she began unloading the story of her "*crime*"

"Six months since, Mr Slickey offered me some offal, from under the counter…nothing important like a leg of mutton, or even a bit of scrag end, just some lites, spleen, cow heel and tripe for the dogs. 'Course I jumped at the chance. Now he says the word has got out and I have to pay him ten bob a week to keep this other fellow quiet…"

"Don't tell me," Arnold was ahead of her, "…now Slimy keeps coming back for more brass to keep this *other fellow*" quiet, right?"

"That's right!" Dora said with surprise, so deeply worried she found it impossible to hold back the tears "How did tha' know?"

"It's what's called blackmail Dora." Arnold said with disgust, "and don't you worry your head no more over it. It isn't thee the little rattlesnake is after; it's Miss Clapworthy, for testifying against him at the Magistrates Court when he was up for starving Heinz near to death."

"But he'll expect his usual ten bob off me at the weekend…"

"...Don't thee part with no more ten bobs to that little turd!" Arnold said, his anger beginning to rocket sky high by the second and with it the resolve to put the mockers well and truly on Slimy Slickey.

"You did the right thing in telling me all about it Dora. Now don't worry about it no more, I'll see to it, and keep it to your self, Miss Clapworthy mustn't be worried over this."

Naturally, being the officer in charge of Craggs Bottom police station, Arnold could not personally bring a charge against the sneaky Slimy Slickey and, much as he deserved it, drag the little rat before the Magistrates Bench. That would mean opening a whole bag of worms, implicating too many innocent villagers who had availed themselves of the little crooks dubious dealings. Not to mention exposing Arnold's own occasional forays under the counter. No, retribution must be brought about some other way. Even as he shovelled the snow from Mrs Shepherd's flagstones Arnold was forming an elaborate plan that would sort the whole matter out without involving an official charge. It would also give Arnold himself great pleasure into the bargain. Fired by this promise of bringing his own brand of justice to bear he fairly leaped into action.

The sharp rap on the door caught Edgar Clough totally unawares. Since gaining some local fame for his prize winning quilt the village cross dresser had gained enough courage to swan around in some of his creations *downstairs* rather than in the privacy of his bedroom. Therefore with the urgent rapping *on* the front door he had no time to divest himself of his Rosalind Russell number in cerise shot silk with the sweetheart neckline. Covered in confusion Edgar called out in what passed for his *"man's"* voice, "I can't answer the door at the moment! Me Mam's out, she's gone to the Co-op..."

176

I know your Mam's out Edgar,"Arnold replied impatiently, I waited till she was out. I want to talk to you on your own. Put summat decent on and answer the damn door."

Having carried a torch for the handsome police man since they were both in the infants school, Edgar knew his adoration would never be reciprocated, but that didn't prevent his heart beating ten to the dozen as he hastily tried to make himself presentable. First he divested himself of his Maria Montez turban and Lupe Velez hoop earrings replacing them with the old dressing gown his father left him when he died. Kicking off his three inch heels, satin court shoes he stumbled excitedly as he unlocked the door to reveal the love of his life standing on the step. His breath coming in short bursts as it always did at the mere thought of Arnold, he felt himself blush like a maiden in the first flush of love.

"Now then Edgar, stop palpitating and take heed," Arnold began in earnest for what he was about to do was indeed very secret, elaborate, and not without a little risk."Thou'rt still in charge of the costumes wigs and make up for the amateur dramatic society aren't you?" He only allowed Edgar time to nod in the affirmative before he carried on. "Well, strictly between you and me, I have this *"friend,"* who shall remain nameless, what wants to borrow a few items for a fancy dress affair in Manchester next Friday night. He's about my build, and wants to go as a gangster, like them you see on the pictures – tha' knows the punch drunk kind, the one's that do the roughing up? Like Maxie Rosenbloom? You know what I mean?"

"Aye, I know exactly what tha' means..." If there was one thing Edgar knew about it was the movies, the stars and what they wore. "Maxie 'Slapsie' Rosenbloom!" Well! If *"thy friend"* is about *"thy height,"* Edgar replied

177

pointedly, indicating he was not fooled by Arnold's story, but that he could be trusted to go along with the intrigue, "...he'll need lifts in his shoes, body padding, wide brimmed Fedora. Cream coloured, tie belted overcoat..." interrupting him the police sergeant added some specifications of his own.

"...Black wig, black eyebrows, black moustache, and dark glasses..."

"Maxie Rosenbloom doesn't have black hair, black eyebrows and a black moustache..."

"...This one does. Can you supply me these things?"

"No bother."

"Right, put the lot in a bag and take it to my house, on Friday afternoon. Let yourself in, the key is where it gen'ly is under the plant pot ...and if you so much as tell one living soul, I'll confiscate all your frocks and high heels." Arnold said with a wink and grin that had the effect of decimating Edgar's composure all over again. Hand on heart and heaving a sigh from the depths of his being Edgar replied with passion, "Trust me!"

As usual, Friday nights in the smoke filled lounge bar at the "Feathers" was packed with the usual sycophantic crowd of mostly middle aged men paying court to Flossie Ingham the brassy landlady as she perched on the high stool at the end of the bar. Her evil eyes fixed almost constantly on the till to see none of the staff did anything dishonest, even though all three of them, Sally, Minnie and Eli were way beyond reproach.

From time to time Flossie's coarse laugh could be heard above the general hubbub as the fawning men surrounding her plied her with double gins and triple entendre jokes. However jovial the scene may have appeared to any outsider, there was no real friendship, no warmth in these exchanges between Flossie and her cohorts. The participants were only interested in their own ends. Never the less they were spending big money for the pleasure of her company, not to mention the promise of some shady transaction that would always be to her advantage. So she laughed dutifully at the smutty quips and flirted with the biggest spender until she called *"Time Gentlemen Please."* At which time, and not a second longer the shutter came down on her brittle smile and she abandoned them all, (all but the particular chosen one for that night only) before she counted the takings. That some of the men had spent a small fortune to be a part of her entourage mattered not. They were brutally dropped like hot coals. This nauseating charade was played out every Friday night when amongst her suitors would be the biggest spender, Herbert Townsend the owner of Townsend's Textiles and smaller fish like some of the Servicemen convalescing at the Military Hospital. But always amongst the rejected sycophants was Slimy Slickey, feeling sick to his stomach that once again his suave wit, debonair looks not to mention a big slice of his weekly takings had been squandered on the object of his desire to no avail. Slimey drained his glass, adopted an unconvincing air of self-satisfied bonhomie to cover the deep resentment that his undeniable charm had been rejected for the umpteenth time. His swagger hardly enhanced for having mixed his drinks all evening, he swept out of the "Feathers" alone into the cold moonlit night.

Apart from a few courting couples the village was deserted. In spite of the bright intensity of the moonlight, there was no one to witness the tall incredibly broad shouldered man close in-behind Slimy as he walked dejectedly past the graveyard. Without warning the back of Slimey's scrawny neck was seized in a vice like grip, and before he could call out, a leather-gloved hand clamped over his mouth. Terror engulfed the little crook as he found himself, helpless as a rag doll being forcibly led behind the out spread wings of the most imposing funerary statue in the darkest corner of the ancient graveyard. Fearing his end was imminent, he was not too lost in the horror of his situation to notice the monument he was being pinned against was appropriately enough the *Angel of Death.*

"If yous values your life, you little freak, I'd advise yous to play dumb and listen to what I have to say, capiche?" The giant's voice was vaguely American, but since Slimy was not familiar with any accent other than his own he couldn't be sure. What he was sure of was that it was full of menace and terrifying.

"Who are you? What..."

"Da name's Heinzie, or *"Heinzie the Swinezie"* but seein' as you count for nothin', you can call me Sir". A slap across Slimy's face put paid to any protest. His monstrous captor, towering above him was of enormous girth. The dark glasses, wide brimmed hat pulled down over a heavy pair of eyebrows, and most terrifying of all, a soot black moustache which obliterated any hint of a human mouth quite vanquished the little crook. It was an image Slimy would take with him to his dying day, which at that moment seemed pretty imminent.

"Da name "Al Sharp" means anything to you?" The voice grunted.

The name certainly did mean something to Slimy. It meant mortal fear. Slimy began to shake with a new dread. Everyone on the fringes of the law in the North of England during wartime had heard of Albert Sharp, head of the black market syndicate with its headquarters in Leeds.

"I see dat it does! Yes sirree, one dangerous man - Al. One definitely not to tangle wid! Oh, my woid no!"

The strange foreign accent was becoming more sinister and threatening with each passing phrase. Slimy felt his bowels change gear.

"It has come to Al's attention that you have been muscling in on his territory. Extortion! Demandin' payola from a certain Armitage dame..."

"Nay bloody hell, it were nobbut ten bob a week...I didn't know it were his territory..." another weightier slap across the mouth turned Slimey into a whimpering child.

"Al left it to my own discretion as to how I should deal wit chew," the voice droned, "Maybe I should blow you away right now and have done wid it..."

"No! No! Noooooooo...!" Slimey was now in real danger of unbuttoning his bum,

"Tell you what I'll do," the big stranger said "bein' as I'm known all over da Bronx for my generous nature, "you pay the Armitage dame all her money back...lets see, six months at ten bobs a week... I make dat a hundred and fifty quids right?

"Right..."

"..a hundred and fifty quid by to-morrow, in cash, in her hand, then may be, just maybe I'll let you live a while longer Capiche?"

"...Right! Absolutely! No bother! ...just as you say Mr Heinzie – sir!"

At last Slimey was beginning to see a glimmer of light at the end of the terrifying tunnel.

"But remember this you little scum bag," the man said as he lifted Slimey off his feet by the lapels, punctuating every word with an ever more severe slap across his gob. "If I have to make another visit to dis God forsaken toilet, it's coitains for you Bozo!" With one last heavy belt across Slimey's chops the man disappeared into the shadows leaving the little crook shaken to the core but at least alive and in no doubt about what he had to do to stay that way.

The following Monday morning proved to be a very satisfying start to the week for Sergeant Wilkinson. First thing, even before elevenses, Dora Armitage came bursting through the front door of the cottage which served as the charge office. No longer was she the frightened old kennel maid. She was now almost operatic with relief and happiness.

"Arnold!!" she sang out, "You'll never guess what! I've got all me brass back off Mr Slickey. He say's the other fellow had a change of heart, and had seen the light, and insisted that Slimey return all my brass. The only thing is, he gave me back a lot more than I paid him in the first place. I felt awful taking it, but he insisted…"

"Don't thee worry over it Dora," Arnold assured her, "Buy thi'sen some War Saving Certificates with the surplus, and say nowt to nobody, alright?"

"So there'll be no need for thee to have a word with him now will there?" She asked.

"That's right old lass, no need at all." Arnold replied pleased to be putting the lid on the affair. No sooner had Dorothy skipped off down the High Street her feet hardly touching the pavement than in walked Edgar Clough to pick up the gangster costume for its return to the Amateur Dramatic Society's wardrobe department, before anyone knew it had been away.

"Was the get-up and wig and everything alright for "your friend" at the fancy dress party last Friday Arnold." Edgar whispered with a sly tilt of the head, proud to be a party to whatever the exciting charade was about.

"Was it alright?" The handsome cop smiled warmly on his old friend, causing his heart miss a beat. "Was it alright Edgar? I'll say it was alright. "My friend got first

182

prize! In fact you might say the whole thing was – Poyfect!
– Capiche?

....

THE SCOURING STONE MAN

Sergeant Arnold Wilkinson and Constable Archie Barker, the two coppers in charge of the converted cottage that served as Craggs Bottom's police station, were cast in the same mould – lenient to the point of dereliction of duty.

Both men occasionally made mild shows of official competence by badgering people who forgot their gas masks or violated the blackout restrictions. But heaven forbid actually charging anybody unless the offender was blatantly evil or dangerous. Anything less was to be dealt with by them and them alone. A kindly word or a heartfelt plea, a telling off here, a boot up the backside there was usually enough to keep the peace. Their gentle touch was none the less, surprisingly effective. Arnold's strong smiling presence was more than enough to defuse any "bother" come chucking out time at the "Feathers" Although he hated paper work of any kind Arnold would fill in the many official war time forms for the old folks. Explain with infinite gentleness the reason they were not able to have a tin of salmon or the extra four ounces of butter because they had already used up their weekly ration. He would put up their blackout curtains, and sit with them when they or their loved ones were off colour, ill or dying.

As far as most of the inhabitants of the village could see, the only reason to keep the pair of them in office was rounding up and accommodating Harry Petty, the local drunk. Every Friday night without fail after Flossie Ingham called *"time gentlemen please"* and the clientele had left the pub Harry, regular as a pound of prunes, would linger on the Main Street to sing hymns at the top of his tuneless voice until escorted home by Arnold or, more likely at the week end, tucked up in the cop shop cell for the night.

Harry earned his living as a pedlar. Living alone in a two bed roomed cottage with an adjacent lean-to, which housed his stock of old fashioned household cleaning materials belonging to an earlier age. Yet here in Craggs Bottom there still was a call for things like carbolic soap, so sharp it would remove the skin from a rhino. Rock salt, wire wool, caustic and washing sodas, ammonia, dolly blue, white and yellow scouring stones. Amongst other weird, wonderful and dangerous cleaning agents, quick-lime for the walls of the out side toilets, paraffin, white spirit and the cause of Sergeant Wilkinson's anxieties – metholated spirits. The reason for Sergeant Wilkinson's concern was when Harry was left alone in his little house after heavy night on mild and bitter, Arnold feared that Harry might resort to a little chaser of meths as a nightcap. Arnold, for all his kindness was not afraid to confront Harry of his suspicions for although the sad old man was wily he was never anything but honest with Arnold and if he had been at the meths. He would admit it.

"By gum Harry, what have you been supping, you've gorra face the colour of a well smacked arse!" Arnold would say, as sternly as he knew how, "I hope that' hasn't been supping any of that there meths tha peddles?"

185

"No, Arnold! Not a drop." Harry would say,"I've given all that up – for lent!"

"Glad to hear it." Arnold smiled as he steered Harry to the prisoner's cell of the cop shop, which in reality was only a smidgeon different from the cosy back bedroom it had been before the cottage had been requisitioned.

Although most villagers would have been hard put to to give a reason, it seemed the entire village felt a great affection for Harry although it would never have done to express it. This tacit concern for his well being was expressed most poignantly by his next door neighbour, Leah Stead. A hardy old widow rumoured to be well over eighty years of age, but still as lithe as a ferret, wise as a barn owl and tough as a colliers forearm. Leah *"looked in on Harry"*, saw to it that he ate properly at least once a day. She served customers from the lean-to when he was out on his rounds – a service that was no small contribution to his weekly turnover. She reminded him when he needed a haircut or a bath. In cold weather she would let herself into his cottage to bank up the fire so there would be some cheer to greet him after a long day trudging his hand cart up and down the steep cobbled streets. For Leah suspected as did Arnold, there was *"something more"* to Harry than the monosyllabic (at least when sober) little hawker so familiar to everyone. It was Leah who burst into the little cop shop one cold Monday morning to alert the police sergeant to Harry's plight.

"Leah me old love! What are you doing, out and about on a day like this? You should be sat up to't fire roasting your shins" Arnold led the old lady through the hatch to the office/kitchen where she was offered a mug of tea.

"Don't concern thi'sen about me lad, I'm as right as a bobbin. It's Harry Petty I'm bothered about," Leah said, in her straight from the shoulder manner. "I have seen neither hide nor hair of him since Friday morning when he set off on his rounds."

"Come to think on it", Arnold replied, "neither Archie nor me brought him in for singing his hymns after chucking out time on Friday night, Where can he be?"

"Oh, I know where he is alright he's locked his-self in. I've knocked and knocked till me knuckles is raw, but he won't answer." Leah said, "It must be summat to do wi' that letter that was waiting for him when he got in from work on Friday neet."

"...Letter? Who's going to write to Harry?" Arnold said, then quickly changed tack realising it sounded heartless. "...I mean to say, I didn't think he had anybody...you know, who would write..."

"Aye, well he didn't want anyone to know about his past. But I think it's about time somebody beside me did." Leah made as if to get moving. "Get thy cape on, I'll tell thee as much as I know on the way round to Harry's."

In the few hundred yards it took for the pair of them to reach Harry's cottage Leah, hardly pausing for breath, presented an event packed account of Harry's entire past life. Her energy, her machine gun delivery - on the hoof mind you, drawing a word picture of such fine detail it left the bewildered policeman reeling in wonder at the life force still erupting in this indomitable old lady.

Harry, it transpired had not always been a reclusive hawker of scouring stones. According to Leah's rapid description he had been owner of a thriving Light Engineering firm in Leeds. He married a pretty but flighty girl from a "good" family from Exeter. The marriage lasted a mere six months. Suddenly, without warning his young bride left him without as much as a goodbye note. Her parents, who never approved of Harry in the first place, either couldn't or wouldn't tell him of her whereabouts, only that she never wanted to hear from him ever again. For months Harry tried hard to contact her, without success. Distraught he took to drink and let his successful business go down the plug. And with unseemly haste sank to the lowest Hogarthian depths. After one prolonged drunken binge, with what little money and what little sense he had left, he awoke one morning to find he had bought the little cottage, handcart, lean-to, hawkers licence and "goodwill" of a door-to-door hawking business. After a brief tour of the district with "Salty Sam" the previous owner showing him the ropes, Harry seamlessly took over the business and "Salty Sam" promptly retired and left him to it.

"Well I'll be...!" Arnold said, "I always thought he was "Salty Sam's son."

"That's what he wanted everybody to think..." Leah said as they arrived at their destination. "Come on Harry!" She shouted as she kicked heavily on the door. "I know there's summat up. Let me in!"

"Harry! Open this door, do you hear?" Arnold shouted through the letterbox. There was no reply. "Sod this Leah – stand back!" The burly copper put his shoulder to the door and the ancient lock yielded as if made of warm putty.

The policeman and the old lady entered the cottage to find the ashes cold in the grate and no sign of life downstairs. Exchanging glances they thought the worst, and climbing the stone chamber steps found Harry lying on the bed comatose with grief clutching a well-handled letter. Barely conscious still in his workday clothes, his hair and beard tangled and matted Harry presented a pathetic picture of humanity. To Arnold's trained eye the almost empty whisky bottle was the one positive clue that Harry had not resorted to more dangerous spirits. Unable to respond to Leah's and

Arnold's concerns he simply lay there as if he had no strength left in his body.

"Nay Arnold lad, it's not what you think it is. What Thou'rt witnessing isn't the result of the devil's brew," If her turn of phrase was somewhat archaic her instant understanding of the situation was deadly accurate, "Thou'rt looking at a man sufferin' from a broken heart."

Unable to acknowledge his visitors and even less able to explain what had brought about this cataclysmic breakdown; Harry simply passed the letter to Arnold. It read...

Dear Mr Petty,

This is the most difficult letter for me to write. The last thing I want to do is to make you feel embarrassed or in any way indebted to me. On the other hand I think – I hope – when you know the full story you will understand and look kindly upon me. For a start, I don't know how much, if anything you know about me. Only recently I have learned you are my father.

When my mother left the North of England to return to her parents in Devon she was pregnant. Shortly after I was born she walked out again. This time she walked out on me. My grandparents raised me leading me to believe that both my parents had been killed in a motoring accident.

Only recently, knowing she is growing older has my grandmother had a change of heart and told me of your existence. I hope you will understand my natural curiosity, and wonder if you would agree to a meeting with me? I am shortly to be posted to the Far East and considering the uncertainties of war I am emboldened enough to hope you will grant my request of a meeting at some neutral venue of your choice. I obtained your present address through a reputable investigation agency, so should you feel unable to see me, for whatever reason, I will understand and respect your privacy. In which case you will hear no more from me and I will bear you no ill will.

Finally, I apologise for the melodramatic content of this letter, but I don't know of any other way to present the facts. I do hope you can find it in your heart to see me.

Yours sincerely, Flt. Lt. Victor. C. Petty

Although he had read the letter a thousand times in the previous two days, on hearing Arnold's gentle, sensitive interpretation Harry finally broke his silence and murmured through his heartbreak...

"...I can't Arnold. I can't do it. I can't let the lad see me like this..."

"Are you sure Harry?" Arnold replied kindly. "It couldn't do any harm, surely!" Harry sank back on the pillow and with closed eyes adamantly shook his head in refusal.

"Now come on. He seems a champion young man. Consider his feelings..." Arnold pleaded.

"What do you think I've been doing for the last forty eight hours"! Harry's voice shook with emotion. "I've thought of nothing else. The best thing I can do for him is to burn that letter. Let him forget about me. He must never see me like this." Harry reached out to retrieve the letter from Arnold, but Arnold held the letter at arms length away from the distraught old man.

"I can't. I can't let him see me like this. Look at me! A derelict! The local drunk – a joke! A laughing stock! A disgrace..."

Leah, surprising both men, exasperatedly burst in. Her voice matter of fact, strong and sensible: "Well at last! Summat I *can* agree with!" "Thou 'art a disgrace and no mistake. I've never seen anybody so damned sorry for his-self in all my born puff!"

190

"But look at me Leah! A hawker, living in a hovel like this, what sort of a..."

"So! Thou'rt a hawker! What be that? It's an honest living. Tha' pays thee way, the house is thy own..."

"Aye, a pig sty..." Harry interjected.

"Only 'cos tha' let it get that way. It's a bonny little house. There's nowt wrong wi' it that a lick of paint and a scrubbing brush couldn't put right."

"It's not just the house Leah, it's me. Look at me - a derelict... not fit to be seen..."

"Good God man, I've had enough of this!" Leah stormed, the veins in her neck standing out with passion as she let him have it with both barrels blazing. "Do you know how much courage it took for that lad of thine to write such a letter? A blind man on a galloping hoss could see he's made of finer stuff than average, and here thou art, fart-arsing around feelin' sorry for thi'sen. A good steeping in a bath of hot water with a handful of washing soda and you'd scrub up looking like a human being. A haircut and shave to get shut of that nasty bird's nest on thi' face at Charlie Allender's costs next to nowt, and tha' must have enough clothing coupons for a pair of decent shoes and a Co-op suit. Now get up off that bloody bed and reply to that letter and arrange a meeting - **BEFORE I LOSE ME TEMPER!!"**

Breathless now Leah finally sat down feeling she must have a cup of tea, for it was the longest speech she had ever made. It was however one hundred percent effective. A letter was in the post the following morning inviting Flt. Lt. Victor. C. Petty, to come to Craggs Bottom for as long as his leave would permit.

Once the word got about - and there was never any hope that Harry's little drama could have been kept under wraps - everyone wanted to have some part in the action to bring about a happy re-union for Harry and his son. The next few days fairly bristled with activity around Harry's cottage. Ellis Clitheroe now well and truly alive and back at the head of the family business had not forgotten his recovery was due, in no small measure, to Harry having rescued the precious pie crust from the ruins of the public convenience.

Ellis offered the services of his two eldest lads to do whatever was deemed necessary to turn Harry's residence into a palace. Wielding buckets of plaster, paintbrushes and blowlamps the two young men were hustled and chivvied along like a pair of tied bondsmen under Leah's hawk eyed supervision. Floor boards newly sanded, smiled at the world for the first time since they were laid. Freshly distempered walls made the rooms appear twice the size. Windowpanes let in beams of sunlight for the first time in years.

Ada Clough and her son Edgar ran up a beautiful set of matching curtains and a new white silk shirt, with strict instructions from Sergeant Wilkinson to all concerned not to ask from under which counter the materials came. Table and bed linen appeared from various bottom drawers around the village. A new bed and a roll of lino arrived from some anonymous source for the second little bedroom. Before long even the old men from the allotments were in on the act. These usually impassive old men now triggered into action by the excitement of it all set about making window boxes, fitting and filling them with a blaze of seasonal colour that showed the newly painted window frames off to perfection. The exterior of Number Three Rudyard's Fold took on an appearance of a glossy picture from the pages of *"House and Garden"*. Arnold gasped in amazement and pride when, after only a few days of intense application the neighbours had changed a hovel into a home.

A similar metamorphosis was being applied to the central figure in this little drama. No matter how much he objected Harry was to have the best treatment the village could supply. Charlie Allinder, who single handedly ran the local barbershop, quaked under the threat of the dreadful repercussions that would befall him if the instructions, delivered in person by Leah Stead herself were not carried out to the letter. Harry was to have the best; most intensive treatment the little salon could manage leaving no room for corner-cutting. Hot towels, shampoos, beer rinses, a gently tapered short back and sides...

"...and none of your usual brutal *"up and over two minute specials"* with them there garden shears. I don't want him resembling a Prussian Field Marshall or a privet hedge" Charlie Allinder stood obediently quaking hoping that Leah's demands were coming to close. He didn't know how much more he could take.

"...and none of that there chip fat of yours that passes for brilliantine! And it tha' so much as nicks his chin when Thou'rt shaving him tha'll need more than styptic pencil for what I'll do to thee Charlie Allinder! I **want Harry Petty to come out of this shop looking like Ronald Colman! IS THAT CLEAR?**

The great day of the meeting between Father and long lost son arrived at last. Although it was an ordinary working day it seemed the entire village turned out. Everyone gathered out side the "Feathers", supposedly about some altogether different purpose, but in reality, all agog to witness the momentous re-union. Jaws dropped, eyes goggled and mouths gaped when it dawned on the crowd that the distinguished, gentleman escorting Leah and Sergeant Wilkinson into the Snug bar was none other than their own scouring stone man – Harry Petty.

"I'm very nervous Arnold." Harry said, as the three friends sat in the corner of the Snug Bar awaiting the taxi that was to deliver his son to him, "Will you and Leah stay with me until he gets here?"

"We'll do better than that, we'll all have a drink while were waiting'" Arnold said as he ordered three Scotches.

"Do you think I should?"

"Sure of it," Arnold replied without hesitation. The three friends sat unusually close. Two of them smiling warmly, the other swamped with a mixture of apprehension, and a feeling almost entirely new to him – a feeling of impending belonging.

"You can afford to smile Harry! " Leah said as the sound of the taxi drew up outside, "Everybody's that proud of thee! There's no'but one person going to be prouder and here he comes - Your son! Flt. Ltnt. Victor C. Petty."

....

OSWALD

"Ah'sll never understand how or why you put up with that terrible man!" Dorothy Armitage fumed as she slammed the phone back on its hook, "even if he is a big wig there's no need to be so snotty, He talks to folk like they was a pile of dog muck!"

"Correct me if I'm wrong Dora, but that can only be Chief Superintendent Oswald Cartwright you were talking to – right?" Elenora laughed as she kicked off her wellies before joining her housekeeper at the kitchen table.

"Right first time! He says to tell you he'll be here on Saturday night to go over the programme with you. He says his time is precious, so would you mind getting on with the rehearsal bang on time. Ooooh, he was that curt!"

"Thanks Dora." Elenora giggled as she helped herself to a healthy portion of Dora's savoury pie. A delicious wartime concoction dreamed up by her and a Home Front recipe containing practically nothing of nutritional value. None the less, tasty and very welcome after a hard day carrying out her veterinarian duties with the police horses at the Leeds stables. "Don't let him upset you Dora darling', he's full of wind and water as they in these parts."

195

"Wind and piss, is the precise phrase," Dora corrected, "You don't have to tell me, he's always been a bad tempered snotty dollop since he was a lad."

"Do you remember him as a lad?"

"Oh aye, He was brought up in the village by his single mother Beatrice. Minnie Clegg's sister..."

"I didn't know Minnie had any family," Elenora was genuinely surprised.

"Oh aye, Minnie and Beatie were as different as ketchup and custard." Dora went on warming to her subject. "Whereas Minnie is kindness itself and loves a good laugh, Beatie was as mean as mustard. Tight fisted! They used to say she would cut a currant in two and save half for later. Hard on Oswald when he was a kid. That's why he's always so tight arsed and distant."

"It hardly seems possible that Minnie could have a sister as mean as you say Beatie was." Elenora said, as she recalled her regular Sunday lunches at her friend Minnie's welcoming cottage.

"When I say mean I mean, mean as in mean spirited," Dora said getting tongue-tied.

"Oswald never went hungry or wanted for anything except perhaps a kind word. He never mixed with all the other lads and lasses. You see, Beatie made him buckle down so that he always came top at school *and* Grammar School! Then when he went away to Police College he eclipsed the lot of them!"

"Too much discipline, too soon?" Elenora ventured.

"Aye, sad really. You can only feel sorry for him" Dora said closing the subject. "Still it doesn't alter the fact that Oswald Cartwright gets right up my nose."

As Craggs Bottom highest achiever one might have expected a show of pride in their successful son. Sadly there were not many who didn't have the same opinion of him as Dora, even fewer who could dredge up a kindly word for him. The feeling was mutual however, for Oswald desperately tried to live down his humble beginnings and never let it be known in the circles he now moved that he came from of all places as Craggs Arse. He longed to be seen as urbane, sophisticated and polished. To this end he spent a small fortune on "*Personal Betterment Courses*" which included Art appreciation classes even elocution lessons, all to little effect for whenever he attended the official functions his rising status afforded him, he came across as highly efficient but something of a phoney – a sad lonely one at that.

By the time he reached his thirties he had already begun to climb in rank within the Police Force and had taken out a mortgage on a large house in the most select part of Leeds, fitted it out with expensive but bland conventional furnishings. Hired a housekeeper who knew her place, addressed him as "Sir" and never so much as discussed the weather with the "master" – there was no mistress of the house, and few signs there would ever be one.

Oswald was alone in the world. The years racing along alarmingly he now found himself well into his fourth decade, aware that life was passing him by, but unable to see why. The tragedy was, had he only realised it, he did have a priceless attribute that lay not in the false front he presented to the world, but in one glorious God given gift – a deep love of music and a natural genius for playing the bass fiddle with such tenderness it threatened to break ones heart.

In spite of her crazily crowded life Elenora found herself,at the outbreak of war recruited into the newly formed ENSA. Given a list of available musicians on whom she could call upon to form anything from a trio to a fairly large orchestra. Much to his chagrin Oswald was high on this list. Commandeered into service with the "*Dixieland Hot Shots*"!

Although the phone message, taken by Dora, was curt to the point of brutality he was secretly thrilled to be on his way to Ambler House to attend the rehearsal. Too grand to admit these "Jam Sessions" were pure bliss and the highlight of his week.

"I still can't understand how you can abide having that miserable man in your band." Dora said, bringing in to the music room a large tray of sandwiches, as the musicians arrived for the run through in preparation for the following evenings gig. "I'm sorry Miss Clapworthy, there's no other word for it, the man's a Pratt!"

"Well I'll tell you Dora. Oswald Cartwright has one magnificent saving grace," Elenora explained, "He plays that bull fiddle like an angel. He has what they call – musical integrity! Sensitive and tender! Now! Can you credit that?"

"Sensitive? My arse! Tender? Oswald? Gerraway!

"It's true – Anyone who has that can't be all bad. Other than that – you're right – he's a Pratt!".

Young Mickey Ryan now a handsome teenager and accepted member of Elenora's select inner circle of musicians was half seated half standing confidently belting out riffs on the drums like an old pro. Jimmy Dreyfuss a convalescing GI from what had been before the war, the Cottage Hospital, and now a Large Military Hospital Complex, stood tuning his clarinet whilst exchanging a few risqué quips with Dora, who of course gave as good as she got. The two brothers Bernard and Otis Briggs, star trumpeter and trombonist from Townsend's Textiles Brass Band, both men regular cup winners in pre-war National contests, now lending their talents to The "*Hot Shots*" and loving it. Graham the saxophonist swapping jokes with Eddie on the euphonium both from the Salvation Army Band, Mickie Ryan on Drums along with Oswald on the Big Bass who in spite of his demand to Dora that the rehearsal must start on time had not yet arrived, and of course their leader Elenora on piano to complete the complement. There was one other newcomer expected, one who would be the cause of many hearts to fl utter andone particular heart to never beat to the same rhythm ever again.

No one noticed Dora's contemptuous sniff as she answered the door to let Oswald into the room. Without a word he unpacked his instrument and joined the others around the grand piano where quickly and efficiently he tuned the strings of his bass fiddle, and ignoring the happy chatter around him began to caress the strings, slowly surrendering to the gentle mellow sounds. Only when the music reached his soul did the personality change occur. Slowly the ghost of a smile replaced the tight-lipped stiffness that was his normal demeanour and a blessed tranquillity settled over him.

This miraculous change would last only as long as the music played, not a moment longer, then he would revert to his normal stuffy, superior self – not tonight though! Tonight something would happen that would change his life forever.

"Gentlemen, can I have your attention, if you please!" Elenora clapped her hands to cut through the happy chatter that always preceded these rehearsals. "Let me introduce to you our guest vocalist for tomorrow night's gig. Miss Peggy Waters. She's a lovely lady so no hanky-panky and no bum notes!" There was a chorus of good natured sarcastic - *"as if we would!"* replies and *"Hanky-panky? Us?"* plus a couple of good-natured yet delicious rude noises from the trombone and trumpet, as the lady herself entered the room. Jimmy Dreyfuss gave a boyish wolf whistle, which earned him a clip around the ear from Dora. All the English boys knew Peggy Waters from her many BBC broadcasts with big name Dance Bands, and treated her with respect as well as the admiration usually afforded a *"glamour puss"*.

Blonde and pretty with a dazzling smile, Peggy was well used to such a reaction from men. She greeted the band with good-natured pleasantness as she handed her band parts to Mickey who immediately began to distribute them. By far the most affected by her dazzling presence, but least able to express the impact she had upon him was Oswald Cartwright. His fascinated gaze followed her every move. Only his instinctive musicianship saved him from making a fool of himself on a number of occasions during the course of the evening.

The rehearsal over-ran well into the small hours. Not because of any musical difficulties, on the contrary, it was a most satisfactory and hugely enjoyable session. Only when she called it a day did Elenora remember Oswald's specific demand that he should not be kept late. As he descended from the podium to pack away his instrument he was still wearing the blissful trance that always descended upon him during a session. But this time the expected change from his Dr Jekyll persona back into his workaday Mr Hyde never came.

"Mickey, what's the matter with Ossie?" Elenora asked in a low voice, as the pair of them sorted the manuscripts ready for the following night's gig, "he usually blows a gasket if we run late. Now look at him, faffing around like an old lady."

"Didn't you notice Miss Clapworthy?" Mick replied delightedly, "He's in love! Didn't you clock him when we stopped for a break, he couldn't take his eyes off her?"

"Well I'll be...!" Elenora gasped, in genuine shock, "Well who would have thought it – Ossie in love?"

Pathetically adrift amidst the happy chatter as the rest of the men clustered around the blond singer, each of them waiting his moment to ask if they might be the one to see her to her hotel. All Oswald could do was to dither on the periphery like a gawky schoolboy - a stranger to the ways of courtship, a loser without a hope of a kindly look from the object of his desire. A wave of compassion swept over Elenora as she watched Oswald flounder hopelessly in the role of would be suitor.

"Oh, Mickie look at the poor sod, he hasn't a clue. There's only one thing for it, we'll have to give him a leg-up." Again she clapped her hands to gain attention. "Thanks for a great rehearsal, We'll be a sensation at the gig tomorrow – see you all there..." then adding nonchalantly, "Oh Ossie, would you mind seeing Peggy gets to her hotel alright, it's on your way home? You're in safe hands Peggy, Ossie has a car, priority petrol ration, and he's a copper."

"Oh that's very sweet of you Ossie," Peggy said, relieved of the chore of fending off the other musicians had been taken out of her hands, "It is "Ossie" isn't it?"

"...er...Chief Super... Oswald... Ossie is perfectly alright, er...Miss Waters."

"Oh, call me Peggy please!" Flashing a glittering smile she took his arm as they walked towards his car.

In spite of, or perhaps because of the Allies imminent invasion of Italy, the following nights gig had more than a sense of impending destiny about it. One amongst many nights during the war when couples clung that little bit closer, knowing but never voicing the dread they might never have another night together. It was a night when men and women would urgently speak to each other of love. From the first quickstep the evening seemed to have a certain something special about it, those who felt the magic would fashion memories that would last forever. This was certainly true for Oswald Cartwright.

From the minute he called at the hotel to accompany Peggy to the gig he was in a strange kind of paradise and it made his head swim. Her perfumed closeness in the car - the surge of pride he felt when she praised his skill in battling through the blackout. The thrill of the intimacy of being allowed to carry her gowns into her dressing room – the ecstasy of actually being   in the shared glow of pink and amber from the twin follow spots as she sang one song after the other to ever increasing adulation. To Oswald it was like being deliciously drunk.

He didn't want the night to end. For the first time in his life he did not recognise merely the music, now he heard the words of the love songs Peggy sang so beautifully. There were even moments during the more romantic ones he was convinced they were directed solely at him.

If Elenora had any misgivings for having set Oswald up with Peggy Waters, they were forgotten on seeing the enchantment in his face as the pair drove off together after the show.

"Oh, yes Mickey, you were dead right," Elenora said with a knowing wink, as she drove back home "Oswald is in love all right!"

"Yeah, he's a different man," the boy squealed with delight, "he even said "thank you" when I handed the band parts out, and you should have seen his face when she sang *"Who's Taking You Home Tonight"* I'd no idea he could smile!"

"Yes. It's love alright." Elenora said, only half jokingly. "But will it last – will love change Andy Hardy?"

The answer sadly was *"No"*, at least not change him for the better. The *"Hot Shots"* didn't have another get-together for a few weeks, not due to a lack of bookings, but rather because of other more essential work some of the men had to perform. Mick continued to work hard doing his chores helping Dora and of course at his music lessons. Elenora too was taken up with her many other occupations - the kennels, the surgery and more annoyingly she was called upon to sit on the Magistrates Bench, which she hated. Superintendent Cartwright's affair of the heart was pushed to the back burner in the busy activities of Ambler Manor. Therefore it was something of a shock when Oswald in his capacity as Chief Cop made one of his surprise nit-picking inspections at the little substation.

He was known to periodically spring these surprise, catch - em' - with – their - pants - down calls, mainly to boost his ego and assert his authority, but subconsciously, according to Dora, "to give Cragg's arse a good kicking".

Maddeningly, there was no denying that Sergeant Wilkinson and Constable Barker had an impeccable peace keeping record. But, and it was a big *"but"*, the number of arrests were far below average compared to similar sized sub-stations under Ossie's jurisdiction. Besides the two local Bobbies were far too popular for his liking. *"Popular"* in Oswald's book, was a word that couldn't be tolerated. For instance – blackout precautions – were they being enforced? Black marketeering – why did it never figure in their reports? Deserters – how come no one was ever sent from Craggs Bottom to the Glasshouse at Aldershot? And so on. Nothing pleased him, least of all the Charge Book, devoid as it was of even a minor charge. Yet this time, for all of the Chief's bluster as he delivered the toughest ultimatum yet to Sergeant Wilkinson and wreaked his usual havoc on the bowel movements of Constable Barker, there was no real, no new substance to his visit. Sergeant Wilkinson, no-body's fool, noticed this at once.

"I want to see," Oswald paused for dramatic effect before delivering his parting shot, "I want to see – take a note of this – **I want to see at least one entry in that Charge Book** the next time I call! **Do I make myself clear?"**

"What do you suppose all that was about? What's eating him?" Sergeant Wilkinson asked his nerve shattered Constable, as he watched through the window his superior officer drive off in the direction of Ambler Lane "I see the dozy bugger is off to give Miss Clapworthy a bad time. Not possessing the same grit, or brainpower as his sergeant, Constable Archie Barker took Oswald's berating to heart, and had to be soothed with a long sit down and a hot cup of tea.

"There's more to this than meets the eye," Arnold said, "If 'tha asks me there's summat bothering him beside the state of our Charge Book. Still you never know whether he's going to set us up, just to see if were on our mettle. He's done it before and he could do it again."

"Archie you'd better pull yourself together, sup your tea and get out on the beat to see if 'tha can't arrest some poor sod."

The Chief Constable drove his car carefully over the deep ruts in the drive that led to the front door of Ambler Manor, creating a cacophony of barking dogs from the kennels. The authority his high-ranking uniform gave him was absent. Looking awkward and unsure of himself he stood on the doorstep. Having used the heavy knocker, which when struck even lightly, the heavy clapper's medieval sound reverberated alarmingly through the old house. He immediately had misgivings; in fact he really didn't know what he was doing calling on Miss Clapworthy in the first place. Or what he would say if she was in. Then it occurred to him that it could be Elenora's Housekeeper, Dorothy Armitage who might answer the door. As he turned to leave, the door opened.

"Ah, Miss Clapworthy," he was deeply thankful it was Elenora and not Dora, "I'm glad I've caught you in. I wonder if you have a minute..." he floundered racking his brain to think of a possible legitimate reason he might have to bother her, he had talk to someone, and he knew of no-one else. "It's about the oats rations for the Police Horse stables... 'er, I wondered if you considered... er... them to be up to standard... the supplier.." His gibberish tapered off into a pathetic incoherent silence.

"Oswald," Elenora asked in bewilderment, "do you mean to tell me you've driven all the way from Leeds to talk to me of the oats supply?"

"Well er.., I had other business at the Sub-station to attend to, and er..." His head dropped so he didn't have to look her in the eye. He realised he was in grave danger of making a bigger fool of himself that he had in front of Sergeant Wilkinson,

"Perhaps you're right. Perhaps the business of the oats can wait...I'm sorry I bothered you." Defeated he turned to go but his well-disciplined officiousness deserted him and he stumbled then stood rooted to the spot.

"Oswald, are you alright?" Elenora asked as she took his arm and gently led him to the large familiar music room. It was then she noticed his eyes were brimming with tears.

"Sit there and don't say a word." Elenora led him to the deep comfortable chesterfield. "What you need is a good stiff drink, and don't dare ask where I got it." She poured him a measure of brandy and stood over him until he drained the glass, replenished it then sat facing him and quietly asked, "Now then Oswald, are you going to tell me what you really came about." The brandy had the required effect. Oswald regained some of his composure and with it came the embarrassment and shame of breaking down in front *of all people* Elenora Clapworthy.

"I apologise for that Miss Clapworthy..." He rose trying desperately to regain some of his familiar characteristics. "...I really do, it won't happen again. I'll be off now." He stood to leave, but Elenora barred his way. She realised that in spite of the brandy, whilst ever he was in his official mode there was no way on God's earth he would ever be able to loosen up and unload what she already suspected.

"OK, as you wish." She said kindly, "But since you are here there is one thing you can do for me. I've got a new arrangement of *"Body and Soul"* I wonder if you would go through it with me? Good! Go and get your bass fiddle, I know you have it in your car, you always do." Uncharacteristically Oswald surrendered to her authority. Without a word he went to his car to get his instrument, still in awkward silence he unpacked it and eager to get his hands on the strings he began to strum.

In the meantime Elenora had set out the manuscripts, seated herself at the piano and poured Oswald another measure of brandy.

"No arguments," she said without looking up from the music, "drink it and come in when you feel the moment is right."

Almost immediately the brandy and the music had the effect Elenora was banking on. The easy style they created as together they played the sublime piece worked it's magic.

. "Right now, keep on playing and start talking." Lulled by the music and the brandy his story began to unfold. The song born of the blues he felt so deeply, released the full pain of first love gone wrong. Through tightly closed eyes Oswald strummed away instinctively as he told of the many phone messages to Peggy Waters that had gone unanswered.

The notes and letters that were ignored, The hours he had waited at various stage doors around the country wherever she might be doing a one night stand, only to be told *"Miss Waters sends her apologies but she has left by the front entrance for another engagement..."* or some such brush off. He told of his last excruciatingly embarrassing move to discover exactly where he stood in Peggy's affections when he tracked her down to a theatre in Lincoln. After waiting for hours at the stage door, he feared the worst when she finally appeared on the arm of a handsome young naval officer. Oswald even found the courage to approach her only to discover he didn't know what to say. Had he found the words, it would have mattered little for she looked straight through him without the faintest glimmer of recognition. He stammered some sort of excuse to Peggy for being there in the first place, finally he made a hasty retreat to embrace his heartbreak alone.

Elenora skilfully segued into yet another repeat of *"Body and Soul"* Tears that had choked Oswald for weeks began to roll freely down his cheeks. A tacit understanding kept them making music together until Oswald gave a final shudder, bravely pulled himself together and attempted a smile, not much of a smile but rare for him, a lovely self deprecating smile.

After another stiff drink and a long silence Oswald was still sober enough to realise that Elenora, who aggravated him so very much at other times, was smarter than him, kinder than him and she had made him see the futility of his infatuation and he was truly grateful. Elenora Clapworthy, out of all the women in the world was the only one in front of whom he could make a fool of himself and still look himself in the mirror no less a man for the ordeal. Eventually it was she who broke the silence.

"Well done Ossie." She said, "You've cracked it. You've loved and lost and faced the truth. Now all you have to do is remember how wonderful being love felt and get out there and find someone nearer your own age who'll love you in return."

"Not yet for a while. I've made a fool of myself. I'll need time to get over it."

"Well you've got plenty of that." Elenora said smiling, "Just relax – try to remember how good you feel when you're strumming your bull fiddle, be like that all the time and you'll have the girls queuing up."

Alas, the minute Oswald started to pack away his instrument his old stuffy mannerisms started to kick in once more as he returned to his former self.

"Thank you for your kindness Miss Clapworthy," he said with the last of his newly found humanity before slipping back behind his familiar cloak of superiority. "I'll be off now..."

"Whoa! Just a minute, are you sure you'll be alright to drive?"Elenora asked. "You've shifted quite a lot of brandy you know?"

"Perfectly alright thank you." Oswald replied, his old officiousness firmly back in place. In spite of her protests Elenora was unable to prevent him leaving. She watched anxiously from the porch as his little Morris swerved recklessly out of the drive and into Ambler Lane waltzing erratically straight into the path of Constable Archie Barker desperate to find a victim to swell the cases in the Charge Book.

"Dangerous driving if ever I saw it!" Constable Barker said to himself, as he took out his notebook. When the realisation sunk in whom he had so rashly apprehended, and the awesome consequences his action would bring about Archie called on Divine intervention.

Archie however wasn't so lost in his terror not to realise that since he had set the wheels of justice in motion, what else could he do but give the Chief Superintendent a ticket? This could well be a ruse to test his mettle. He had no choice but to carry out the order of his superior officer to get at least one arrest in the charge book.

....

FLOSSIE INGHAM

Perched like a hungry vulture on a high stool at the end of the bar Flossie Ingham, the "Feather's" malevolent landlady kept a suspicious eye firmly on the cash till scrutinizing every single transaction made by her staff.

Sundays included, she would sit fluttering thickly massacred eyelashes exclusively at her fawning male admirers, her rasping smokers laugh, grating on the nerves of the more sensitive clientèle. Flossie had little time for the locals - her charms and favours were for the black marketeers, misfits and petty crooks who could supply her with under counter contraband. Most of these fools did not realise Flossie's main purpose in life did not really centre around them but was merely to feather her own tacky little nest, yet still they hung around nightly, content with the futile chase, eager to grub for any meagre little *"come on"* she might drop their way. These degenerates were Flossie's clique.

There were of course others, a number of Tommie's, walking wounded from the local barracks and the ever expanding US military hospital on the edge of the moor, who's curiosity drove the patients to see for themselves *"the hard faced floozy"* who ran the tavern. Flossie, for all her self serving cunning hadn't the sensitivity to realise the main attraction was the barmaid, the young and lovely Sally Hancock a complete opposite of herself, beautiful, sweet natured, fragrant and chaste (as opposed to *chased*)

Being a small tightly knit community most of the locals were aware of Flossie's sexual *"carrying on"* but since it all went on after hours, behind locked doors and in her own time no-one did much about it apart from wonder how anyone could be so thick skinned to ignore the tittle-tattle, and of that there was aplenty. What she couldn't ignore nor abide, was the disdain and superiority of what she called *"the brainy buggers"*. These included all professional people, lawyers, doctors and especially that *"jumped up dog breeder"* referring of course to the well loved Elenora Clapworthy. From the beginning the two women were fated to clash. Their first stormy meeting was when Flossie arrived in Craggs Bottom to take over as licensee of the village's favourite pub.

"Hey Mrs Clatterworthy, or whatever your fancy name is, how much are you asking for one of your guard dogs?" Flossie's opening gambit was a sure fire hackle raiser on two counts (a) Elenora's surname was a name she often joked about herself, but not a name to be abused by the likes of Flossie the Floozy. (b) Her precious Alsatians were not mere commodities to be bought and sold by heartless any bodies. They were adored thoroughbreds to be respected.

"Come on, how much you askin'? And don't give me any of your fancy prices!"

"I beg your pardon?" Elenora's response was ninety degrees below zero.

"Them there Alsatians what you breed, are they any good as guard dogs?"

"The very best!" Elenora replied from a dizzying height.

"Well I'll take one, and don't try palming me off with the runt of the litter."

Elenora fixed the over-rouged slut with a killer look, "They are not for sale."

"What're you talkin' about?" Flossie screeched, capable of turning from vamp to fishwife in an instant. "I know you sell 'em. I know somebody what's got one off you!"

"I'm particular as to who may own one of my animals!"

"How do you mean?" Flossie's eyes narrowed suspiciously, "my money not good enough for you?"

"Since you ask – no!" The conversation was at an end.

Even Flossie, with a skin like a rhino knew when she had met her match. The surprising out come of this fiery exchange was that the "Feathers" ended up with the season's pick of the littler. The change of heart was in no way due to a softening of the heart towards the landlady. It was due to Minnie Clegg, the "Feather's" washer up, cook and bouncer, who successfully pleaded the case for the premises to have a guard dog.

"Eli'll take care of him, Miss Clapworthy." Minnie vouched, you can be sure of that. Flossie'll have no truck with looking after a dog; she'll hardly come into contact with him"

"Eli?!" Elenora had forgotten that Eli almost lived on the premises. "Of course..." Eli Pearson the pot man, cellar man and general dogsbody was known to Elenora, and in spite of drinking himself into oblivion every night, she had a soft spot for him. One day shortly after he first arrived in the village, he turned up at the surgery early one morning nursing the mother and father of all hangovers and gently cradling an injured cat that had been run over by the Co-op coal wagon. Anyone who would do such a thing was fine in Elenora's eyes.

"God knows Eli could do with a bit of company, not to mention a bit of affection." Minnie added, "He gets little enough around here. She treats him little better than a slave. Do you know, she refers to him as '...*that broken down old drunk?*' I mean ter say is that any way to talk about a nice old man like Eli?"

"Well in that case. so long as none of my animals are dependant on Flossie Ingham I'll let the "Feathers" have a pup."

"...Don't thee worry, Miss Clapworthy, Flossie will be only too glad to have the protection without the responsibility, and as I say, one of thy lovely little puppies will be a God send to Eli!"

With a new purpose in life Eli remained sober enough to build a sturdy, roomy well-ventilated kennel with a tough, tarpaulin covered roof, proof against the worst weather the Yorkshire moors could throw at it. As Minnie predicted Caesar, as Eli named the pup was idolised and grew into the most handsome, intelligent animal Ambler Thorn Kennels had ever produced.

Six years on, and the devotion between man and dog grew by the changing seasons. As Minnie had said he would, Caesar brought great solace into Eli's life, and became the object of affection he so badly needed.

Although Eli's intake of alcohol didn't alter – he was still legless by eight every evening – both Elenora and Minnie reckoned that it was a small price to pay to see Eli proud, if not exactly happy, at least with a reason to remain sober long enough to groom, exercise, feed and lavish Caesar with loving attention each morning.

It came as a surprise therefore when Eli appeared in the surgery waiting room just as Elenora was about to close for the day.

"Eli! What a nice surprise." Elenora greeted him with a warm handshake and led him into the surgery.

"Hope there's nothing wrong with Caesar?" she patted and fussed over the handsome dog with affection.

"Oh no," Eli replied dolefully, "There's nothing wrong with him, he's fine. I just wanted a word with you. That's if you've got a minute?" Elenora sensed her visitor had made a great effort to appear sober and unemotionally businesslike. Behind his well-scrubbed exterior she suspected he was nursing some grievance.

"Well if nothing ails our lovely boy here," Elenora said brightly, "let's go through to the lounge, maybe you'll join me for tea?"

"Oh, I didn't mean to disturb you..."

"Oh, please Eli, you're not disturbing me, I'll be glad of your company." Such kindness was rare. The shock of being treated like a human being did nothing to ease the flow into the interview. He faltered clumsily as he entered the comfortable living room with its reminders of pleasantries he had long since forgone. He began, ever so slightly to shake. Sensitive to her visitor's emotional condition Elenora took the bit between her teeth.

"Tell you what Eli, sod the tea let's have a proper drink. Scotch OK?" Without waiting for an answer she poured them both a measure, which did the trick. After a lifesaving swig Eli launched straight into his reason for his visit.

"I'm thinking of leaving Craggs Bottom Miss Clapworthy," Eli began, "and I wonder if you could find Caesar a good home?" There was an awkward moment whilst he took another swig to give him the courage to carry on. "You see where I'm going I won't be able to take Caesar with me." Immediately alarm bells began ringing in Elenora's mind. "...I'm moving into a Council flat in Bradford... and they don't allow animals." So far his story didn't convince. Elenora felt sure Eli would never abandon Caesar for something as banal as a housing byelaw. There was something about Eli's stated reason for leaving more disturbing, more disquieting.

"She won't miss him, and she can't object and say I stole him," Eli had this part of his story well rehearsed. "I made sure his licence was in my name. It was my own money that paid for him, and his pedigree is signed over to me."

"Yes, I remember very well making sure that it was in your name, but why Eli? Why are you doing this?" There was a long silence from Eli. He fixed her with a look of deep sadness. Could she be mistaken?

Could *"going away"* in this context be a euphemism for something else altogether? Did Eli mean to do himself in?

"But you know Miss Clapworthy, until I'm absolutely sure he's settled in a new home, and the new owner is right for him and will be good to him, I'll not do it – er, leave I mean. That's where I hoped you might be able to help. Of course I wouldn't want anyone – you know who I mean – to find out about my intentions."

"Your secret is safe with me Eli, and I'll do my best to find a new home for Caesar" Elenora said, "but it won't be easy finding the right place for a fully grown animal in wartime – rationing you see Eli? Nobody wants the bother of finding food and all that." She knew very well of course there would be little trouble finding a place for a bright animal like Caesar, but she was determined to put the mockers on Eli's plan to do himself harm. If that was what he intended doing. She would stall him as long as – well, as long as it took. In the meantime she meant to find out something about the reason for Eli's obvious despair.

"Let's do a deal Eli." She said, "Promise you won't do anything – sudden – like leaving Craggs Arse until I find a good home for Caesar. Then we'll talk about it, OK? A deal?" Elenora knew Eli would not *"leave"* until there was a mutually approved home for Caesar, and she intended making the possibility of finding such a place never ending.

"Right Miss Clapworthy it's a deal!" Eli agreed. They shook on it and Elenora watched through the window as Eli made his way slowly back to the "Feathers" and a life of living Purgatory. The following morning as Elenora was having her usual bowl of porridge, the phone rang. It was Minnie Clegg.

"Oh Miss Clapworthy, me and Sally's ever so worried. Eli is nowhere to be found. He wasn't there when we opened the pub last evening. Fortunately we weren't too busy so we managed without having to tell Flossie, and of course she was that taken up with fluttering her eyelashes at all them sleazy buggers at the far end of the bar, she never even missed him."

"He's not ill is he Minnie?"

"Well, he's not in his cottage. I had a look last night after we called "*Time*"

"Just one thing, did he take Caesar with him?"

"Aye, I suppose so. Caesar's not in his kennel."

"That's good. If he's got Caesar with him, neither of them will come to much harm. Can you meet me at Sally's in ten minute's time? We'll put our heads together." Sally and Minnie would surely be the best starting point, being as they were the only human contact the old man had in his miserable life as resident drudge.

"I've been worried about him for some while now, especially just lately, this last year or so." Sally confirmed after Elenora had hinted at Eli's suspected intentions.

"Why especially just lately?"

"Well just recently – oh, Miss Clapworthy, I'm not sure I should say this, it's not really any of my business..."

"...in for a pound Sally lass!" Minnie put in.

"Well you know there are rumours about the shady dealing that go on at the "Feathers""

"The Black Market deals?" Elenora asked, "...Yes, bit of an open secret isn't it?"

"Well, recently we think, Minnie and I, it's become a lot more than just the odd lamb chop under the counter from Slimey Slickey," Sally continued, choosing her words with care, "It has become sort of serious lately involving cases of stuff and gallon tins of what we believe to be petrol. More serious is what we think is dealing in forged documents, clothing coupons, even Identity cards and other things it doesn't bear thinking about. But so long as Flossie didn't involve us in her affairs, we were able to turn a blind eye..." Sally paused long enough for Elenora to realise the enormity of what they suspected. "Things came to a head yesterday afternoon as we were getting ready to open the pub for the evening session. Flossie told Eli to take a suitcase full of *"stuff"* to a certain party at the Great Northern Hotel in Bradford. *"Stuff, what sort of Stuff?"* Eli asked her. *"What difference does it make to you? You'll do as you are told"* Flossie threatened.

"I've put up with a lot from you" Eli answered her, *"but I'll not do anything illegal."*

"You'll bloody well do as I say," she was screaming at him now, but when she realised Minnie and I were hearing all this she calmed down a bit. *"It's only a bit of chocolate. A few Hershey Bars I managed to get hold of. Now behave yourself and get off to the Great Northern. Here's four pence for your tram fare. Get back as quick as you can."* She pressed the coppers into his hand and he left with the suitcase.

"Oh, I'm beginning to understand a lot of things now." Elenora said

"Please Miss Clapworthy," Sally pleaded, now almost in tears, "you have to believe me, Eli is the most honest straight...he wouldn't do anything...he couldn't..."

"So that's when he took off, and hasn't been seen since?"

"Yes, he didn't deliver the suitcase though; he hid it in the kennel, collected Caesar and took off. I found the suitcase this morning when I was trying to find out what was going on." Sally's concern showed in her lovely eyes, "I'm afraid he might do something desperate."

"What I can't understand is why an intelligent man like Eli can allow himself to be so under the thumb of a slag like Flossie." Characteristically when dealing with the likes of Flossie, Elenora's terminology took on a more colourful tone. "It doesn't make any sense"

"No, not to me neither," Minnie added, "unless..."

"Unless what Min?" Elenora asked.

"Unless the old buzzard has some hold on him. I mean some emotional hold." Minnie warmed to her theory, "I remember when he first arrived in the village, not long after she took over as landlady. He turned up out of the blue and started work as the cellar-man. I think he must have known her in the past."

"If it's going to be any help in finding him," Sally took over from Minnie, "I think he hails from Kendal in the Lake District..."

"...And I can tell thee he knows more than a thing or two about the licensing trade, you just have to look at the 'maculate way he keeps that cellar."

"If only Eli realised how **un** – alone he is, he would see himself in a whole new light." Elenora added. "Somehow, girls between us, we will make him aware! First he has to be located."

"Aye, where can he have got to?" Minnie speculated,

218

"Especially with Caesar. He'll have to have gone somewhere where there's food and water for the dog."

"We must get Sergeant Wilkinson on the job" Sally said, "even if it means there being charges brought against Eli."

"What charges?" Elenora asked, "Eli never delivered the suitcase, did he? That's it then! Send for Arnold." Sergeant Wilkinson was promptly summoned.

"Arnold," Elenora said, after quickly filling in him in on the story of the missing pot-man. "The question is, where's Eli now?"

"Well I'll tell you if none of you say a word." Arnold said, "He's in the cell at the cop shop."

"Nay, Arnold," Minnie said in a voice full of disappointment and disgust, "Surely you haven't arrested him, have you?"

"Arrested him?" Arnold was genuinely shocked and hurt that anyone would think he'd do such a thing. "Nay Minnie, you know me better than that."

"What's he doing in the cell then?"

"Well let's see," Arnold said, looking at his watch, "quarter to eleven. He'll be having a slice of toast and a cup of tea in the charge office with young Archie before he set's off for the pub. Now then," Arnold continued in a decisive tone of voice, "We'll all go up to the "Feathers". I want a word with Flossie, and I want you all there when I do"

"Arnold please," Elenora said, "for Eli's sake, there won't be any scandal will there?"

"Nothing like that Miss Clapworthy," Arnold answered reassuringly, "you know me, I go in for happy endings."

Flossie swung around in astonishment as the four of them entered the public bar. Eli was already setting up the tables and chairs ready for the mid-day opening time.

Without a word Minnie and Sally went about their usual chores. Arnold smiled broadly and removed his helmet.

"Mrs Ingham, just a few words," he said politely but with underlying force, "I won't keep you more than a minute or two."

Flossie's face, even through the thick layer of cheap make-up paled noticeably.

"Mrs Ingham." Arnold couldn't help but enjoy the turmoil churning around inside Flossie's stomach. "I don't suppose Eli - Mr Pearson has had time to tell you...well, to put it in a nutshell, yesterday afternoon he was stopped by Constable Barker, and asked what was contained inside the suitcase he was carrying, just routine of course, wartime precautions and all that, you understand."

"I know nothing about what that drunken fool gets up to..." Flossie began to squirm as her brain ticked over at a feverish rate, trying to think of a way to load the blame onto Eli.

"I wouldn't put it past him if he had the Bank of England in that suitcase..."

"Oh, Mrs Ingham, you should be very grateful to Eli," Arnold continued in his most charming manner, Mr Pearson explained that the contents of the suitcase were a gift from you to the children at the orphanage. Eli explained how you had collected chocolates and sweets from all the American GIs who visited your pub over the past few months, and he was just on his way to deliver it. What a lovely gesture. All that chocolate for the kids, Easter coming on too!" Although the charming smile remained intact on Arnold's face, Flossie registered the steel in his eye, which told her she had been given a very narrow escape.

True to her nature Eli received no thanks from Flossie. He humbly went about his life as he had done previously, but thankfully aware she would think twice before involving him in her nefarious dealings in future.

He also had been made aware however, that his two work mates along with Elenora and Arnold Wilkinson were quite a force for the good and were in his corner.

Some months later Elenora marvelled on seeing Eli battle with a tsunami of all hangovers, as he deftly manhandled a heavy barrel before expertly sliding it down the ramp into the cellar.

"Finding someone to look after Caesar as well as you do doesn't get any easier Eli Pearson!" She said in a nonchalant, throw away voice. "It's proving very difficult, nigh on impossible! I think you might have the job much longer than you anticipated"

"I think I can live with that, Miss Clapworthy." Eli replied with just the ghost of a smile.

....

...NORTH WINDS DO BLOW

Noble Kellett's father Everhard, his mother Rebecca and of course his young wife Amy, were all of one accord – any war was nothing but a *"mugs game"* and no place for their precious son and husband to be seen in, dead or alive!

Indeed Everhard was the chief architect of the elaborate plot to shield his son from the shell shock and gassing he had himself suffered in the previous conflagration. That of course was some twenty years earlier in that *"abomination of Mankind"* as he often referred to the Great War of 1914 -1918. Since that time he had become a fervent, almost fanatical pacifist. A vociferous Anti-war Campaigner swearing he would never allow his son to become *"Cannon Fodder"* as he believed so many of his own contemporaries were.

The decision for his son to do a bunk, disappear, or in official terms - desert, was in Everhard's mind long before his son was shipped to France with the BEF. Of course to the Kellett's the word *"abscond"* held no shame or disgrace as it did to the majority of the citizens of these beleaguered islands in the dark days of 1939.

Everhard realised that if his son merely went AWOL the authorities would never give up until he was found, punished and sent back to the front. No, Everhard decreed, his son Noble would *volunteer* rather than wait for the call up, willingly go to do his duty. Then when the opportunity presented itself, like perhaps during the first skirmish with the enemy, he would disappear whilst in the midst of battle. If possible, be pronounced missing or dead, and make his way back home and bingo! Here he would stay without fear of being hounded until peace returned. Everhard avoided exploring the almost impossible details of this highly fanciful plan. He would leave the critical moment of actual abscondence to his son.

The Kellett's had one fantastic trump card in this game of intrigue. The ancient cottage they had occupied for countless generations on the edge of the complex of higgledy-piggledy dwellings surrounding the coach yard at the back of the *"Feathers"* pub had a long forgotten - except by Everhard – dry, warm and well ventilated secret *"hide-away"* beneath the cellar floor; they believed it to be a genuine priest hole dating from the days of the persecution of the clergy. If Everhard avoided delving deeply into the proposed actual moment of his son's desertion, not to mention the difficulties of the clandestine journey back home for his son after the event, he certainly did apply meticulous attention to the details once his son arrived.

"Don't think for a minute, it'll all be over in a fortnight." Everhard pontificated, "That's what they thought last time, and look what happened, it went on for four years. We'll have to make do with nobbut three ration books. Oh, aye, we'll have a bit of a struggle with the rations but never heed, we'll manage..."

"Aye, were better off than most," his wife chipped in, "we've plenty of vegetables in the garden and even more in the allotment. Enough fruit to bottle. We have the hen run churning' out eggs by the day, and the hutches are running wick with rabbits. We'll not starve!"

223

"...So lad, you'll be able to sit it out until peace is declared!" Everhard enthused; double sure he had thought of every eventuality that could go wrong.

Noble's faith in his dad was such that he was loath to pick holes in the foolhardy plan. He would go along with it knowing the imagined scenario had about as much chance as a cat in Hell of working out. Feeling it so outlandish he only mildly questioned his own heart as to the morality of the plan.

With his battalion posted to France with the BEF Noble, much as he would have liked his fathers barmy plan to work, was in spite of his lack of faith in the hair brained scheme secretly on the lookout for an opportunity to become *"missing"* or *"dead"*.

Miraculously, beyond all sense or reason that chance presented itself with remarkable ease! When the German Army made its devastating advance on the Allied armies, pushing them back onto the beaches of Dunkirk, There the thousands of battle weary troops amassed awaiting rescue on anything large or small that could float and was capable of crossing the English Channel.

The week-end *"Captain"* of the little craft that picked Noble from the sea was although undoubtedly courageous, only a teenage boy and not very experienced. Finding it impossible to negotiate the established shipping routes to dock successfully at any of the seaside ports. With little ado he bid a cheery farewell...

"Good luck Boys this where you get off!" The brave young lad off loaded his human cargo on the nearest beach, probably somewhere near Eastbourne.

Avoiding the hastily set up check-in posts intended to receive the men separated from their units, Noble simply walked inland and made his way north hitching lifts from any vehicle that was not of a military nature. A couple of days later he made it without detection to the outskirts of Leeds. Lying low in the railway sidings until dark he set off on foot on the last few miles for home. Carefully avoiding the built up areas around Pudsey, Stanningley and Bradford. He arrived home shortly before dawn. Filthy with the oil and sand of the French coast still in his hair and clothes, footsore and exhausted, but he was safe and undetected.

After a good meal and a hot bath he inspected his quarters in the cellar where he was to sit out the war snug and in peace. Mr Kellett Senior had furnished the secret room with a comfortable bed. A cable had been buried beneath the ancient flagstones so his son might enjoy electric light and heating. Everhard even went as far as providing a radio.

"Of course," Everhard explained, "Tha' can come upstairs to sleep and for thi' meals, and even go outside for a breath of fresh air once it gets dark of a night. The only thing tha' has to remember is *not to get careless*, then tha'll be undetected till Kingdom Come." Noble wasn't the only one to come under Everhard's scrupulously strict regime. Kellett senior began to run an obsessively disciplined household. Not even the slightest hint of Noble's presence was allowed to leak out. He lectured his wife and daughter in law regularly – *"...no extra washing on the line..." "...the table to be set for three people only..." "...extra care with the blackout curtains..."* Above all he insisted on minimum discussion with the neighbours about the loss of their son and even rehearsed scenarios that might be useful in the event of someone nosing around.

For the first few weeks after her husband was registered as *"Missing"* Amy badgered the local Authorities with convincing performances – *"...was her man captured by the enemy?" " Was he alive?" "...Was* he lying in some French ditch?" "...Would they let her know – please, because she was sick with worry? In the meantime the object of her concern was safely hidden away enjoying all the comforts of home.

When, six months after the Craggs Bottom fugitive went to ground the message arrived from the War Office confirming that, "...241609516 Private Kellett N. was feared missing presumed killed in action..." The Kellett conspirators knew they had pulled it off. And they had done it with great aplomb! Or had they?

As the months passed Noble was unable to share his family's jubilation. He not only began to feel distanced from the world outside but also from his wife and parents. It wasn't something he could fully understand himself, let alone explain even to his wife. His opinions about the futility of war had grown no less. Nor had he any misgivings about cheating the Conscription Board. Never-the-less, there was no way he could put into words that in spite of the success of their joint venture he suspected there was a flaw in their subterfuge. He was coming to the belief that he himself was that flaw. Noble spent long hours laid up in his hide-away agonising about it and growing ever more distant from those he loved upstairs.

In early January a knock on the door heralded the end of Everhard's complacency and the beginnings of his son's understanding of his growing problem. It was mid-day. Only Noble and his mother were at home. Following the scrupulous drill his father had initiated Noble disappeared like a flash down the cellar steps and into his sanctuary.

"Sorry to bother you," a young soldier stood awkwardly on the doorstep. Rebecca well versed in not giving anything away remained cool and pleasant, "I'm looking for a Mrs Kellett, Mrs Amy Kellett. I understand she lives around here somewhere?"

"What's it about lad?" Rebecca asked, cagily, pretending to dry her already dry hands on her apron.

"Nay, it's just that I served with her husband in France." The young man had an honest, open face. "Nobby Kellett and me were mates and I swore to me self that I'd look his wife up ... well, aksherly, there's summat important I have - I must tell her."

"She's at work lad," Rebecca replied, "she minds sides at Townsend's Textiles, but she'll be in tonight."

"Right enough Missus, if it's alright by you. I'll call back this evening...Oh! By the way, my name is Lynch, Private Ernest Lynch." Rebecca closed the door, and watched from behind the lace curtains as the young man passed through the open courtyard at the back of the "Feathers". When it was safe to do so she hurried to the cellar.

"I wish I'd known it was Ernie Lynch Mam," Noble said morosely, his hunger for contact with the outside world worrying him more than his mother thought it should. Noble's doubts about his self inflicted incarceration seemed to his mother to be growing ever more obvious by the day. "I would have liked to have seen him." Noble said sadly. "It would have been alright, Ernie's one of the best. How did he look? He was in a bad way the last time I saw him." More disappointed than he himself thought he had a right to be Noble returned with a troubled heart to his hide-away to wait the evening.

"Course you realise you won't be able to talk to him tonight Noble don't you?" Everhard said when he and Amy arrived home from the mill.

"Oh Dad! Why not? Ernie wouldn't blow my cover..."

"No lad – nobody... *Nobody* must know you're here! Everhard stressed emphatically."You must remember in the eyes of the world you're a deserter and

227

the fewer people know of your whereabouts the safer you'll be."

"Your dads right Noble," Amy's heart ached in sympathy for her young husband. She knew her words would only widen the rift that had grown between them but she had to agree with the old man, "You can't let your friend know you're here, not just for your own safety, you must think of the responsibility you would be placing on his shoulders if he knew you were on the loose. It wouldn't be fair on him love."

Noble remained silently nursing his disappointment. In the end had to concede that his wife was right. If he gave the game away he realised it might open a whole new bag of worms, not just for him and Ernie but he would put his parents and Amy in jeopardy with the law.

"I suppose you're right," Noble said reluctantly, "But when he gets here don't forget to ask about the other lads who were with us." "Get his home address as well. When this lot is over I'll want to get in touch with him."

"Come on now love," aware her son was in turmoil, Rebecca was as gentle as she could be but anxious he get him out of sight before their visitor returned, "You'd better get back into your little hidey-hole." But Noble didn't go back to the cellar; he positioned himself on the cellar steps so he might hear his old friend and perhaps even get a glimpse of him without himself being seen.

"Come in son. Ernest isn't it?" sitting in the dark on the cellar steps Noble heard his father greet his old mate. "You will have a bite to eat with us won't you? It isn't often we get visitors. This is me Missus, and this is our Noble's wife Amy."

"Very pleased to meet you, I'm sure," awkward and stiff, Ernie went through the ritual of the formal introduction, "I hope you will accept my deepest sympathy on the very sad..."

"No need for that son," Mr Kellett hastily cut in, "We've all gotten used to the idea by now. Time is a great healer, and besides we've never given up hope of him turning up after it's all over. After all he was nobbut declared *"Missing"* – only *presumed* dead! So don't be embarrassed..."

"...come in to the living room Ernest..." Rebecca leaped into the fray sensing her husband's pedantic explanation was in danger of over egging the pudding. "...Take your greatcoat off love... make yourself at home...sit yourself down." She fussed around their visitor in a motherly fashion until a little of his awkwardness disappeared. Private Lynch was relieved to find the family's attitude to their missing son made the difficult task of getting started on the delicate subject he had to pass on a little easier.

"I hope you don't mind but there is something I must tell you." Although his shyness was monumental Ernest Lynch knew he had to conquer it, for what he had to impart was bigger burden than he had ever encountered in his life before. "You see, it's only because of your Nobby that I'm here to tell the tale. You know we was at Dunkirk together?"

"Aye lad, we know that... well, we guessed you was." Everhard answered clumsily.

"We was ordered to form a line from the beach out to the sea, because some of the rescue vessels couldn't get in close enough. Well of course, we made a perfect target for the machine guns of the Gerry planes. I caught a bullet in the guts and one in me wrist. I was losing blood. No way could I have stood in line. To make things worse the tide started to come in, we were up to our waists in water and I started to get weaker. Your lad

Nobby - Noble held me up, then as the water got deeper, without a word he lifted me onto his back and he stood holding me on his back for hours. Can you imagine what that must have been like for him?"

Ernie paused and looked down in an effort keep his story factual and unemotional, desperate not to allow his emotions to colour his telling of it. So far he hadn't broken down as he did whenever he went over the events in his mind. He hadn't reckoned on the give-away tension in his tightly clasped hands as he fought to control the shaking.

"We saw the newsreels at the time." Amy said gently, sensitive to the young man's feelings. It must have been terrible for you all. All that time in the water."

"It must have been for Nobby, he was bearing my full weight, and do you know Mrs Kellett, he never once complained, in fact he *joked* to keep our spirits up – *Joked!"*

"Aye, that sounds like our Noble all right!"

"You've never seen anything like it." Ernie picked up the threads once more. "Fortunately someone was belching black smoke; it acted a bit like a smoke screen. There were all sorts of little boats, some of 'em hardly fit to go on the park lake never mind cross the Channel but there they were, picking people out of the sea, conveying them to the bigger ships further out. A little sailboat came right up alongside us, very low in the water, a sort of private yacht, well, more like a week-end dingy really. Still holding me up out of the water, with his free hand Nobby grabbed the side of the boat and pulled it towards us.

The chap in charge shouted out that he couldn't take any more, 'cos the water was up to the gunnel's it was in danger of sinking. It was too! The side of the boat was only inches above the surface. But your son shouted back, *"I'm sure you have enough room for another little 'un!"* Before the feller could do anything about it, Nobby managed to roll me on board and push the boat away. That's the last I saw of him, the sea lapping at his face as the boat, with me in it pulled away."

If the emotions around the Kellett's table were in something of a whirl it was nothing compared to the turmoil going through the mind of the other member of the family sitting alone on the cellar steps'.

"Your son could just as easily have dropped me and got on that boat instead of me." As if he were giving evidence in a court of law, careful not to omit even the smallest detail Ernie continued to plead his case. "But he didn't, he saved my life Mr Kellett. I've thought about it a lot since it happened, and I think it's…what they call it…? *'…Courage over and above the call of duty'* "Since I've got back on my feet I've had a word with my Commanding Officer and he agrees with me. I've made a statement and filled in some forms to apply for Nobby to receive a posthumous decoration. You see I want him to get recognition for what he did…"

Until this particular evening Ernie Lynch had probably never said more than two sentences at one time and so many words, all heavy with unaccustomed emotion quite overwhelmed him. His chin sank onto his chest he said no more. The tears that coursed silently down his face spoke more eloquently than any words.

Everhard took Ernie to the "Feathers" to treat him to a pint and proudly introduce him to the locals as - *"Our Noble's best mate what was with him when he went missing"* thus substantiating the elaborate fiction. "I can't tell you how much I appreciate you telling us all you did lad" The old man was unable to hide his joy to have such iron clad confirmation. As he waited to see Ernie off on the last tram of the evening, Everhard felt it hard to hold down the pride he felt inside. "We'll not forget you son, and I promise you, we'll keep in touch. Because don't forget - our Noble is only *"**pronounced**"* Missing - only *"**presumed**"* killed. Don't be surprised if he turns up large as life after the war is over!" He watched and waved as the tram careered recklessly down Grantham Hill. Not sure if his elation was entirely due to the undoubted success of his long-term plan or the confirmed heroism of his son. Everhard turned and walked home as if on air. Noble, on the other hand enjoyed no such feelings of elation.

For so long now doubts about the morality of his dad's plan for him to go AWOL had plagued him, he had never once felt the slightest suggestion of dishonour.

Until now!

Now he now felt unclean. He had cheated his mate. He had made a mockery of Ernie's trust in him. Not only that, he felt he had relinquished his responsibilities as a – well – as a human being. His self disgust was becoming intolerable. Alone at the far end of the garden where the thick foliage had been encouraged to grow. Undercover of darkness, Noble Kellett sat trying to sort out his tangled thoughts.

"He's down past the hen run, by the apple trees." Amy explained when her father in law returned home after seeing Ernie onto the tram. "He's very upset."

"Upset?" Everhard's incredulity at the ingratitude of his son's behaviour puzzled and hurt him. "What the bloody hell has he got to be upset over?"

"I just think he's bothered about not being able to explain everything to Ernest." Amy replied, she herself not fully able to come to terms with the change of feelings Ernie's visit had brought about, "I'll give him an hour or so to be on his own, then I'll try to reason with him."

Midnight came and went and still Noble showed no sign of returning indoors.

Everhard and Rebecca prepared for bed, Everhard in a huff at their son's ingratitude.

"Here he is, a good three years after absconding, safe and comfortable…little likelihood of ever being detected! With every chance his bravery will be acknowledged by a posthumous decoration into the bargain! And the little bugger's *'upset!?…'*

"Calm down Everhard, for goodness sake calm down!" Rebecca said trying to pacify her husband, for in truth she had more than a little sympathy with her son in his dilemma.

"…The ungrateful little bugger!" Old man Kellett muttered, as he made for the chamber steps, "Amy, tell him not to act so bloody daft, and to come inside it's going to snow before morning. There's been a ring round the moon for the last couple of nights. He'll catch pneumonia sitting out there all night."

Making her way silently through the overgrown garden she found her husband sitting on the dry stone wall where, he could see without being seen, across the little stretch of common land to the back court yard of the "Feathers"

"Aye, here I am," Noble said in a desolate, self pitying whisper, "watching the world roll along without me."

"I've brought you a blanket." Amy said softly, "Its bitter cold Noble, your dad thinks were in for snow before morning." Noble took the hot drink she poured from the flask. The bright moonlight was beginning to give way to a sky heavy with snow.

"For the last hour or so I've been sitting here, and you know Amy, although there's not much ever going on in Craggs Bottom, what little there is, means *something* to them folk… Eli Pearson the cellar man, rolling into his little cottage drunk as usual… there's Minnie Clegg shouting to him to wrap up well and keep warm …that tall GI lad from the military hospital fiddling with the back door and tending to that lovely Alsatian… then before he set off back to the hospital I watched him carefree as little kid chuck a stick or summat into our bushes. All signs of life chugging along Amy… everybody in the land of the living – everybody except me!"

Amy wrapped the blanket around him and sat next to him on the dry stonewall, next to him but not close. She had not been close to him for some time now, and it broke her heart. Noble was alone in his struggle

"I'm so mixed up in me mind Amy. I've done a lot of thinking tonight. You know, listening to Ernie believing I was dead made me feel like a right hypocrite. It isn't that I've changed my mind about playing silly buggers with guns and all that. I'm still as anti war as I ever was. I still believe me dad is right when he says that them there Politicians and generals and warmongers should all be put in a big field to get on with it. Wipe each other out if they feel like it but don't force us ordinary folk to do it for 'em. If only it was as simple as that." He whispered as he watched the cold clear moon riding high in the sky with its beautiful aurora – a sure harbinger of snow to follow.

"You see Amy lass, I still believe what the Bible says – 'Thou shall not kill.' Killing is a sin. But tonight I've come around to thinking that shutting myself off from life is as big a sin. Listening like a thief from the cellar steps to Ernie telling his tale about his rescue and hospital and then his time with the Desert Rats made me feel like I'd cheated him. Now all I can think about is that I should have been with them lads in the desert.

Amy's tears flowed silently. She tried moving closer to her husband, but he remained apart and distant. With the best intentions in the world she had conspired to distance her husband from the world and his fellowmen.

234

What she hadn't reckoned on was that same cold distance would come between the two of them. Unable to bring him any solace she left him to his anguish. She went indoors to cry herself to sleep and pray for forgiveness and maybe a miracle.

The following morning the threatened snowfall had covered the entire mountaintop in deep and sculptured drifts. A bright yellow sun illuminated the mountain hill village - an inappropriate cheerful backdrop to the bombshell Noble was about to loose on his family.

"I'm going to give meself up." He announced unemotionally as they all gathered for breakfast. The pronouncement came as no surprise to Amy. Rebecca too showed less astonishment that might have been expected. Only Everhard was open mouthed at the revelation.

"So as not to implicate any of you for hiding me away for so long, I'm going to make my way to the West Country to give myself up, I'll tell 'em I was holed up down there suffering from shock. Plead amnesia or summat. I'll write to you as soon as I can. Nobody around here need ever know." Without pausing in his deliberations, he took his weeping mother in his arms and calmly continued. "We have to face the fact that I will have to do time in the Glasshouse. It's unlikely they'll do to me what they did to deserters in the last war, especially as I'm giving meself up. If they do, so be it. I missed out on being with Ernie and the lads in the desert. I'll be damned if I'll miss out being with them when they go back into France."

Listening intently to his son as he stared out of the window at the virgin snow covering the valley Everhard, instead of the expected tirade cleared his throat and quietly looked his son in the eye.

"You've obviously made up your mind lad. Even though it's not what I would have wished for you, if it's what you want…! Now that's it! We won't say another word about it except to say – you'll not be able to set off for the West Country until the snow's been trodden down. We can't have you leaving incriminating footprints in the fresh snow. So let's all sit down and have some breakfast."

The enforced delay of Noble's departure was providential in other ways none of them could have imagined. One benefit the change of heart had brought about was that the destructive air of defeat that had crept over him since the early days of his incarceration lifted as if by magic. No longer distanced from his father, mother and young wife, in their eyes he was *'back again'*. Most importantly he looked on Amy with love in his eyes.

Although Everhard would never live long enough to admit that his scheme to save his son from the *'degradations'* of the battle field, he did have humility enough to recognise that valour came in other guises. All the confirmation he needed all those years ago at his son's Christening when he himself insisted against much opposition - on naming his baby son 'Noble' was now proved justified. Old Kellett looked once more with new eyes upon the courageous man the boy grew up to be.

………………………

TWO RINGS AROUND THE MOON.

Elenora Clapworthy leaped out of bed with her usual whoop of delight and joy on sensing the muted light and muffled tones of the world told her it was now under a thick coating of snow.

This celebration of the weather was nothing new. Every year she looked forward with more anticipation than was normal for a rational human being of mature years. For to Elenora the snow brought with it memories so precious it was impossible to explain to any one, not even her dear old friend, Dora.

Dora for all her cheerfulness and wicked wit, was also capable of delivering doom-laden *'sayings'* and *'homilies'* all delivered with a dead pan expression, all of which few people, least of all herself understood..

"What did I tell thee?" Dora demanded, as she doled out a ladle full of hot porridge for her mistress, "What did I say? I said, *'A ring around the moon, will bring snow soon'"*

"So you did Dora darling, and look how right you were."

"Aye but what I didn't tell thee was," Dora said in her gloom-doom-Armageddon-cometh type voice, "there

237

is another true old saying round these parts - '*Two* rings *around the moon, brings both snow and* **WOE!**"

"Two rings? I didn't see two rings."

"Neither did I" Dora said un-dramatically, "But I'm just saying…"

"I've never seen two rings…"

"Neither have I…"

"You just made that up you old Pariah, trying to blind me with scientific folklore."

"Aye well," Dora said, you'll please me if you'll kindly wrap up well before you set off over them moors with the dogs this morning."

"Consider it done!" Elenora chuckled as she donned her corduroy trousers, wellies, tweed flat cap, classic Aquascutum lined greatcoat and finally wound the seemingly never ending knitted scarf around her neck. "Will that do?" She asked as she stood for inspection.

"I suppose so." Dora said, with begrudging complicity.

"You just '*suppose so*'? It's more than Scott wore when he tackled the Antarctic!"

"Aye but he only went to the South Pole; he didn't have to contend with Craggs Bottom Moor in January!"

As in previous winters it took much threatening, pleading and bribery to coax Heinz to venture across the threshold of Ambler Thorn manor and into the bright sunlit winter morning but as ever, once across he forgot he was an aged mongrel and frolicked like a young pup in this lovely stuff called snow.

Together mistress and canine beat a virgin path through the deep drifts they made their way up to the village where as usual, they would call for Caesar the Alsatian guard dog from his kennel at the back of the 'Feathers" before setting off across the moor.

In the near distance ahead of them Elenora watched the ancient service tram fitted with the snow plough clanging up Grantham Hill pushing the snow to one side making the road clear for the usual Sunday traffic. To her left, further up the hill a figure came into view waving to her. It was her talented protégé, pupil and pal Mickie Ryan. Every Sunday morning he made his way from the housing estate to help Dora in the kennels, and coax renewed life into the temperamental coke fired boiler which heated both the house and the out buildings.

"'Morning Miss Clapworthy!"

It was clear to see by his dazzling exuberance he was unable to conceal the news that he had the results of his winter exams, and that he had obviously done well.

"Top ! You came top!" Elenora matched his excitement, "Top marks? I don't know why I should sound so surprised. I knew you'd do it. This calls for a celebration. When I get back we'll uncork a bottle of vintage Tizer. When you get down to the house, have look in the manuscript cupboard, there's a stack of old sheet music tied up with red ribbon. Amongst them there's a rag time number called *"Georgia Camp Meeting"*. You'll love it, I promise. Get it off pat, and you can play it at the next gig."

Mickey though, hesitated, sensitive to the fact those old tunes, from a time long before he was born were a jealously guarded personal part of Elenora's past. Once when the pair of them had been rummaging through the cupboard he asked about them; her eyes told him to back off, it was sacred stuff. They were never mentioned again, until now.

"I thought that particular pile tied with the red ribbon was not to be touched by anyone but you?"

"Ah well, me old cock sparrow," she answered with a wink, "You're not just "anyone" are you?" The boy felt a

239

glow of deep pride, aware he had made enough progress in her eyes to be granted access to the holy of holies.

She turned to continue on her way leaving her young friend with a smile on his face so broad it threatened to split his face as she and Heinz carried on up the hill towards the "Feathers" humming *'Georgia Camp Meeting'* very, very gently.

Giggling to herself as she recalled her earlier conversation with Dora, and the crazy dubious North Country proverb *'**Two** rings around the moon, brings both snow and woe'* Crazy because – well - witness the glorious, bright morning! Dora's wonderful dry humour and Mike's good news heralding - *snow and woe?* Bullshit! All was well with the world whilst ever there were folks like Dora and kids like Mickie Ryan in it.

She and Heinz happily struggled through the virgin snow drifts, theirs the only footprints to disturb the snow that almost made impassable the constrictive service lane that led through the narrow gate posts, to the back of the "Feathers" The open area at the back of the "Feathers" Court Yard was just large enough to turn around a coach and eight horses. Apart from the stables there were a number of cottages haphazardly dotted around the yard as well as the ash-pits and middens originally intended purely for the staff of the pub. Far from being a sordid service area, the residents of these residences had become a tightly knit community.

Over the generations they had cultivated their little plots, made gardens, planted fruit trees and vegetables. Some of the more ambitious, like Everhard Kellett even cultivated a small orchard and hen-runs and rabbit hutches hidden amongst the trees affording him all the privacy he yearned, especially since the loss of his son at Dunkirk.

Elenora put a warning finger to her mouth to keep Heinz quiet so as to avoid waking the residents. After all it was Sunday morning and still early. Calling to release the beautiful Alsatian was a regular Sunday occurrence, especially careful not to rouse the landlady Flossie Ingham, with whom she had no wish to have any dealings anyway. This Sunday there was something amiss. It was too quiet. Every previous Sunday since he was a young pup Caesar recognised her approach and could usually be heard stirring in anticipation of his romp across the moor. But today was different. There was no sound from Caesar's kennel.

Pulling back the old carpets that covered the door of the kennel, her breath caught in her throat when she found Caesar on a cruelly short chain, muzzled and deeply unconscious on his straw bed. His breathing shallow but still discernable. A large wad of pink lint lay by his side. She detected the sweet smell of chloroform. Cold fury that anyone could do such a thing propelled Elenora into action.

Dragging the dog's limp body from the stale interior of the kennel, a wave of relief swept over her as the animal began to respond to the fresh cold air. A swelling on his head where he had obviously received a heavy blow worried Elenora. Caesar was groggy, disorientated, but alive and on his feet.

"Eli! Eli, wake up!" She called as she crossed the yard to the gate of Eli's tiny one up and one down. She went no further. The cottage door was wide open; snow had drifted inside and lay there undisturbed by any footprints, leading neither in nor out.

Turning her attention to the back door of the 'Feathers', only now did she notice it was not merely ajar but was hanging almost completely torn from its hinges. What if the intruders were still inside? Elenora realised she had no choice but to enter the pub and see for herself. Careful to avoid touching any surfaces, for fear of disturbing any possible fingerprints She made a mental note that hers were the only footprints to disturb the snow that had drifted in partly covering the linoleum strip running down the passage. In spite of his natural timidity Heinz remained by her side, trembling, whining and begging his mistress to go no further. Ignoring his pleading Elenora edged her way inside calling out to her archenemy, "Flossie! Flossie! Are you there?" There was no answer.

"Flossie! Eli! Anybody there?" Listening for any reassuring sound of movement Elenora inched along the corridor, past the cellar door, towards the main lounge bar. She tried peering through the decorative leaded lights of the lounge door panel but the kaleidoscopic images gave no hint to what awaited her on the other side. Apprehension made it hard to swallow as the door slowly swung open to confirm her worst imaginings. Elenora stood for an age stunned by the scene that lay spread before her. There, behind the bar, lying in a pool of her own blood Flossie Ingham lay dead in a pool of her own blood.

Elenora experienced a genuine feeling of guilt for for her absence of compassion There was little if any compassion in her regard for Flossie when she was alive and not much now she was dead. Confused as Elenora was at her own lack of feeling she gazed at the victim, sprawled on the floor, eyes wide open in death - not as one would have expected, bulging with terror, for terrible must have been her final moments, but with a slightly apologetic, gormless expression of surprise. Elenora averted her eyes. Was she being heartless? A second glance at Flossie's body confirmed her estimation was right the first time. Gormless was the appropriate word.

Edging around the corpse in order to reach the telephone Elenora used her hankie to lift the phone so as not to disturb any prints there might have been. She paused to remind herself she must take extra care not to let either of the Oglethorpe twins who took turns to man the switchboard at the local exchange know the reason for her call. The two maiden ladies were notorious for relaying juicy bits of information within seconds of receiving it to anyone who would listen. To Clarissa and Hazel Oglethorpe nothing was sacred, no secret secure.

"Craggs Bottom telephone h'exchange speaken..."

"Would you put me through to the Police station Clarissa please?"

"H'its not Clarissa, h'its me - Hazel what's on duty this mornin'." Hazel answered in her impossible official *telephone voice.'* Unable to conceal her curiosity she ventured the question; "...may Hi arst what the purpose of your call his?"

"No, mind your own business Hazel; just connect me to the Cop Shop."

"H'ay was h'only tryin' to be 'elpful..." Hazel sniffed, in a huff.

"Don't be helpful Hazel! Put me through **at once!**" Elenora replied in a deep threatening voice. If the Oglethorp girls were a hazard, what Elenora hadn't reckoned on was Constable Barker's mental inability to interpret thi loaded message intended to circumnavigate the sensation hungry ears of the terrible twins was Elenora's next problem.

"Craggs Bottom police station 'ere. Nah then what can I do for thee?"

"Archie is that you...?"

"Aye, Constable Barker speakin'" Whenever he was left in charge of the police station, Archie felt he was no longer on the bottom rung of the pecking order and it was evident in his tone of voice. It went into an *'I'm in charge here, so watch it!'* mode. "Okey-dokey! Now! Tell me what can I do for you?"

"This is Elenora Clapworthy. You and Sergeant Wilkinson had better get round here to the 'Feathers' as quickly as you can. There's been..." then, remembering Hazel was still ear wigging at the telephone exchange..."...there's been... an incident."

"Oh, Miss Clapworthy...'erm...er... Good Morning Miss Clapworthy..." The deferential tone he now adopted quite cancelled out his *'in charge'* voice. Miss Clapworthy, he reminded himself was respected by all the bigwigs in the council. Not to mention being on social terms with his superior, Chief Superintendent Cartwright. Even the mere thoughts of such omnipotence made Archie's head swim. So superior - in Archie eyes – was Oswald Cartwright only God himself was ahead in rank.

"I wonder if I might enquire as to the nature of the er... you see Miss Clapworthy, Sergeant Wilkinson doesn't come on duty till after nine o'clock, he likes to have a lie in of a Sunday morning, and in bad weather he goes round to all the old ladies houses to shovel the snow, and there's only me here at the station, and I have to make the breakfast for the prisoner..."

"...**Prisoner!?**" Good God! Could Archie have apprehended the murderer on his own? "What prisoner Archie?"

"Harry. Harry Petty. You know Harry, he's our regular." Constable Barker referred to his prisoner-in-charge with more than affectionate pride, "By gum, he wa' in a right sorry state when I brought him in last night. Paralytic! Staggerin' up and down high street at one o'clock in the mornin' singin' at the top of his voice..."

"Harry Petty! Is he the only prisoner you've got?"

"Well, yes." Archie sounded hurt. The only misdemeanour's Archie liked having to deal with were minor traffic offences, pilfering from the allotments, having a light showing from the edge of the blackout curtain, and of course the weekly apprehension of Harry Petty. "He can be a handful can Harry. I don't mind tellin' thee ..."

Heaven only knows what Archie's reaction might have been had she filled him in on the real nature of her call. Desperate to share with someone the terrible responsibility of having discovered Flossie Ingham stabbed to death and here she was, listening to a critique of the village drunk's al fresco concert. Elenora could hardly believe she was having this conversation. However her sense of the ridiculous kicked in and in spite of the enormity of the moment she found it hard not to laugh. Battling to retain a calm demeanour, she tried an authoritarian approach. "Where is Harry now Archie?"

"He's sittin' at the table waitin' for his breakfast."

"Lock him in the cell, and go at once and wake Sergeant Wilkinson."

"Harry'll be very upset if he doesn't get his breakfast..."

"...**At once Archie!** Lock Harry in his cell. Do it **now!!** Then Go round to Sergeant Wilkinson's and wake him and tell him to get round here. Tell him it's urgent. Imperative!"

"But he'll kill me if I waken him up of a Sunday mornin'..."

"I'll kill you if you don't! Tell him it's a matter of life and death – *your* death - if you don't **do as I say - now!**" She bellowed and hung up before Archie had time to protest any further.

Elenora was still struggling with her own lack of compassion, together with the irresistible sense of the ridiculousness of the situation. There was never any love lost between her and Flossie and from the stories that circulated, it was predicted that Flossie Ingham would indeed come to a sorry end. A final glance at the body as she edged past on her way from the immediate scene of the crime confirmed she had it right. There was no question the word *'gormless'* on the corpse's face was perfectly apt. Elenora's self-castigation for lack of compassion vanished for good.

Hoping she had conveyed the urgency of her message and that Archie would act upon her order to wake Sergeant Wilkinson she made her way to the back door from where she had entered to await his arrival.

Once in the clean air of the bright winter morning she was better able to consider the terrible nature of her discovery. Who, she wondered, in his or her right mind would first anaesthetise then choke a dog before delivering a heavy blow to its head? There was something deeply bizarre about that! In her mind Elenora mulled over the first stormy meeting between Flossie and herself. It was Eli who tipped the scales and persuaded Elenora to allow one of her famous Alsatians to go to the 'Feathers'. Pathetic, lonely Eli Pearson.

Eli may have seemed an unlikely candidate to come up to Elenora's exacting standards to be allowed ownership of one of her beautiful Alsatians. Being always in some degree of inebriation ranging from slightly tipsy to totally wasted. Yet whatever state he was in there was always a gentleness in his nature.

"...'appen it could be the best thing for Eli, you know Miss Clapworthy. God knows he could do with a bit of company." Minnie said at the time. Finally persuaded, Elenora agreed and as expected, Caesar was ignored by Flossie and attended with constant and loving care by Minnie, Sally the barmaid and Eli.

With almost human intelligence Caesar quickly became undisputed master of his territory, tireless in his vigilance. Allowing only legitimate access to the confines of his personal realm, he need only mildly growl to convince the occasional inebriate undercover of the blackout to think twice before attempting to use the back wall of the pub as a urinal. .

"Until last night that is," Elenora said to Caesar as she gently fondled the animal's ears. "Someone managed to shorten your chain, didn't they boy?" Once she began to apply her highly intelligent brain to the evidence she very soon realised that for someone to apply the wad of chloroform... then when Caesar was unconscious hit him over the head. Whoever it was,he or she must surely have been someone who had the dog's full confidence. It certainly looks bad for Eli. Now we must ask ourselves, who else other than Eli would dare take such a liberty?"

Although she didn't realise it at the time, Elenora Clapworthy had embarked upon a strange and exciting journey, a journey that would lead her into intrigue, mystery, suspicion even mortal danger before its eventual end.

....

As she stood in the bright winter sunlight pondering these possibilities Elenora suddenly felt a desperate need to share her terrible discovery with someone.

"Minnie! Minnie! Are you awake?" Elenora called. The urgency in her voice was such that the old lady's blackout curtains parted immediately and Minnie's mob-capped head appeared at the tiny bedroom window.

"Is that you Miss Clapworthy? What ever is the matter? Is it Caesar? He's very quiet?"

"No Minnie, Caesar's alright. Come down as quickly as you can." Whilst she waited for Minnie to appear Elenora glanced around the court yard. The bright clear sunshine offered little warmth, certainly not enough to threaten the drifts that had swirled up against the hotchpotch of cottages, out buildings, privies and ash pits that bordered the little courtyard leaving the cobble stones in the centre of the space for the most part exposed. Again, the fact that the door of Eli's cottage was ajar and the snow had drifted inside was somehow significant. At the moment she didn't know why. He was either still asleep, oblivious to what had occurred, which would go a long way to proving his innocence or he had done a bunk which would definitely point to his culpability.

"Eli! Eli!" She called, "wake up! Are you there? ... Eli?" She so hoped, for his sake he would answer her repeated call, but there was no response.

Aware she must remember to tell the police that there was no disturbance of the snow previous to her own in the entrance to Eli's cottage. She went inside. The little house was empty. As she feared Eli had done a bunk

"What's going on, Miss Clapworthy?" Minnie emerged from her front door, a heavy overcoat over her flannelette nightgown and Wellington boots pulled hastily on over her thick knitted bed socks. The tough old lady strode purposefully through the drifts to join Elenora by the back door of the pub then seeing the mutilated hinges exclaimed loudly,

"Bloody hell! There's been a break in!" Minnie's urge to investigate was halted by the ominous tone in Elenora's voice.

"Don't go in there Minnie! It's worse than that!" The apprehension at such uncharacteristic gravity coming from the Vet demanded an explanation.

"Flossie's dead." Elenora said. "Stabbed, I've phoned for the police. They should be here any-time now."

"Dead...? Dead...? Nay! Does tha' mean... Nay, not that" Her next question confirmed to Elenora that Minnie's thoughts ran along the same lines as her own. "Where's Eli?"

"I don't know Minnie. He's not in his cottage. The two ladies were interrupted in their speculation by the appearance of Sergeant Wilkinson, hurrying into the yard. The give-away signs the friendly cop gave out at having been roused from sleep, were still very evident around his half closed eyes. His uniform jacket hastily done up in the wrong buttonholes, his shirt flap protruding from his gaping flies and helmet obviously dumped cock-eyed on his head whilst on the move.

Riddled with anxiety for fear he had called his boss out on a wild goose chase Constable Archie Barker trotted like a naughty child close on the heels of his boss. In spite of the calamity that hung about them Elenora found it hard to subdue the words *Keystone Kops* from forcing their way into her brain at the sight of the two guardians of their community in such disarray.

"Morning, Miss Clapworthy! Morning, Minnie! What's going on?" Then sensing the atmosphere, and seeing the back door of the pub hanging on its hinges, realised the gravity of the situation. "Ay, ay! a break in 'eh?"

"Worse than that Arnold I'm afraid," Elenora said, "I'm sorry to be the one to tell you, but Flossies dead...

"Good God!"

"I found her about fifteen minutes ago when I called to take Caesar for his regular constitutional over the moor. I should tell you before you go in, the footprints on the steps and in the corridor are mine and Heinz's - going in and coming out."

"That was quick thinking of you Miss Clapworthy. Thank you." Arnold said with admiration, "Well, we'd better take a look Archie. Come on lad, brace thi'sen and take a deep breath."

Constable Barker though was made of softer metal than his Sergeant. Archie's normally rosy complexion turned an unhealthy grey on hearing the earth shattering news. The thoughts of what might be facing the timid young Constable inside the pub made his knees buckle. A break-in was just about within the bounds of his imagination, but a dead body!? A dead body - MURDERED! That was altogether something else. His pallor changed once more, from grey to deathly white.

"I think you'd better leave Archie out here with us Arnold," Elenora said, tactfully assessing the extent to which Archie's nerves would stretch, "one less set of footprints if you see what I mean?" She added quickly to cover the boy's embarrassment.

"I see what you mean." Arnold said as he entered the pub to assess the scene of the crime. He wasn't long before he re-emerged into the fresh cold air, deeply grateful to have Elenora and Minnie on hand.

"What a bloody mess!" Arnold said, himself now shaken and ashen faced, "I've made a phone call to headquarters in Leeds. Well have Superintendent. Cartwright on the job I'm afraid." If Ossie being present caused the Sergeants nerves to play up it was nothing compared to the effect it had on the boy Constable's entire system, especially his bowels.

"Aye well," Minnie said, knowing all too well how unbearably officious her nephew Chief Superintendent Oswald Cartwright could be, she thought it best to warn the Sergeant. "If that snotty little bugger is coming Arnold, hadn't tha' better fasten thi' fly 'ole buttons and smarten thi'sen up?" Arnold blushed a little, grinned apologetically and promptly made the appropriate adjustments.

"God in Heaven help me," Archie looked skyward and offered his plea to the firmament. "I don't think I can face Chief Superintendent Cartwright, Arnold." In spite of the keen winter air a film of sweat broke through on Archie's brow and upper lip. So far his morning had gone briskly downhill. First of all he burnt Harry's toast, which made his prisoner more than a little peeved. Then that telephone call from Miss Clapworthy, which proved to be mind-bendingly serious. Now within minutes he would have the Almighty Cartwright breathing down his neck.

"Oh, dearie me! Oh heck, I don't feel well at all..." The constable's eyes rolled back to reveal the whites. "I'm going to have to go to the toil..."

"Nah then Archie, pull thi'sen together!" Arnold said, "You're acting like a big fat lass. Gerra grip on thi'sen!" Sergeant Wilkinson tried to sound officious, but it came out more like a plea. "...And smarten thi'sen up, they'll be here from head office before long. I want you to stand guard at the front door of the pub and make sure nobody gets inside, or disturbs the footprints..." The threat of head office only served to remind Archie his impending bowel movement was imminent. "But Arnold, what about Harry?" he quivered.

"Harry? What the 'ell has Harry got to do with it?"

"Well I left him in charge of the station while I went to wake you up!"

"You left the prisoner in charge of the station? That'll look bloody lovely on the report sheet! I don't believe it! Are you bloody barmy or what?"

"Well I didn't know whether we were going to prefer charges of drunk and disorderly or not." By now Archie was fighting back the tears.

"Prefer charges! Prefer char...! Talk sense you dozy pillock! He's never disorderly when he's drunk; he's only disorderly when you burn his toast! When was the last time we charged Harry?"

"I can't remember."

"There you are then! Bloody Hell Archie! Get round there and send him home. Lock the station door after you, and get back here as soon as you can – before Cartwright gets here, else he'll have your guts for garters. If he doesn't, I bloody well will!"

"Can I go to the toilet first Arnold?"

"No you can't! Go to the bog once you've sent Harry home, God-dammit!"

In spite of the enormity of the calamity that hovered over the little group as they stood by the back door of the pub Elenora felt compelled to turn away in an effort to control the laugh that threatened to expose her as a heartless hysteric. As she did so she found great solace in noticing both Minnie and Arnold also trying to conceal the same brand of gallows' humour.

Archie scuttled off, choking with terror and panic. No sooner had he got to the gateposts at the exit of the courtyard on his mission to relieve himself and the prisoner - in that order of urgency, than three police cars sped aggressively through the narrow entrance forcing him to leap sideways into the drift at the side of the lane.

As he went down in the snow Archie just had time to notice that in the passenger seat of the leading car sat his nemesis. Police Chief Superintendent Oswald

252

Cartwright.   The great man himself didn't even notice Archie.

....

In spite of the inconvenient time of day, Ossie Cartwright resplendent in his immaculate dress uniform swept nimbly from the police car almost before it came to a halt. It was deadly important to him that more than all the other sub-units under his authority he make an impression in Craggs Bottom.

There were still many who remember him as the quiet, awkward orphan brought up by his maiden aunt Beatrice, the sister of none other than Minnie Clegg who stood there in the tiny group before him.

The only flies in the ointment being, on this cold and frosty morning there, amongst the gathering crowd were two people he would most like **not** to confront but knew he must – his Old Aunt Minnie and Elenora Clapworthy, both of whom were able to cramp his style in the worst way. Yet the only person in the small gathering who showed any respect for him was, oddly enough, Elenora Clapworthy. Her high opinion of him however sprang not from his grandiose position as a high-ranking copper but as a sublime master of the bull fiddle he played with such tenderness in her brilliant little jazz band. There was a tacit understanding between them that they never let the two sides of his split personality emerge at the same time.

In his musical mode Oswald showed a surprisingly opposite side to his personality. There was no sign of the overbearing pomposity he displayed in his daytime role as Chief Superintendent. Together they would make wonderful music, jamming the night away enthralling troops of all nationalities in increasingly crowded barracks, hangars and transit camps as the Allies assembled their mighty armies for the imminent invasion of Europe

Unfortunately this mutual interest in Jazz didn't alter the fact that once away from the bandstand and with his Bass Fiddle back in its case Oswald Cartwright reverted to being the most exasperating, self-important prig ever to breathe pure Yorkshire air. His flawed flowery turn of phrase didn't impress her one bit, and if his occasional Spoonerisms were to be detected it would invariably be in her earshot.

The trouble was, having supplied the West Riding Constabulary with generations of working police dogs from her famous kennels, as well as being the permanent Veterinarian Surgeon in Attendance at the Police stables it was impossible to avoid having dealings with him and his department.

The other serious threat to Oswald's image this particular morning was in fact a real life Aunt, an embarrassing reminder of his more than humble beginnings. His only defence against her was Oswald's firmly held belief that *'Familiarity bred contempt'* and could *'jeopardise his standing in the community'.*

After all he reasoned, why should he let his Aunt Minnie interfere with his peerless organising abilities (as he himself saw it) Oswald had been landed with an inhuman workload, which included the supervision of these outlying sub-stations. Usually these *"hick Stations"* were manned by what he considered to be incompetent *'Hillbillies,'* either over age or medically unfit for military service, as was the case here in Craggs Bottom. His contempt was obvious as he strode grim faced towards Sergeant Wilkinson who unlike himself had not shaved that morning.

"Now then, what do we have here Wilkinson?" Oswald demanded, satisfied to see the sergeant gulp with apprehension, obviously overwhelmed by the enormity of the situation. Oswald's own manner made it plain that it was just another routine case he would soon have neatly tied up and closed. He had other more pressing matters to attend to than this sordid little crime of passion. Already, from Sergeant Wilkinson's briefing on the telephone, Oswald had relegated this affair to a minor category. "First degree murder? Yes," he loftily conceded "nevertheless, sergeant, straightforward and routine".

Without acknowledging any of the locals, Cartwright fired orders at his men like bullets from a gun. With a cursory glance at the door and its mutilated hinges he entered the building radiating an air of superior efficiency. Ten minutes later with same unruffled smugness he emerged to allow the forensic people access. He would soon have this in the bag.

"Sergeant Wilkinson. Where is your subordinate?"

"Er... my what sir?"

"Your subordinate man! Your Constable...what's his name?"

"Oh, Arch...Constable Barker. Well sir, he's 'er ..." Arnold rummaged around his brain for an excuse for Archie's glaring absence. He could hardly tell the Chief Superintendent the truth that Archie had gone back to the Cop Shop to relieve the village drunk from desk duty.

"He's gone er... to..."

He's gone to fix up a barrier around the scene of the crime." Elenora offered, "Then you ordered him to stand guard at the front of the building, didn't you Sergeant?" At the same time Elenora tipped the wink to Minnie to run and make sure Archie complied.

"Thank you, Miss Clapworthy. But if you don't mind, the sergeant ought to be capable of answering for himself." Turning to the unfortunate sergeant he plunged into a rapid fire barrage. A grilling, intended to intimidate rather than to get at the truth. This completed he showed by his supercilious smirk that he had *"made the bugger sit up and take notice"* He made a walking tour of the area making sure it was his own men from Leeds and not the *"yokels"* who did the real investigation.

He would eventually have to bring this initial investigation to a close, he knew. But not yet, not before ostentatiously ordering the goggle eyed neighbours to stand back from the scene. Not too far back though, he was enjoying being centre stage far too much to dismiss his enthralled audience altogether.

Minnie Clegg, his closest blood relative was the next to be questioned. This he knew only too well could be tricky, but he was determined not to let her get the better of him. Elenora in the meantime was careful to remain at a distance knowing by the hint of fear on Oswald's face and the animated body language of his Aunt Minnie the interviewee; this was one time the long arm of the law was in danger of over reaching itself.

"I left the pub as soon as I'd done washing 't glasses and pots at me usual time of eleven o'clock." Answering the questions put to her with mounting impatience since her interrogator seemed set on covering the same subject at least twice over.

"Did you leave by the back?"

"Of course I left by the back door. Do you think I'd be barmy enough to leave by the front door and walk all the way round when you know full well I no'but live over yonder next door to Eli."

"Did Mr Pearson leave at the same time?"

"No I've telled thee three times now. I saw him coming out of the privy at the end there..."

"Was he inhebra...?"

"Course he was ...Pissed as a parrot!" Poor old sod. I remember tellin' him, I sez -, "mek sure tha' keeps thi'sel' warm to-neet, I wouldn't be capped if it doesn't snow afore morning!" I sez.

"Did he then enter his cottage – alone?" Cartwright's tone seemed to Minnie dangerously loaded with innuendo.

"No, he did not! He had Mae West on one arm and Dorothy Lamour on the other!" Minnie snapped sarcastically. "Of course he was alone! Who'd want to go to bed with Eli? Have you seen the state of him? You'd have to steep him for a fortnight in Jeyes Fluid 'afore you could get within three feet.

"Where then did you go, Mrs Clegg?"

"Where then did I go?" Enough was enough. Her rag was up, and this idiot of a nephew of hers couldn't see it. "I've told thee umpteen times *where then did I go*" Minnie repeated in disgust, "I went home, got into bed with cup of hot milk, a hot water bottle and half a dozen Royal Naval Ratings!"

Fortunately for him he realised he had driven her to the edge of control and she could be of little further help to the enquiries.

"That will be all for now, thank you Mrs Clegg."

"I should bloody well think so." Minnie's voice carried far and wide. "In any case tha' should have questioned Miss Clapworthy before anyone else; she was the first on the scene."

"I have my methods Mrs. Clegg." The superintendent replied defensively backing down.

"...Methods my arse!" Minnie snapped, "you've kept her standing about just so everyone can see how bloody important you are!"

Arnold's air of omnipotence had taken a blow from which it would take a while before it recovered. He

257

decided to throw in the towel whilst he still had a little control.

"That will be all for the present Mrs. Clegg. Just one more thing, I must ask you not to pleave the recinct...er... leave the precinct, as you may be needed for further questioning.

"Pleave the recinct?! Pleave The recinct?! Minnie insisted on having the last word, "...and where would I be pleaving for? - Conte Marlo?!"

Elenora found it hard to keep a straight face. No matter how hard Ossie tried to be Eliot Ness the more he came across as Dagwood Bumstead. The Chief Superintendent was relieved to turn his attention from his old Aunt to his next victim, Sally Hancock.

Elenora, seeing that she was to be overlooked again sought out her old friend Dr Sharp the Coroner, an old friend in charge of the Forensics on the case.

"Good Morning Elenora." Dr Sharp's greeting was hearty in spite of the seriousness of the occasion.

"Good morning John. Well this is a fine how do you do isn't it?"

"Yes, bit of a shock for you old girl, finding the body. You all right?"

"Oh yes, but I'll be glad when Ossie gets through with his questioning." Elenora replied with a knowing smile.

"Yes! I noticed he was making a bit of a meal of it." Dr Sharp was all too familiar with the Chief Superintendent's foibles. You been grilled yet?"

"Not yet I think he's saving me till last."

"Of course, he's out to impress," the doctor observed accurately. "But there's really no need for it, he's already convinced the cellar man – Eli Pearson is the guilty party."

"Hmm... bit premature if you ask me. What do you think John?

""Oh I think it must be Pearson my dear. Such a lot of evidence pointing towards him I'm afraid."

"Yes I must say, it does look bad for him." Elenora replied, adding as if it were merely small talk, "Tell me John what was the time of death?"

"Shortly after midnight. Multiple stab wounds and the weapon is missing."

"Missing? Isn't that unusual for a crime of passion?" Elenora asked with an air of innocence.

"I don't know. Is it?" Dr Sharp replied. "Well whatever. Not my department. Ossie seems convinced Pearson is his man."

"You wouldn't think so the way the way he keeps on covering the same old ground." Elenora laughed, "He's almost driven Minnie Clegg to another first degree murder – his own!"

"That's Ossie for you." The coroner replied with a chuckle as he signed the clearance chit for the removal of the body. "Well that's me finished Elenora, I'll see you at the trial, if not before. We'll have that little drink then!"

Still Elenora was kept waiting. The Chief Superintendent now partly recovered from the pounding he took from Minnie and once again fairly bursting with importance bestowed his investigative skills on the young barmaid Sally Hancock. Sally he noticed, was the prettiest girl in the small crowd who had gathered to watch the exciting events in spite of the zero temperature. Had he asked any of them he would have been told that Sally was very dear to them all.

"Mrs. Hancock, tell me if you please, what time did you leave work last night?"

"Just after eleven o'clock."

"...and had Mr. Pearson...Eli already left?"

259

"Oh yes. He was a bit worse for..." Sally hesitated, not wanting to make Eli's case any worse that it seemed already

"...drink, were you going to say?"

"Worse for wear I was going to say. It's a long day for him and he's not a young man. Yes, I have to admit he had a drink or two during the evening." Sally was annoyed at the way Eli was being prematurely depicted as the villain of the piece.

"But not too inebriated to go home unassisted?"

"Well he doesn't have to go far, he only lives over there." Sally said with rising anger pointing to Eli's hastily abandoned cottage with its door still ajar. "It must have been a terrible shock for him finding Flossie's body like that..."

"...You are assuming he merely discovered the body and did not commit the crime himself." Ossie said, in a meaningful challenging manner. "Perhaps you know something more to this effect Mrs Hancock?"

"No! It's just that Eli couldn't do anything like what you suggest." Sally said, her eyes filling with tears. "He's a sweet harmless old man..."

"...not an habitual drunk, so inebriated he didn't know the time of day or night?"

"No! No! Well what if he does have the odd drink or two! That doesn't mean..." Sally broke down and began to sob. For she could not deny Eli drank himself into oblivion every night.

"That will be all for now Mrs. Hancock." Ossie had scored valuable Brownie points by making Sally shed tears, but at the sight of them he wished the interview over. More than anything he would have wished to come across to this lovely young girl in a heroic light - as a seeker of truth. Not as he had so successfully managed to do, as a heartless bullying smart arse. Maybe he would

260

have more luck with Elenora Clapworthy. An idle wish for he knew in his heart he was no match for her. Still his professionalism demanded he must try.

"This shouldn't take long Miss Clapworthy. I imagine like me, you have other more important things calling on your time" This was as informal as he was going to allow. He expected Miss Clapworthy to fall in with his professional approach and keep their personal interests well and truly separate. She for her part had no intentions of disappointing him. The role he had appointed himself as Chief Superintendent of Planet Earth was far too entertaining to sacrifice.

"As you say Inspector…"

"Chief Superintendent, if you please."

"Quite. I do beg your pardon Chief Superintendent." Elenora affected a deadpan expression that with anyone less conceited would have been detected. Not Ossie, he took it on face value. Preening like a turkey having survived Christmas he launched into his interrogation.

"Now Miss Clapworthy, I understand you arrived on the scene at approximately…."

"Exactly at five minutes past nine."

"What was the purpose of you visit? I believe you were on friendly terms with the deceased?"

"No. In fact I didn't particularly like the woman. I come most Sunday mornings to take the dog for a run across the moors."

"I understand there was a pad of pink lint that had been used to anaesthetise the animal lying on the floor of the kennel."

"That is true but I rather think the blow to Caesar's head did more to incapacitate him than the chloroform did."

"Thank you Miss Clapworthy, of course you would be able to recognise that kind of thing... being a Veterinarian Surgeon, wouldn't you?"

"I don't know Superintendent, would I?"

"I think you would. You would also have access to such substances."

"Oh, I hardly think..."

"Don't worry Miss Clapworthy," He said, magnanimously letting her off the hook, "at the moment you are not the prime suspect."

"Oh well, that's a blessing."

"But you must realise we have to cover all angles."

"Of course Superintendent."

"No we...I... think it's an open and shut case." Although he knew it was strictly against procedural practice Ossie couldn't resist this chance of impressing her with his superior understanding of the case. "I know who our man is. It's only a matter of time before I... we get him. I have already ishiniated...initiated a Man Hunt."

"It does look bad for Eli I agree Superintendent." Elenora said in a suitably deferential tone of voice. "But I think when the full facts come to light you'll hardly think him capable of anything as subtle and devious..."

"Subtle? Miss Clapworthy I don't think doing a bunk a subtle move!" Ossie answered. "No, barring miracles, I believe the main facts have already come to light. The suspect broke down the back door to make it look like a break in ..."

"But surely," Elenora ventured, "assuming he saw the door hanging by its hinges and then discovering the body of his employer, wouldn't he realise he was suspect number one, get frightened and flee?"

"Of course! And he could also have got frightened and fleed... er...flod... damn it - fled *after* killing the victim?" The more Oswald fought for his words more feather legged he got and in turn lost his composure.

"Now if you don't mind Miss Clapworthy, allow me to develop the theories revelant... relevant to the case in my own professional way   Suitably chastened Elenora allowed herself to be grilled. Repeatedly going over the details... finding the back door of the pub torn from its hinges... seeing Eli's door ajar... finding Caesar almost strangled and unconscious.

The more she repeated her story the more she sensed her interrogator was teasing her by holding back some other vital clue no one else was privy to. She became more convinced than ever Eli was not the culprit. But there was no way she could convince Oswald of it, nor could she prove it – yet. Risking the Chief Superintendent's further displeasure Elenora made one last stab at pointing out other glaring facts that seemed in danger of being overlooked.

"The snow didn't start to fall until five a.m., the footprints are *leading away* from Eli's cottage, if he had murdered her at midnight would he have gone back home to wait for five hours before taking off?" Elenora rattled on not too absorbed in her own rhetoric to notice Oswald's surprise at her very lucid understanding of the evidence.

"..as I see it," now with bit between her teeth Elenora let Ossie have it. "Eli had risen early to answer nature's call and on his way to the outdoor privy noticed the back door of the Pub hanging off its hinges, entered the pub, discovered the body, panicked at the gory sight and expecting the blame would fall on him, he took flight. Finally I think you will find irrefutable proof that Eli Pearson was incapable of harming the guard dog Caesar... "

"Enough! Enough, Miss Clapworthy! I will decide what is and what is not irrefutable proof!"   Oswald was almost catatonic with anger. First he had suffered the terrifying wrath of his Aunt Minnie, and then made a total mess of his interview with the pretty young widow Sally Hancock. Finally what was already a tricky relationship with Miss Clapworthy had taken a further catastrophic nose-dive.

"That will be all for now! Please keep yourself available. You may be needed for further questioning. Without another word he turned on his heel, climbed into the waiting Austin and testily ordered the driver to make a speedy exit from the scene of the crime. Eager to be rid of the loss of face he had suffered so far he went on to question the rest of the witnesses including Herbert Townsend and Slimey Slickey. A minor consideration seeing as he considered he already had the whole thing practically sewn up.

Unaware of the cold Elenora remained standing in the middle of the courtyard of the pub as she watched the police cars drive away. Her unease soaring as she mulled over the depressing possibilities. Oswald seemed blinkered and set on bringing the case to a swift conclusion. A balls-up was in the making, a balls-up of such proportions that could put his own career in jeopardy and send an innocent man to the gallows. Something must be done. The more she thought about it the stronger her resolve grew to save both pursuer and pursued.

....

Elenora stood in the centre of the back yard of the pub pondering on her next move. It was not a difficult choice – a cup of hot, strong tea in Minnie's cottage.

"Well! What do you make of this little lot?" Minnie asked eager to get Elenora's take on the extraordinary

264

morning they had just undergone. Tut-tut-ting in disbelief she went on. "I can't believe that's all there is to it. I know our Ossie is a bit of a wazzack, but to just drive off like that without giving any thought or considering any other suspect other than Eli has me flummoxed and right,"

"Yes it's amazing." Elenora agreed, "I know it looks bad for Eli but everyone except you and me seems to have already decided Eli did it!"

"Nay - not everyone! Sally believes he couldn't have done it. Not in a million years, and Arnold knows Eli couldn't have."

"In that case Arnold must conduct his own investigation independently of the Leeds big boys," Elenora said, "...and we – you, Sally and me will give him all the help we can. Where is Sally by the way?"

"She's gone to report the mur... you know what - to Mr Sanders the brewery manager, she'll be here in a minute or two as soon as she has left Brandon with Leah Stead." Minnie said, "I've made enough pie for all three of us." "I don't want Sally to be on her own, not to-day. You neither."

"God Minnie, we are lucky to have you in our corner." Elenora said.

"We're lucky to have one another... here comes Sally now. Come in Sally love."

"What's going to become of Caesar by the way?" Minnie asked.

"Oh, he's coming home with me, until Eli gets...you know, - back in circulation."

The three friends ate heartily and surprised themselves at the buoyancy of their spirits in the face of the cataclysmic event that had taken place. Elenora put this positive attitude down to the fact that none of them had ever held any affection for the victim, and in spite of

Eli's unfortunate position they all loved the prime suspect and believed in his innocence.

No formal agreement to had taken place. It was purely an arrangement to pool their knowledge of the events. No appointment of a leader either, merely a shared understanding that a monumental miscarriage of justice must be averted.

There was also a tacit understanding that even if they did not discover the identity of the real murderer they must at the very least clear Eli's name. At the same time Arnold might get some long overdue credit for being a treasured member of the community instead of the "*Hill-Billy*" dolt he had been made to look. Who knows, they may even save the reputation of Chief Superintendent Ossie Cartwright? After all, both Elenora and Minnie knew he may be a social climber blinded by his own importance but he was not a bad man at heart.

"Right, now then!" Elenora started the ball rolling, "First things first. We're all agreed that Eli couldn't have done it? Now just because we all love the old bugger we must be careful to have no bias n his favour."

"Right oh" Sally agreed. "First of all why would he break down the back door, when he had a key...?"

"...Noted..."Elenora said as she scribbled down every detail as it came up.

"...and why did he take off **without** Caesar? He'd never have done that in a thousand years..." Minnie added enthusiastically.

"Exactly! I think that's because he didn't know Caesar was still in his kennel - unconscious, on a tight chain and a bump rising on his head! Isn't that it Caesar old darling?" The beautiful Alsatian looked up at Elenora his intelligent eyes she felt sure, confirmed her theory.

"There is one thing..." Sally again. "...we mustn't forget MOTIVE!" If anyone had a reason to see Flossie dead, it must surely have been Eli. Her treatment of him was appalling…"

"Oh, God forgive us Sally love, they're lots beside Eli wanted to be shut of Flossie, the list must run into hundreds!" Minnie was passionate in her answer. "For a start theres me! Many a time I could gladly have banged her head against the wall.

"…And everybody in the village knew there was no love lost between her and me!" Elenora confirmed, "which brings us neatly to Flossie's clique of sycophants who spent most of their leisure time sucking up to her in the lounge bar every evening."

"That's still quite a number," Sally in her role as barmaid was in a position to witness the dodgy black market transactions that took place every night and lunch time during opening hours. Being scrupulously honest herself and wishing to have no part of these dealings she was always careful to avoid knowing the identities of most of these casual miscreants. "So I'm afraid I could be no help in naming a lot of them."

"The same goes for me, I'm afraid!" Minnie added. "In fact I made sure I didn't "see" a lot of things that went on!"

"So Minnie and me are not much help there Miss Clapworthy."

"Yes…but let's not forget ladies, we hold the vital trump card in that regard" Elenora said in a cod Hercule Poirot accent. "My little grey cells tell me the list of suspects is far, far smaller than you imagine Mes petites!" The blank expressions on Sally's and Minnie's face told her that neither of her fellow detectives knew what the hell she was talking about.

"Alright, the trump card is this - The person who killed Flossie is someone who had Caesar's total trust and confidence otherwise they would never have been able to get near enough to tighten his choke - chain, anaesthetise and slug him over the head ! Which you see, narrows the field down to us three and Eli unless there is someone else you may know of…"

"Bugger me! That's bloody brilliant Miss Clapworthy!" Minnie beamed admiringly.

"I'll say it is!" Sally agreed.

"Not really girls, it's nothing that even Ossie couldn't have deduced if he hadn't had his head so far up his own arse this morning."

"So come on, who else could have felt safe going into Caesar's kennel last night?"

"Well Caesar was able to tolerate Slimey Slickey the butcher, which is a deal more than I could." Sally offered, "Slimey would often provide him with bones, only as a means of making up to Flossie, with little effect I might add, but yes, Slimey was able to get to him without any fuss."

"Then there was the High and Mighty Herbert Townsend." Minnie added, "Caesar put up with that nasty old drunkard because he was used to him being around after the pub closed…""Prior of course, to spending a night of lust in Flossie's boudoir - Townsend of course not Caesar! - If you know what I mean?

"…who needs a diagram when we have you darling?"Elenora answered. "Is there anyone else you can think of – *anyone* who could get near enough to do that awful thing to Caesar?"

"No," Sally pondered, "can't think of anyone else."

"Well aye, there is somebody,that lovely young American lad Buddy Martin. One of them there *"walking wounded"* from the Hospital." Minnie added warmly referring with great affection to the handsome young GI. He's always hanging around. There's absolutely nothing he won't do. Change light bulbs… wipe the table tops…he

268

was even replacing the old screws on the hinges of the back door last night..."

"Well, we know what the attraction was there don't we?" Elenora said with a smile, "It was Sally he was after. Am I right?"

"He needn't have bothered". Sally answered. "Not my type."

"Maybe he wasn't *your* type," Minnie said with a laugh, "but if I'd 'ave been forty years younger, he wouldn't 'a stood a chance. I'd 'ave had him between two slices of bread! He's gorgeous!"

"Well girls," Elenora said summing up. "We've made a start. We know of three other suspects other than we three. Next question! Any suggestions as to where Eli could be hiding right now?"

"I haven't a clue." Concern returned to colour Sally's answer, "I just know he won't last long outdoors in this weather."

"Let's hope that Eli is discovered before the Man Hunt that Ossie started discover him." Minnie added. "When did Mr Sanders say the pub must open again Sally?"

"Tomorrow lunch time" Sally answered, "I thought it was in rather indecent haste, but he said life must go on..."

"Oh aye lass, the brewery can't rest easy unless the till is ringing every second..."

"He asked if you and I could manage until he could organise something more convenient. I told him we could."

"You know, maybe it's a good thing you are carrying on as per, we'll see how it affects the other suspects. I mean if one or the other of them didn't turn up, breaking the habit of a lifetime. It might mean something?"

269

Elenora's analytical faculties went into overdrive. Suddenly remembering the time when she had feared that Eli was planning to *"do himself in"* She recalled the conversation with Minnie and Sally, all about why Eli had taken off and they feared for his safety*....* It all came back to Elenora ... *why would an intelligent man like Eli allow himself to be so under the thumb of a slag like Flossie* ...Minnie had speculated at the time *"...the old buzzard Flossie had some previous hold on him...* Minnie had been emphatic***..."I feel sure he must have known her in the past!"***

Retuning to the present dilemma, Elenora asked.

"Did you say that he came from Kendal or somewhere in the Lake District?"

"Yes," Sally answered, "I remember him often talking lovingly about the Lakes."

""First thing in the morning I am going to do some probing on the phone and try go get some answers." Elenora said as she prepared to leave Minnie's cosy fireside for home. Each of them promised to take all precautions in case the murderer showed up again.

"I'll be as right as rain," Minnie said, "in fact I wish the bugger would turn up, I haven't been the chucker–out at the "Feathers" all these years and not learned a thing or two about unarmed combat."

"Brandon and I will be OK." Sally assured them, "We have Leah Stead on hand..."

"Not to mention the ever attentive eye of Sergeant Wilkinson." Minnie added teasingly. "But, what about you Miss Clapworthy? Are you going to be able to sleep tonight cut off from the village in that rambling old ruin Ambler Thorn?"

"Safe as houses!" Elenora answered, "Don't forget, I'll have both Heinz and Caesar guarding me. So until tomorrow morning, lets all keep eyes and ears open. I'll join you in the pub at lunch opening time."

In the fast failing light of this incredible day Elenora made her way home. Trudging through the deep snow drifts that were, she noted, still undisturbed by human footprints therefore she assumed...

"...*Ossie's Man Hunt has obviously not yet reached my neck of the woods then*" she thought aloud, seriously wondering yet again if her friend the Chief Superintendent was up to the job.

Once indoors she fed the two dogs, made herself a hot drink then went to bed. In spite of her head reeling with unanswered questions she immediately fell into a deep, healthy sleep.

The next morning she leapt out of bed eager to make the phone calls that might throw some light on Eli's past. Within an hour there were three telegrams with pre-paid replies to the leading breweries in the North West. One of them struck gold.

To:- Clapworthy re. Pearson: Eli: Mr Not in our employ for number of years. No knowledge of whereabouts. Best we can offer – forwarding address: c/o Olive Barraclough Miss, 61, Bracken-ridge Close, Grange-over-Sands, Lancs. From: - Agnes Long (Miss) Personnel Dept). For: - Coniston Lakes Fine Ales & Co Ltd.

Next a long distance telephone call to Grange over Sands, sadly failed to reveal Eli's present whereabouts, but the delightful Miss Olive Barraclough turned out to be a joyous explosion of information that might yet provide the story with a happy ending. The first jaw dropping revelation from this vociferous, bubbling lady was that Flossie and Eli had been, in a period before they moved to Craggs Bottom

- MAN AND WIFE!

"...he was a lovely young man and such a hard worker." Once Miss Barraclough got started there was no stopping her, *"...can you credit it Miss Clapworthy... at twenty one years of age he was made the manager of the brewery's flagship hotel in the swanky resort of Bowness-on-Windermere. What do you think of that?"*

"It doesn't surprise me at all Miss Barraclough."

"That's when I met him..." Miss Barraclough paused to heave a nostalgic sigh, but she soon picked up her story again. *"We became engaged! For a couple of years his success went forward in leaps and bounds. I was studying law but as soon as I graduated we planned to marry."*

For someone who had been cruelly jilted, there was not the slightest hint of self-pity in Olive Barraclough's voice. Quite the contrary, she seemed to treat the whole affair philosophically and with infectious good humour. Elenora warmed to her enormously.

"Then he met Flossie Ingham! Fell blindly in love with her, and although he was too sweet a person to ditch me outright, I knew I was yesterday's newspaper! I put all hopes of being the future Mrs Pearson behind me. After a bleak registry office ceremony Flossie, now firmly set in her role as the landlords wife, immediately made herself cognisant with all the finer details of the trade. Coldly ambitious and a blatant flirt... may I be blunt, Miss Clapworthy...?"

"...Absolutely, please do Miss Barraclough!"

"She showed herself to be more than a mere flirt, she was a downright trollop!"

"Well said Miss Barraclough!"

"Thank you Miss Clapworthy! You may think I'm being bitchy, and that I have an axe to grind and you would be right to a certain extent, but without a word of a lie Flighty Flossie was cultivating a string of rich

businessmen into her clique, all to be exploited shamelessly. All of us around them knew what was happening – all except poor old trusting Eli! ...shall I go on?

"*Please* Miss Barraclough do go on!" Miss Barraclough was only too eager to go on.

"*...the first affair she had with one of these fellows broke Eli's heart, but since Flossie showed no signs of leaving him he tried to get over it, or at least live with it, for although he wasn't blind to her infidelities, which she not only **admitted** to but **flaunted,** as I say, he was absolutely totally besotted, wouldn't hear a word against her. It seemed in those days the more shameless her behaviour the more he idolised her! There's no accounting is there? – I am soooooo enjoying this, please don't stop me now Miss Clapworthy!*" It was obvious Miss B. had wanted to off load this heartfelt saga for so long her rapid-fire delivery could have put Rosalind Russell to shame. Only a world catastrophe could have stopped her.

"Keep going Miss Barraclough, but whatever you do keep breathing!" Elenora strained to stifle her own enthusiasm that threatened to disrupt the other lady's flow. Renewed and encouraged Miss Barraclough picked up the thread once again.

"*Eli took to the bottle! The once shining hope of the hotel management world was now on the skids. Flossie managed to acquire full charge of the hotel and get her rapacious hands on the all important order book. Letting this happen was a big mistake on Eli's part! Amongst other shady dealings this bottle blond Jezebel began ordering supplies from sources other than the tied brewery! That Miss Clapworthy in the eyes of the licensing trade is punishable by instant dismissal and unforgiving shame within the trade. Shall I go on? Please let me, I'm almost finished.*"

273

"Oh! I wouldn't dream of trying to stop you!"

"Without turning a hair, Flossie showed little shame at getting herself and Eli sacked by the brewery…" Now on the home run, Miss Barraclough raced for the finishing post. *"Flossie made no more ado, she enlisted the services of her many shady "Gentlemen" contacts. Strings were pulled. Flossie adopted her maiden name – Ingham and disappeared from the Lake District…"*

"…surfacing as the landlady of the "Feathers" here in Craggs Bottom with a bundle of glowing albeit phoney testimonials…" Elenora eagerly added.

"Bulls eye!" Miss Barraclough exclaimed triumphantly

"…and Eli, now a desolate, broken man and persistent drunk…" Elenora seamlessly took up the story, "…departed shortly from the Lake District to take up residence in the little cottage at the back of the "Feathers", not as husband and co-licensee, but as anonymous cellar-man, pot-man and general dogsbody."

"That's it exactly!" Olive concluded, *"I told him at the time he should have been a man and stood up to her. But he knew Flossie would have sent him packing – that would have simply finished him off altogether. Oh, thank you for contacting me and hearing me out. You see Miss Clapworthy I still think of him with great affection, I always will… but it's just occurred to me that you will have to pay for this call and it must by now have amounted to a small fortune. I'll be forever grateful if you would keep me informed. I would so like to hear he was alright and safe"*

"Miss Barraclough, what a fabulous lady you are." Elenora said, "You bet we'll keep you informed and please, if he turns up at your place please let us know first before you tell the authorities." Elenora, breathed a satisfied sigh In spite of being all too aware they were no nearer to finding Eli she felt heartened and optimistic.

No sooner had Elenora hung the earpiece of the telephone back on the hook, as if on cue her housekeeper, Dora, appeared in the kitchen doorway. Dora didn't usually go in for dramatics or histrionics, but here she was with the strangest look on her face like Mrs Danvers about to set fire to the East wing of Manderlay.

"I didn't want to alarm you while you was on the phone but I think there's summat you should know about..." unable to put into words what that *"summat"* was, she thought it easier merely to step aside and let her boss see for herself who was standing behind her. It was Eli Pearson!

"I found him in the boiler-house just now... I think he must have been there since..."

"I didn't know where else to go Miss Clapworthy." Eli said, his whole body shaking. his knees wobbled he began to sink to the floor. Elenora and Dora were quick to support him. They took an arm each and led him to the big wheel back chair and gently sat him down. "I didn't do it, Miss Clapworthy! I didn't do it!"

"I know you didn't Eli – we believe you. Dora, Minnie and Sally and most importantly Sergeant Wilkinson, we all believe you!"

"I could never have done that to her...I was frightened...when I saw...I just had to get away..."

"We understand Eli... look at me! ... Look at me! ...We understand all that... we all know there was no way on earth..."

"...but when I saw the back door of the pub hanging off its hinges, and I didn't hear a sound out of Caesar, I got fright..."

"...That's what we assumed..."

"...then when I went inside the lounge bar and saw Flossie... dead in all that blood... I knew they'd think it was me. I had to get away...

"…It must have been dreadful for you Eli…

"…But what did they do to Caesar…they didn't do anything to him did they…?"

"Caesar is fine." Elenora whistled and the two dogs came bounding into the kitchen, one of them wild with joy at seeing his beloved master.

"The reason he couldn't raise the alarm was that he was inside his kennel unconscious. But as you see he is as right as rain. Now try to calm down Eli. First of all let's get Dora to make you something to eat and drink…"

Knowing his dog was alive and he himself was amongst friends Eli became much more settled. The next bit of news he was to receive would lift his opinion of himself a good few notches higher than it had been for years.

"I've just had a long phone conversation with a lovely lady called Olive Barraclough. She is totally in your corner Eli, and as determined as we are to clear your name and get you back on track.

"Then I'd better give myself up, hadn't I? I suppose they are looking for me?

"Yes Eli. There's a Countywide search in operation. Led by the Leeds Police force, but don't give yourself up to them. You must give yourself up to the Craggs Bottom branch. Sergeant Wilkinson will see no harm comes to you and also it will give us a little more time to make some further investigations ourselves."

Arnold Wilkinson arrived at ambler Thorn within minutes of receiving Elenora's call. Breathless the friendly cop burst into the kitchen to see Eli having his first meal in days.

"Thank God you're alright Eli," Arnold was genuinely relieved to see the cellar-man, "you had us all worried. Now you know I have to arrest you?"

"Oh I know that," Eli answered, "but now that I know Caesar is ..."

"...I have to arrest you." Arnold's kindly approach was far from frightening to the old man, "But I have a plan!" Although Arnold knew he was about to bend the law – again - there was nothing new in that. It might save a great deal of grief later on. "Now I'm going to arrest you and put you in the cell at Craggs Bottom cop shop. I'm not going to let the Leeds lot know about it until later in the day. They won't like it, but at the very least you will be viewed in a better light for having given yourself up."

"Whatever you say sergeant..."

"Good I just need some time to follow up some of the clues the Leeds Boys neglected." Arnold said. "They were so sure it was an open and shut case they nearly disappeared up their own arses they were that eager to get away from here on Sunday and again this morning..."

"Has Chief Superintendent Cartwright been this morning to the scene of the crime?" Elenora asked.

"No, he sent his minions." Arnold was frustrated and angry with the treatment he had received from his superior."

"But they were as useless as Ossie – they treat this case as though Eli was already guilty."

"Are you going to the pub now?" Elenora was already on her feet. "If you are, do you mind if I come with you?

"Not at all, any help will be welcome. In fact your presence could prove useful if we come across any of the search party on the way to the station. You could vouch for the fact that Eli voluntarily gave himself up"

Eli gladly fell in with Arnold's plan. Now that he had his dog and these wonderful people, and his dear old friend Olive on his side he was a changed man. After depositing Eli in Archie's custody Elenora quickly filled

Arnold in on who she, Sally and Minnie had decided were most likely to have had access to Caesar's kennel in order to silence him. Although it was a vital aspect of the case Arnold had hardly had time to consider it, he was more than grateful the three ladies had done so. And since the Leeds police force seemed to have decided it was an open and shut case he was going to need someone like Elenora on hand to help him conduct a full investigation. Especially seeing Constable Barker – Archie, was usually of no more use than a rubber hammer to a cabinet-maker.

....

On arrival at the "Feathers" Arnold and Elenora were a little shocked to see the Monday lunch time session in full swing. In spite of the deep snow covering the whole of the countryside, the village was heaving with sightseers from all over the West Riding eager to see for them selves the scene of the goriest crime of the century. The press too, both National and local were having a field day

Slimey Slickey hovered approximately where he did when Flossie was alive – forever on the fringes of her group of sycophantic lickspittles. Without her as the focal point he looked desperately uneasy, but then - he always did look uneasy. Under the present circumstances that unease looked mightily like guilt. He would dearly have loved to be anywhere else on earth. But what with Sergeant Wilkinson and that veterinary woman clearly still probing into the cause of Flossie's death? He thought better of it, he had enough cunning to realise his absence would be more suspicious than his presence. Much better, Slickey thought, to pretend he was merely as shocked and disturbed as the rest of the community.

Herbert Townsend's thinking was on almost the same lines as Slimey's but, of course, they could never console each other. Townsend, being a Mill owner and his wife a leading member of the community he and Slimey Slickey never exchanged words in spite of, or more like because both had been suitors vying for the attention of the dead woman. Therefore guilt hung over him as it did over Slimey like a wet Monday morning drizzle.

Buddy, the young American GI was pleasantly merging with the crowds. Cheerfully helping Sally and Minnie who were deftly pulling pints for the morbidly curious crowds all baying to be served in the same Lounge bar that the dreadful deed had occurred. Buddy applied himself in any way he could, filling shelves, collecting empties, mopping up any spillages. He seemed buoyant and bright as if nothing untoward had taken place.

Also present Mr Sanders from the Brewery showed little sympathy for the deceased. The increase in sales due to the lurid attraction of the event kept the till ringing like it never had before. To his business like mind that was the most important thing. It did not escape his notice however that Sally and Minnie were the most efficient bar staff he had ever come across. Sally's organisational abilities and foresight in recruiting Ada Clough and Big Nellie Fawcett to help deal with the sudden increase of business also made a great impression. He would remember this when the dust settled.

"There are a couple of things have me baffled," Arnold said over the hubbub as he drew Elenora to a quieter spot - inside the front porch of the pub. "Tell me what you think. When Ossie questioned me yesterday - Sunday morning, he asked me if this front door was locked. Well, it was, and he left it at that, he wouldn't let me go on to tell him that it was locked *but only on the latch key.* Now I know for a fact that this door is heavily locked and bolted every night normally."

"So…?

"So, we know the killer **entered by** the back door, why did he not **leave by** the same route?"

"Good question…"

"Another thing… follow me…" Arnold led Elenora through the crowded Lounge Bar to the back of the pub where the damaged door still hung, crippled on its hinges. "What do you make of that?"

"Well, it seems obvious to me," Elenora said, "one hefty kick at the base of the door was all that it took for him, or **her**, and seeing as I was one of the few people who could have nobbled Caesar, I am a number one suspect too don't forget ! – One good kick and he or she was in!"

"Exactly!" Arnold went on," So if the back door offered an unimpeded exit, why after the deed was done, did he go to the trouble of unbolting the two big bolts and the mortise lock on the front door?"

"Could it be because Flossie was not alone? Was she sharing her bed with a lover, a suitor?" Elenora paused to muster her thoughts. "Supposing Flossie heard a noise, came downstairs to investigate, and was confronted by the intruder, Flossie screamed, was then stabbed to death. How am I doing?"

"Great!" Arnold said as he began to get the picture. "Keep going!"

"The scream alerted her companion, who came downstairs. Realising there was someone else in the house the murderer fled through the back door – the way he came in…"

"…Then the lover seeing Flossie dead in a pool of blood immediately realises that he was in a very bad position." Arnold picked up the story. "He knew he would be the prime suspect. He makes sure his hands are covered so as to avoid leaving his finger prints, unbolts the *front* door and lets himself out, closing the front door behind him leaving the door locked with only the latch key!

"Brilliant! Arnold, you'll make chief of police yet"

"Yes but who was it that let himself out? Let's see. Now we know both Slickey and Townsend – amongst others – drooled nightly over Flossie, but which was the most likely to have been invited into her bed?"

"Either and all, if you ask me," Elenora answered, "but my money is not on Slickey. Ever since you stopped her using Eli over the Hershey Bar business, remember? I think she used Slickey primarily as her handler of dodgy goods; he did her errands and was the fence for their dirty black market dealings…but her lover? I hardly think so."

"Miss Clapworthy!" Arnold said, with genuine admiration, "You are brilliant! OK! So for now, let's assume the person who let himself out of the front door was Herbert Townsend, how can we prove it?"

"Ask him!" Elenora said, simply "ask him what time he arrived home in the small hours of yesterday morning. Better still threaten to ask his missus what time he arrived home! That should stir things up a bit. What we need is an independent witness," Elenora said, slightly defeated, "someone who actually saw somebody leaving by the front door. But it's hardly likely there would be anyone around at that time of night…"

"Hardly likely, Miss Clapworthy, I agree, but not impossible!" Arnold almost did a cartwheel with delight as he remembered the one man in the village who might have been out and about in the small hours of Sunday morning. Harry Petty!

"Harry? But wouldn't Harry have been in his cups by then" Elenora offered, "too smashed to remember anything?"

"Just the opposite," Arnold said, "when Harry's well oiled that's when he at his best – remember the Big Air Raid when Clitheroe's Pie Crust demolished Uriah's Urinal? He was rat arsed at the time, but he remembered every last detail. He's in the tap room at the moment, do me a favour, keep him topped up with mild and bitter, I want a word with him when I get back. In the meantime I must get Constable Barker to go over what Harry said when he brought him in for singing in the street." Without another word he took off for the police station where his second in command was proudly holding Eli in custody.

"Archie lad, think hard," Arnold said breathlessly, not allowing himself time to go off the boil, "Where was Harry when you arrested him for disturbing the peace in the small hours of Sunday morning?"

"Where he usually is, in the main street…"

"Where exactly…?"

"On that bench, out side the front of the "Feathers" singing like he gen'ly does…"

"Was there anyone else about…"

"Well, nobody I recognised. But there was a big fellow hovering around in the shadows, listening to Harry singing. But when he saw me coming he scarpered" Archie answered,

"Archie, think, rack your brain could it have been Herbert Townsend"

"Well it could have been but I couldn't be sure." Archie replied apologetically. Although Arnold felt disappointed, he didn't really expect a positive outcome from Archie.

"You're sure Archie, there's nothing else, just Harry singing hymns?"

"That's all, except... well there is just one thing..." Cowering, Archie looked afraid expecting Arnold to chastise him for being flippant.

"What Archie? Come on, I'm not going to clout you."

"Harry wasn't singing hymns. You know he always ends up singing *"Jerusalem"*? Well on Saturday night he was singing *"Hold Your Hand Out, You Naughty Boy!"* Archie squirmed as if expecting his boss to round on him for his stupid answer. "I know it sounds daft Arnold, but you did ask me if there was anything unusual..."

"That's right Archie I did. Don't worry you did your best son." Disappointed that he was no nearer a conclusion Arnold returned as quickly as possible to the "Feathers" where at least he could take comfort that Miss Clapworthy would lend an intelligent and sympathetic ear.

"Well, I've given Harry another pint of mild and bitter," Elenora explained when Arnold returned "that should get Harry's alcoholic level high enough and keep him nicely sloshed and articulate until you can question him. "Archie any help?"

"No, I'm afraid not. It seems Harry was true to form singing his head off as per usual. There was someone else hovering in the shadows, but Archie couldn't identify him.

"Let's hope Harry can. Only other unusual thing, on Saturday night was that Harry changed his repertoire from religion to Music Hall!"

Elenora and Sergeant Wilkinson pushed their way past the crowds into the Taproom where Harry greeted them in his usual friendly but slurred way.

"Arlon Winkinson! Miss Clapperty!" Harry slurred, glowing with alcohol induced good nature. "Come over here and sit thee both down."

"Harry, just before Archie took you into the cell on Saturday night," Arnold began, "when you were still on Main Street giving your usual rendition of *"Jerusalem"* …"

"No, no, no, Alond! Willim Blake would hardly have been in keeping on Sat'dy night…

"Why is that Harry? Why wouldn't William Blake's hymn be in keeping?"

"… I winnised something very naughty, I saw with me own eyes a very respeckable pirro… pillow… of the comm'nity sneaking out of the front door of this very 'stablishmint" So I decided on a song more ippro…appropriate. "That's when I rem'bered one of my dear old mother's fav'rite songs. *"Hold Your Hand Out You Naughty Boy"* It was when I got into the second line of the song that's when he started to get … 'Noyed"

"How do you mean?"

"…It was z'if he took the words of the song pers'nally, like as if I was goading him,you see it was the words, they went like this – '***…last night in the pale moonlight, I saw yer! I saw yer!..***'" I saw his shoulders scrunch up, he turned round to face me, he started to walk towards me, menacing, murder in his eyes, and he twisted the tea towel into a tight rope…"

"What happened then Harry? Did he …"

"He didn't get a chance, young Constable Barker showed up… I was never so glad in all my life when I heard Archie coming to arrest me. The big fellow dropped the tea towel and scarpered and I never thought anything more about it until just now. I have to be pissed to remember all that stuff.

"Now who was it Harry? **Who was it came at you with a twisted tea towel?**"

"Mr Herbert Townsend the owner of Townsend's Twisted Tea Towel Textiles. And here's the very tea towel with which he would have done the dirty deed"

Feeling very pleased with himself Harry produced from his pocket the pre-war linen tea towel on which was emblazoned the Brewery's elaborate logo.

"Thanks Harry! Thanks a million. "Now finish your drink and get off home and no singing in the street, remember it's only the lunch time session and it's not a holiday. You're not working to-day because your cart couldn't cope with the deep snow"

"So the tea towel answers the question of what was used to prevent the fingerprints getting on to the bolts and the front door key." Elenora said, "it also suggests old man Townsend was capable of strangling someone to cover his tracks, but it doesn't prove he actually did Flossie in!"

"No I'm afraid it doesn't. But it does show that he is involved. He is guilty of something. So is Slimy Sidney Slickey, the other prime suspect"

"...Not the only other suspect Arnold, don't forget the rest of us - Sally, Minnie, me and the American kid – Buddy Martin."

"Well, if I was a betting man I'd plump for Slickey – or Townsend." Arnold said, "So I'll just have a word with that little creep Slimey."

"In the meantime there's something been bothering me," Elenora said, "I'll catch up with you before Sally calls *"Time Gentlemen Please"*

Sydney Slickey was propping up the bar in an effort to give the impression that, although he had been on friendly terms with the dead landlady, he was not in any way mourning her departure.

More likely he wanted to appear like the rest of the locals. As if he merely felt a certain communal concern.

"Nah then Mr Slickey," Arnold said, "I wonder if you could answer me a few questions?"

"I told the Bobbies from Leeds all I know Sergeant Wilkinson, which was very little. I know nothing else." Slickey squirmed, oozing guilt, as he always did in the presence of Arnold. Only this time the stakes were much higher, and he knew it.

"Come with me, where it's a little quieter, and we can have talk Sidney?"

Arnold led the little SPIV into the front porch away from the crowds.

"Now Sid," Arnold's familiarity did nothing to ease Sidney's loss of composure. His top lip was starting to gather little droplets of sweat which threatened to spoil the carefully applied mascara his pencilled moustache depended on for its existence.

"I understand you have – or did have an arrangement with the late Mrs Ingham, Sidney?"

"What do you mean by arrange..."

"You would run little errands for her," Arnold couched his question as if he were the sole person privy to the information.

"I would occasionally do the lady a favour..."

"For a fee I believe...?"

"Well, a fellow has to make a living, all strictly above board..."

"But am I right in thinking that you would have forfeited your fee had the lady in question looked more kindly on you?"

"How d'yer mean? Sidney asked, as rising panic sent a visible judder through his limbs.

"I mean," Arnold pressed on "Had the lady showed you more kindness, paid more attention to you instead of simply using you as a lackey, you might not have felt so rejected?"

"What you sayin'?" Slickey thought perhaps a show of bluster might help his case. "What the fuck are you suggestin'?"

"I'm not suggesting anything Mr Slickey. I'm merely trying to get a clear picture of who had a reason, or not, for murder. And rejection is a pretty strong motive."

"You've got nothing on me, and you know it Sergeant..."

"... Well apart from black market goods, forged documents, receiving dubious materials... all of the above serious crimes, shall I go on? " Suddenly Arnold grabbed Sidney by the lapels and adopted his ultra tough voice, deep and threatening, "There's a good hour between now and this pub closing at two o'clock. I'm going to get to the bottom of this. I want you to stay here until I say you can go. Its either that or I take you in to the station. Understand?"

Arnold dropped the little sneak's lapels with disgust, and walked back into the Lounge bar to question Herbert Townsend.

On seeing the sergeant approaching him the mill owner made a move as if to leave.

"Oh, Mr Townsend," Arnold was all charm and politeness once more. "I wonder if I may have a word with you."

"What is it about Sergeant Wilkinson?" Townsend's tetchy attitude - attack being the best defence - prompted him to adopt a high handed position.

"If it's about this ugly business that happened here on Saturday, I told the Leeds Enquiry all I know. There is no more to say."

"Yes, sir, I have a transcript of your statement. I merely need to check one or two things..." Arnold looked the red faced industrialist straight in the eye. "... For instance, the time you left on Saturday night?"

"I left these premises around eleven thirty, I told all this to Superintendent Cartwright."

"...Not *twelve* thirty?

"For the last time I repeat - eleven thirty!"

"...and you left by the front door – this door in fact?"

"**Yes!**" For all of Mr Townsend's bombast he knew he was rapidly losing ground and he wanted to be away. Agitatedly he turned as if to leave.

"Mr. Townsend!" In spite of Arnold's normally kindly nature he was capable of assuming a powerful bearing. This was one of these moments. In Herbert Townsend's eyes it was an awesome sight.

"I must ask you stay and answer these questions. If you refuse I will arrest you on suspicion of murder. That will mean taking you in to the Police Station. For a man of your standing in the community that could be a needless embarrassment. I'm sure you don't want that do you?"

Arnold had miraculously lost any trace of his homely broad Yorkshire accent and this new articulacy was very intimidating to Herbert Townsend. He was no longer dealing with a yokel. He thought it best to comply.

"Ask your damned questions then and get it over."

"I have a witness who saw you leaving by this front door at twelve thirty on Sunday morning in a most surreptitious manner..."

"...Who'll take the word of a incessant drunkard like Harry Petty?"

"I didn't mention the name of the witness Mr Townsend. You did!" Arnold delivered his damning line without any sign of triumphalism. But it had driven home with outstanding effect.

The big self important man shrank under the same weight of defeat, shame and guilt as he showed that particular morning a few years earlier when he had spent a terrible night of fear six stories up stranded in the crippled lift at his mill.

"Besides Sir, there was another witness – Constable Barker saw you run off, not however before you left behind a piece of damning evidence – the tea towel with the brewery's logo, which you used to prevent your fingerprints being left on the mortise key and bolts on the inside of the door. Be wise sir; remain here at the scene of the crime until Sally calls *'time gentlemen please.'* And I give you permission to go."

Mr Townsend's bombast completely deserted him. Without a word he went back to his usual bar stool and ordered a stiff drink, in an effort to quell the serious bout of jitters and await he knew not what might befall him. By this time the Monday lunchtime opening of the "Feathers" was almost halfway through.

The thing that was bothering Elenora was this:- The previous afternoon, Minnie had been singing the praises of Private Burgess (Buddy) Martin the tall blond GI Adonis and apple of her eye. What was it she said? *"There's absolutely nothing too much for him to do to make him self useful - change light bulbs, wash the floor, put shelves up. **Only last night he was even mending the hinges on the back door...**"*

Was it not wildly coincidental that the same evening the boy had been repairing the hinges that same door was so brutally burst open? She made her way to the back door, only a makeshift door had been erected by the police as a temporary measure. The original ancient door was propped against the wall, as it had been when she found it prior to her terrible discovery on the previous day.

True the ancient oak door had been kicked in but to her way of thinking there was only a minimal amount of damage where the screws had torn through the woodwork. It had offered little resistance.

Elenora realised she had discovered what the investigation led by Chief Superintendent Cartwright had failed to see. The back door of the pub had not only been kicked in it had been weakened earlier! Had Buddy Martin been repairing the door? Or had he been sabotaging it!? If she was right, and it looked very much as if she might well be, she needed to do something quickly to substantiate her theory. What was more worrying was that Minnie and Sally had all this time been harbouring, encouraging, and even in Minnie's case cosseting a murderer?

"Minnie!" She called over the cacophonous noise of the busy pub, "I know you're up to your eyes at the moment, but it is important. Can you spare me a moment?"

"...Just coming!" Minnie banged two newly filled pint glasses down on the bar, rang the money up in the till then turned her attention to Elenora.

"Nah, then doy! What can I do you for?"

"Buddy Martin? What do you know about him?" Elenora asked, "Apart from the fact that he is the most beautiful male creature since Michelangelo's David?"

"Oh. Buddy!" Minnie replied rapturously, "...grandest lad his mother ever had! Doesn't say a lot, I don't think he's the sharpest knife in the drawer, but then, what's a hunk like him need brains for?"

"I know he's an in-patient at the American section of the Hospital, but what is wrong with him. Was he wounded? He looks as fit as a butcher's dog to me."

"Oh, no!" Minnie replied, "He wasn't wounded or anything like that. From what I can gather, he had a breakdown. One of the medical officers told me they are pleased that we allow him to spend so much time here in the pub pottering around. '*Occupation*al *Therapy'* he said it was."

"OK Min," Elenora said, "...just one other thing, how did he get along with Flossie?"

"He didn't." Minnie replied emphatically. "Mind you not many people got along with Flossie did they? The fact that he was an extra, unpaid helper suited her down to the ground. So she was only too pleased to put up with him, but as for liking him? Well, she never had much to do with him. But he used to watch her a lot. He seemed to have what they call nowadays a '*fixation'*"

"Minnie you are a fund of information! See you later"

Arnold, in the meantime had been back to the little sub station to formally arrest Eli as number one suspect. He was just about to call up head quarters in Leeds to inform them of this so they might call off the manhunt when Elenora burst in.

"You couldn't just postpone informing Leeds for just a little while longer could you Arnold?" Elenora asked.

"Why Miss Clapworthy what...?"

"I've just found out something that throws a whole new light on the case..." Arnold listened in amazed admiration as Elenora explained her findings on the nobbled back door. This information together with Minnie's portrait of the young GI was surely enough to throw suspicion him on.

"Yes I suppose it is. "Arnold's mind was racing overtime, "but the thing is this, once I ring Leeds it will be out of my hands, they will take over, Transfer Eli to Armley Gaol..."

"...That is why we need time for you to talk to Buddy Martin, Ideally get a confession. As I see it Arnold, the other two most likely suspects, Slimy and Townsend are mighty guilty of something but so far there is no proof that either of them did Flossie in."

"You're right" Arnold said decisively as they set off back down the Main Street. "Come on, back to the 'Feathers Miss Clapworthy.' Was the kid still there when you left?"

"Oh yes, happy as a pig in Chiffon helping Minnie and Sally,."

Both Slickey and Townsend stared shamefacedly deep into their drinks both of them in their separate Hell registering fear as they saw the Sergeant and the Vet re-enter the still crowded pub.

"Sally, do you think you could spare Buddy for a few minutes" Arnold asked, "and will it be alright if we use the kitchen.

"Whatever you say Arnold," Sally answered. As soon as the young GI joined Arnold and Elenora the pair lost no time.

"Buddy, it is Buddy isn't it?" Arnold asked, in his most gentle manner. "You don't mind me calling you Buddy do you?"

"No sir," Buddy answered smiling broadly. Not at all Sir, my given name is Burgess but I prefer Buddy."

"Would you mind repeating what you told the Leeds investigation squad on Sunday morning regarding the incident that took place here on the previous night?"

"Not at all Sir," Buddy looked straight ahead as he repeated robot fashion almost word for word his previous statement,

"So correct me if I have it wrong. You left here with the rest of the clientele at closing time and returned to the hospital?"

292

"Yes Sir."

"...And you didn't leave the hospital until the next day? When did you hear that Mrs Ingham – Flossie had been murdered."

"The next morning – Sunday when the Leeds Police Force questioned us all."

"How did you feel about it. Were you shocked? Saddened?" Elenora asked.

"Neither. I didn't feel anything."

"You didn't feel upset Buddy?" Elenora persisted.

"She had it coming." Buddy answered nonchalantly his smile fading into an unfamiliar look of cold distaste as he gazed into the middle distance. "She had it coming for a long time."

"Why do you say that Buddy? Was it something she did to displease you?

"Everything she did displease me." Buddy's answers were clear, emotionless and well considered. But the boy's whole demeanour was changing, he appeared to becoming disconnected, darker and and distant. "I didn't tell the other lot earlier, but I don't mind telling you Miss Clapworthy. She did what that other dirty whore had done..."

"What other whore?"

"Her! Her!" Buddy scrabbled in his breast pocket as he searched frantically. Eventually he brought out a much handled old photograph of an early middle aged woman. "Her! Take a good look! That's my mother! She was a whore too!" Buddy now mightily disturbed leaped to his feet his voice rising hysterically, clearly losing control, "Do you know what she did? She locked me in that cupboard for hours when I was a kid, whilst she...she... with men... a lot of different men..." The boy began to hyper-ventilate, Arnold physically supported him until he

293

recovered a little. The young GI began to shake alarmingly. "I don't want to talk about it any more."

"Did Flossie ever..." Arnold asked

"No! No! I don't want to talk about it. I don't want to talk about her." His voice rose higher with each word until he was almost screaming again. "Minnie! Minnie! Tell him to stop asking me questions!" Looking around and not being able to locate Minnie, the young boy began flail around dangerously. It took all of Arnold's strength to subdue him. Buddy had lost control and was now dangerously manic. Elenora dashed to fetch Minnie who quickly judged the situation and took the disturbed boy in her arms. Her motherly attention had an immediate effect. He regained a troubled calm. But was now unrecognisable as the sweet bright-eyed boy they all knew.

"Minnie, tell him to stop asking me questions. I want to go back into the lounge bar and help you wash the glasses. Tell him! No more questions."

"He'll not ask thee any more questions if you don't want him to." Minnie shook her head and with her wise old eyes indicated to Arnold and Elenora that Buddy was beyond reasoning with. Arnold telephoned the Military Hospital. A doctor and ambulance he was assured would be sent at the earliest.

"I'll sit with him until they come." Minnie said,.

"You sure you'll be alright Min?" Elenora asked concernedly

"Oh, aye!" Minnie answered, "Buddy wouldn't harm me." She led Buddy to the easy chair. Almost immediately he closed his eyes and fell into an un-natural troubled half sleep.

Elenora and Arnold exchanged glances acknowledging their mutual frustration at not being able to tie up the ends. It was deeply disappointing. True they had *almost* cleared Eli's name. They had exposed a certain amount of guilt resting on both Slickey and Townsend and Buddy's alarming condition had come to light most dramatically in the last few minutes making his guilt appear obvious.

Alas it was not conclusive.

Elenora's disappointment was not so much for herself but for Arnold. He had suffered such cavalier treatment at the hands of the Leeds detectives in general and Chief Superintendent Ossie Cartwright in particular. She knew that between them she and Arnold had come so close to redressing this unfair balance by proving that Eli had dropped from first to fourth suspect.   But the evidence they had gleaned was inconclusive. If only there were more time, but both Arnold and Elenora knew they must make that phone call and give Eli up to have the man hunt called off. Now the time had come when Arnold must hand the case back to the Leeds boys. To delay any further would be tantamount to withholding evidence, and both Elenora and Arnold were aware they had pushed their luck to the limit already.

Deep in thought Elenora chose her next words with care.

"Before we throw in the towel Arnold, one last thing we can do for Eli. First of all, when they come for him imagine what the scene outside your little cop shop will be like with all these crowds baying for blood. It will be like one of those Deep South movies.   Don't you think it would be best to tell them to pick him up here at the pub where at least he will be surrounded by friends?"

"You're right of course." Arnold answered, resigned to the fact that they had failed by a hairs breadth to bring off their heroic effort to clear Eli's name. "I'll go fetch him here, then ring Leeds."   Once more Arnold hurried back to the sub station. Within minutes he had Eli safe inside the kitchen of the pub where Minnie sat with the young GI tenderly wiping the fine film of sweat from his brow as the ambulance arrived from the Military hospital with a doctor and attendant in answer to Arnold's phone call.

Still this seemingly interminable lunch time session plodded along through the couple of hours the licensing law permitted. Elenora turned to Arnold once again.

"Right all we need now is to see Chief Superintendent Ossie Cartwright's face when he arrives and realises what a shambles he made of the case and sees what super copper you are Arnold Wilkinson! You may not have entirely cracked it but you came within a hairs breadth of doing so."

"Not just me Miss Clapworthy, WE! You and me, together."

"OK, WE. Between us we have gathered enough new evidence to have turned this case around enough to have almost cleared Eli's name"

"Yeah, sure! If only we had found the weapon. Wouldn't that have been the icing on the cake? But I'm afraid, seeing Cartwright eat humble pie isn't going to happen.

"Never mind at least..." Suddenly she felt an urgent tug of her sleeve.

"Can you come outside for a minute Miss Clapworthy?" It was young Mick Ryan, her protégée. Not normally lost for words, he started on an explanation but the urgency of his errand robbed him of his voice, made his pulse race and eyes sparkle.

"There's someone needs to see you, to talk, er... sort of confess something of importance...they don't want Sergeant Wilkinson in on it until they have spoken to you" he whispered.

"Mick, you're not making sense. Who is it needs to see me?

"It's… It's… Oh, I think you better see for yourself."

He led her by the hand out of the pub, past the disabled back door still leaning against the wall, into the cobbled courtyard of the pub surrounded as it was by the pretty little cottages, including Eli's with the police notice still flapping in the breeze forbidding entry.

The cottage further along hidden in heavy foliage was the home of the Kellett family. The ancient stone cottage was set further back from the rest of the dwellings, deep in the fruit trees, bushes and overgrowth as if deliberately courting secrecy. The thick growth of ivy that covered the cottage now heavy with snow added even more mystery. Mick led Elenora towards the front door.

Everhard Kellett, the stern patriarch stood on the threshold awaiting them.

"Thank you for coming Miss Clapworthy," He greeted Elenora with an old world politeness. "We have summat to tell thee that concerns the terrible happening last Saturday neet at the pub. I'd like you to come in, but before tha' does I must ask thee to prepare thi'sen for a bit of a shock."

Elenora exchanged glances with Mick. She was glad she had him along.

"It's alright tha' can bring the lad with you, he knows what this is all about and he can be trusted. Do come in."

Elenora stepped into the tiny kitchen to find Amy, Rebecca and Everhard. The shock was almost physical when who should step out from the cellar but the presumed dead son - Noble Kellett!

Elenora caught her breath.

"Aye," Everhard confirmed, "Your eyes don't deceive you Miss Clapworthy. It's not a ghost. It is our Noble alright."

"Noble, we all thought you... Although I don't know if I'll ever get over the shock I couldn't be more pleased to see you are very much alive."

"I know Miss Clapworthy, and I do apologise for the shock..."

Noble stepped forward, his open, honest features yearning to be understood. Taking a deep breath he began to tell of his long and voluntary incarceration in the cellar. Of how he intended sitting out the war, until his conscience got the better of him

"You see," Noble began after a deep breath, "when I came back from Dunkirk I went AWOL. I won't try to deny it. It was a deliberate and well-considered plan to escape the war. I could have stayed undetected indefinitely hidden in the cellar until the war ends. The only problem is, me conscience started playing me up. What I witnessed in the small hours of Sunday morning at the back door of the pub was a clincher. When I learned there was a manhunt on the go for Eli Pearson, I also knew for certain it couldn't have been him. You see Miss Clapworthy; the moon was so bright on Saturday night before the snow came you could have read the newspaper by its light.

What I saw meant nothing much at the time, but in the small hours of Sunday morning. I saw somebody messing around in the kennel; Then I saw him kick the back door open and go inside. At the time I thought he was a little heavy handed but I thought no more of it when I saw who it was. Not long after, he came out again smiling and humming a little tune as he passed by the end of our orchard on his way out of the back court yard gate. He threw something, into our fruit bushes. Once we heard there was no weapon found at the scene of the crime we guessed that what he threw into our orchard might well have been that very weapon!"

There was a heavy silence in the Kellett's living room whilst Elenora took in Noble's incredible story.

"Of course, the knife! If it was the murder weapon it is still where it landed, buried under the snow." She said at last. "And could you identify the person you have just described? "

"Yes. It was Buddy the GI, without any doubt."

"Noble, are you prepared to swear to this in a court of law?"

"Yes."

"Of course you realise it will look very bad for you with the Army Authorities..."

"So be it." Noble replied unemotionally. "I would never be able to live with myself if Eli took the blame, and all the time I knew the truth."

"Right!" Elenora stood up. What she was about to suggest was at the very least mind-boggling. But if they could pull it off, the future happiness of the Kellett family might be secured. .At the same time the final piece in the Murder mystery would fall into place. What she was about to propose, she knew, was dizzyingly risky. It would bend the law to breaking point. "Now everyone pay close attention." Almost luminous with excitement she laid before them her plan

"Am I right in thinking that Noble meant to take off for the West Country today to give himself up to the Military Police?"

"Yes, the reason he left it until now was to wait until the snow was trodden down and he wouldn't leave any tell tail footprints."

"And the reason for going to the West Country was...?"

"…So that Mam, Dad and Amy would not be charged for harbouring a deserter." Noble spoke out gallantly, "I figured that if I volunteered to give my self up I would only serve a few months in the glass house then be sent back to my regiment."

"Good! I've got it." Elenora said with more than a little triumph in her voice. "Now then Everhard - supposing I put it to you that it was *you* not Noble who saw Buddy Martin on Saturday night. That it was *you* not Noble who saw him tend to the dog, kick down the back door of the pub. *You*, not Noble who saw him come out about five minutes later and throw an object into the orchard… *You* were the one who saw the whole affair *not* Noble"

"But, it *wasn't* me." Everhard protested. "It was our Noble."

"Don't be dense Everhard - *supposing* you *say* it *was* *you* who saw it all. Would your conscience allow you to do that?"

"Aye it would. And me conscience would be clear because if our Noble says it is the truth, then it is!"

"In that case doesn't it make sense to not involve Noble at all? Let him take off this morning for the West Country? All Noble would have to do is serve his time in detention then re-join his regiment and the human race once again. You, Rebecca and Amy would no longer be culpable of harbouring a deserter, and Eli would be a free man." All four of the Kellett family stood with their mouths open.

"I can see the sense in your plan Miss Clapworthy," Noble was the first to come down to earth, "I know that it *was* Buddy I saw, but I didn't actually see him kill Flossie. Is it possible I might be damning an innocent man?"

"The police already have substantial doubts about his innocence" Elenora said, with confidence. "The only

300

thing they don't have is the weapon which should still have his fingerprints on it which would confirm guilt.

Noble turned to his wife; slowly a smile replaced any residual doubt he may have had. The look on his face told her all she needed to know.

"I take it we are all in agreement?

"Aye we are!" Noble looked with glowing admiration on this wonderful woman who had shown them how to get their lives back again.

"In that case there is no time to lose." Elenora said, "We'll go back to the pub now Everhard. You can make a police statement *of what you saw from the orchard."* Elenora said pointedly.

"Aye! I get your meaning Miss Clapworthy." Everhard replied with a wink letting her know he knew exactly was expected of him.." **We must not tell Arnold of our plan**. It would be too much to ask of him being a police officer to bear the responsibility of being in on any bending of the law like this. **This is strictly between us!** Noble, As soon as we leave for the pub, you must say your goodbyes to your Mam and Amy. Then set off to the West Country to give yourself up. We'll see you just as soon as you have cleared the Gerries out of Europe. You're a good man Noble Kellett!" She allowed father and son a short time to say farewell.

Drinking-up time back at the pub! Sally asked Big Nellie to clear the crowds out into the street where the sensation seekers made their way to the little police sub station, only to find it deserted, since Eli, the object of their morbid interest was now sitting in the kitchen of the 'Feathers' having a cup of tea.

At this high moment of the drama, as If on cue, Elenora entered with Mr Kellett senior. Confident, cool and composed Everhard signed a flawlessly written statement stating he had witnessed seeing Buddy throw the 'object' into the orchard.

Constable Barker was sent to find the 'object', which as expected, was the murder weapon. It was exactly where Everhard said it would be, and for once Archie had enough sense to make sure that any fingerprints that were on the weapon were not smudged, nor were any of his own added to even the smallest part of it.

Even as these events were taking place two more parties, important to the outcome of this story arrived at the pub after closing time demanding entrance.

First: a very elegant middle aged professional lady from the Lake District – A Miss Olive Barraclough here to stand by an old friend in his hour of need. Not without a certain amount of clout in the legal department should it be required.

The final person needed to make this dénouement a heaven sent, blissful affair was, at that moment banging impatiently on the front door demanding entry.. It was of course Chief Superintendent Ossie Cartwright on his virtuous mission to catch the culprits drinking after hours.

The door was unlocked to allow him entry. He strode purposefully, dramatically straight into the crowded kitchen before he delivered his condemnation.

"Just as I suspected...!" He announced jubilantly, **"a blatant breach of the licensing laws! Drinking outside the permitted hours! Which one of you is the responsible person in charge here?"** The answer, heavy with triumph, came from the one he dreaded. It was the voice of his aunt Minnie!

"That's right lad we are drinking, Tea!" Like a blow to the solar plexus looking around he could see - everyone present were indeed drinking only *tea!*" They were drinking tea but in the private area not in the Public area of the pub everyone was in the kitchen where it was perfectly legal. To compound the total collapse of his world, Elenora and all the major players in this drama were gathered as if it were the finale of a play with a happy ending. Ossie had made the biggest fool of himself and he stood exposed looking like the pillock that he was.

"Ah! Superintendent Cartwright! Ossie!" Elenora was the first to break the spell. "So glad you could come. Perhaps we can bring you up to date. Your excellent man here at Craggs Bottom Sub Station, Sergeant Wilkinson, has done some splendid work on this case in your absence. Work, that had it been done by you and your men after the discovery of the body yesterday morning would have saved a great deal of expense in mounting a County wide man hunt. Not to mention distress to the falsely accused. Most of us here today find it very remiss, not to say appalling that you personally could not make yourself available be here to clear up this mess. Yet were only too eager to come over here to pursue the minor offence of *Drinking After Hours!*" Ossie remained dumbstruck. Elenora picked up the thread. "Still now you are here have nice cup of tea with us all whilst Police Sergeant Wilkinson fills you in all the goodies you missed out on.

Arnold was only too pleased to tie up all the ends, and let Craggs Bottom get back to normal. The pieces fell into place nicely. Elenora, Minnie and Sally got most of their wishes fulfilled. One of those wishes was that Arnold got the credit due to him for his remarkable work on the case. Justice fell in abundance in other ways. Not least in the admiration in the eyes of Sally Hancock as she fondly linked her arm in his.

Noble Kellett was on his way to turn himself in to the military and his not-so-Everhard-father became reconciled to the fact that his son's honour was still intact.

303

Eli Pearson's name was now cleared. He and his first love Olive Barraclough were reunited.

Early days yet to know whether it would be wedding bells for Sally and Arnold and Olive and Eli. But it would be a very bad bet to lay money against it happening.

Elenora knew as indeed Ossie did, that he could suffer serious consequences for his conceit and stupidity. That is if ever the full extent of his neglect became known. At best he would receive a reprimand of mammoth proportions, at worst dismissal from the force.

Elenora showed not the slightest hint of triumph at his downfall. She knew, in his better moments there was goodness in him. Besides, she held that anyone who could play the big bass with such love and genius couldn't be all bad. With this in mind there was one more outstanding item to attend to, before she finally left the "Feathers." She drew Chief Superintendent Cartwright to one side.

"Ossie, don't forget rehearsals for the "Hot Shots" next Saturday evening. Drop everything else. We have to shape up for Sunday's gig at the Mechanics Institute!"

"Oh, Miss Clapworthy, I don't..." Ossie faltered miserably a sure give-away that his omnipotence had taken a monumental nose-dive, from which it may never recover.

"Thank you for asking me, but I don't think you will want me in the band after my fall from grace becomes common knowledge."

"Ballocks!" Elenora replied, " Who says it's going to become common knowledge?" "You don't seem to realise how much kindness there is in the good folk of Craggs Bottom. Forgiveness too. Besides, It's not what I want, it's what you're going to want if the worst happens and it all leaks out. For your own sanity you need to be strumming that bull fiddle next Sunday night and maybe every night thereafter. So we'll see you seven o'clock Saturday night. OK?" Ossie's eyes brimmed with tears of gratitude. He found it hard to find a voice.

"OK?" Elenora repeated. All Ossie Cartwright could do was to nod his head in the affirmative.

Young Mickie Ryan blazing with admiration grinned up into Elenora's face as they set off through the drifts back to Ambler Thorn with the two dogs Heinz and Caesar all four of them gambolling like young pups in the snow..

THE END

41010206R00173

Made in the USA
Charleston, SC
20 April 2015